Also by Amanda Stevens

THE DOLLMAKER
THE DEVIL'S FOOTPRINTS
THE WHISPERING ROOM

The Graveyard Queen

THE RESTORER
THE KINGDOM
THE PROPHET
THE VISITOR
THE SINNER

Look for Amanda Stevens's next novel
in The Graveyard Queen series

THE AWAKENING

available soon from MIRA Books.

AMANDA STEVENS

THE SINNER

MIRA

ISBN-13: 978-0-7783-1784-5

The Sinner

Recycling programs
for this product may
not exist in your area.

Printed in U.S.A.

THE
SINNER

One

The caged grave was an anomaly in Beaufort County. In all my cemetery travels, I'd come across only a handful of mortsafes, all of them in Europe. They were a Scottish invention, cleverly devised and manufactured in the early nineteenth century as a means of thwarting the nefarious grave robbers who dug up fresh human remains for profit.

But body snatching wasn't a modern-day concern, and from what I could see through the tall grass, the cage didn't appear that old. No more than two or three decades, if that. The heavy iron grates had rusted in the salt air, but the rods and plates were still intact and I could see the dull gleam of a steel padlock on the gate.

My pulse quickened as I made my way along the overgrown pathway. It wasn't every day I stumbled across such a fascinating find. Although *stumbled* was perhaps a misnomer because I'd been drawn to that desolate spot for a reason. Lured from my work in Seven Gates Cemetery by a presence as yet unknown to me.

For the past several months, I'd been working in

a small graveyard that was located near the ruins of an old church in Ascension, South Carolina. Until now, there had been nothing unusual about the restoration. I gathered trash, cleaned headstones and chopped away overgrowth until sunset, and then I went home to a cool shower, a solitary dinner and an early bedtime.

It had become a welcome routine. Even my nights had been uneventful and mostly dreamless. The dog days of summer left me so drained that I slept the sleep of the dead as the Lowcountry sweltered in the August heat. The small air conditioner in my rental provided only the barest relief and so I'd taken to sleeping in the hammock on the screened porch. There was something intrinsically soothing about the sea breezes that swept in from the islands and the songbirds that serenaded me from the orange grove.

Here in this coastal oasis, Charleston seemed a million miles away and so did John Devlin. I told myself that's what I wanted. After the events that had unfolded over a year ago in Kroll Cemetery, the gulf between us had widened until I'd felt I had no choice but to give Devlin the space he seemed to need.

His leave from the Charleston Police Department had turned into a permanent resignation, and the last I'd heard he was working for his grandfather, a situation I couldn't have imagined a year ago. A lot of things had happened that I could never have imagined, not the least of which were the changes I'd undergone. The one constant, however, was the ache in my heart. After all this time, Devlin's absence from my life still pained me.

Which was why a challenging restoration in a new location was a welcome distraction. Seven Gates had come at just the right time after a long, lonely winter of hibernation. Spring had brought resolve and renewed commitment to my work, and the peace and quiet of the cemetery had restored my rocky equilibrium. But I should have known the calm wouldn't last for long. It never did.

A shadow passed across the landscape and I glanced skyward where a buzzard floated in lazy circles over the treetops. The day was hot and still. The Spanish moss hung nearly motionless from the live oaks and the resurrection fern clinging to the bark had curled and browned in the heat.

As I stood watching the vulture, my heart started to pound even harder. Nothing stirred. Animal, ghost or otherwise. And yet I knew something—someone—was there, hidden among the shadows.

Why did you bring me here? I silently implored as I turned to scour the woods behind me. *What do you want from me?*

No answer. Nothing but the silken rustle of the palmettos.

The mortsafe was an intriguing find, but I didn't think it the sole reason I'd been drawn to this place. Nor was the isolation of the interment. Quarantined graves were hardly unique, and in bygone days, any number of reasons—suicide, thievery or suspicion of witchcraft—could have kept the deceased from a consecrated burial in the churchyard. No, something more was at play here. A mystery that had yet to reveal itself.

A stray breeze ruffled the damp tendrils that had escaped from my ponytail, and despite the heat, I felt the dance of frosty fingers up and down my spine. Another vulture joined the first and I tracked them for a moment longer before dropping my gaze to comb the shadowy tree line. I could have sworn I heard chanting coming from somewhere deep in the woods. A distant singsong that dissolved into silence as the wind died away.

I turned back to the path, trudging onward as I slapped at the mosquitoes and gnats rising up from the grass to flog me. The palmettos barely stirred now and no other sound came to me. The utter silence of the clearing engulfed me.

The fingers that tickled the base of my neck now slid with icy precision across my scalp. The hair on my arms lifted as the still air suddenly became rank with the sulfurous odor of the nearby salt marsh. The chanting came to me again, hushed and distant, no more than a whispered repetition that vanished the moment I glanced over my shoulder.

I hurried my steps, driven by a force I had yet to understand. Not once did I consider the alternative of fleeing back along the path to the cemetery. I had come too far and the prodding from the watcher in the woods was too strong.

As I drew closer, I could see the cage more clearly through the weeds. It was a heavy device with a series of rods and plates padlocked together to safeguard the buried remains. In the old days, the contraption would have protected the grave until decay rendered the corpse useless to the medical schools and anatomists that employed the body snatchers. Then the mortsafe would have been unlocked, removed and placed over another grave.

Not so this cage. The edges were anchored in cement, making the safe virtually immovable by human hand or Mother Nature. Thorny vines with heart-shaped leaves coiled around the rods and weeds jutted up through the grates. So thorough the camouflage, a casual passerby wouldn't have glimpsed the cage at all. No telling how long it had remained hidden and forsaken until the watcher in the woods had summoned me here to find it.

I was near enough now that I could see the sunken dirt beneath the grid. At any other time, I would have searched for a marker or headstone, but now I gave the grave only a cursory examination because something else had caught my eye.

About ten feet to my right, I'd glimpsed another cage. From what I could see through the weeds and vines, the device appeared identical to the first except for one grisly addition.

Inside the mortsafe, a pair of hands rose up out of a freshly mounded grave to grasp the iron grate.

Two

The hands were tiny and delicate. Pale with a chalky bluish tint beneath the crust of dirt. Smooth and unblemished save for the dried blood around the broken nails. Not the hands of a child, I realized, but of a small woman. Young and Caucasian.

I tried to tear my gaze from the horrifying scene, but I couldn't look away. I stood motionless, sweat soaking through my shirt as a suffocating dread settled over me. I was stunned by the discovery and nearly breathless with fright. I even had a moment of déjà vu that took me back to the Oak Grove murders and to the gruesome discoveries I'd made there with Devlin.

But even in such a distressed state, I had the presence of mind to take stock of the situation and make sure I was in no immediate danger. Except for that unknown presence in the woods, I seemed to be alone.

My evolved senses were so attuned to the environment, I could hear the ruffle of feathers high up in a treetop and the distant lap of water against its banks. I could smell the brine from the saltwater marsh and the woodsy aroma of the evergreens, but nothing human came to me. No lingering energy. No telltale malodor of sweat and excitement.

Almost against my will, I drew a deeper breath, testing the air for a hint of decay, which might have given me an indication of how long the body had been buried. The absence of putrefaction suggested a fresh death. The flesh on the backs of the hands and on what I could see of the arms jutting up through the dirt appeared somewhat supple, leaving me to wonder just how recently blood had flowed through the poor woman's veins.

Perhaps only a matter of moments before I had come upon the grave. If only I had arrived sooner…

You might also be dead, a little voice whispered. *Locked inside one of those metal cages for all eternity.*

Shaking off a stifling claustrophobia, I refocused my attention on the properties of the mortsafe. Like the first cage, the edges had been anchored in cement so that it couldn't be easily moved. The metal rods and lattice had rusted in places, but the padlock looked fairly new, having been placed on the gate so recently that the salt air hadn't yet corroded the steel.

The more obvious observation and by far the more chilling had occurred to me immediately, but I'd managed to push the revelation to the farthest corner of my mind. Now as I stared at those dainty hands, I had to face the horror head-on. The woman inside the grave had been buried alive.

Buried. Alive.

I shuddered and moved in even closer until I was

staring down through the grate directly over the hands. They were filthy, the nails caked and ragged from digging. Through the grime, I could see the curlicue of a tattooed word on the inside of her left wrist and the gleam of a silver ring on her right hand. The intricate design made me think that the jewelry was old, perhaps even an heirloom. The kind of piece that could easily be traced. I couldn't help but wonder why the killer had left it. Had he or she been that certain the body would never be discovered?

Killer.

The silence deepened as the reality of my find gripped me. Only a few moments had passed since I'd first come upon the hands, but it seemed as if I had been standing there for ages, wasting precious time. A homicide had been committed and the sooner I called the police, the sooner they could identify the victim and start searching for her murderer. I knew the procedure, knew what I had to do. Yet I still hesitated because I sensed this was just the beginning of something dark and sinister. A riddle from the dead that would test me in ways I had never before experienced.

And so I remained rooted to the spot, breathing deeply and drawing out those last moments of calm before the storm hit.

As it turned out, I had very little time to vacillate. From somewhere in the woods, the warning tremolo of a loon sent a sharp thrill along my spine and I spun once more to rake the tree line. It occurred to me in the split second before the crack of a rifle sent me scrambling for cover that the killer might still be nearby.

I hit the ground as something hot seared my face. My hand flew to my cheek and I drew back bloody fingers. I'd been hit. *Shot.*

Propelled by fear and self-preservation, I flattened myself in the dirt and covered my head with my arms, certain that at any second another bullet would rip through my scalp. That would be the end of me because neither my gift nor my calling could save me from a mortal wound.

Eyes squeezed shut, I braced for the impact as the reverberation from the first shot died away in the stillness. As always in moments of extreme crisis, I thought about Devlin. If I died here in this desolate clearing, would he sense my passing? Would he come here to search for my body? Or was my absence from his life such a relief that he would ignore the twinges of premonition and gut instinct that had been honed during his years on the police force?

As the disturbing notion flashed through my head, I again became aware of the absolute stillness and I tried to corral my senses. What could I see, hear, smell, taste? *Focus!*

When nothing moved in the weeds, I lifted my head to reconnoiter. Touching a finger to the blood on my cheek, I realized the wound was superficial and had come from nothing more sinister than a smilax vine. And in hindsight, I decided the shot had sounded from the direction of the marsh instead of the woods, leading me to believe that a gator was most likely the target, not I. In my already height-ened state of agitation, I'd overreacted.

Even so, I remained prone in the dirt for several minutes longer as I tried to quiet my flailing heart. Using the weeds for cover, I listened for the tell-tale sound of a sliding bolt or the snap of a twig be-neath stealthy footfalls. When nothing came to me, I eased to a kneeling position and then to my feet as I dusted off my jeans and walked back over to the second mortsafe.

I almost expected the cage to be empty, those pale hands having withdrawn back down into the grave. But no. They were still there, still clutching the metal grate.

A breeze swept over me, cold and unnatural. My head came up and I made a slow turn to once again survey the clearing. As the tall grass parted in the wind I saw now what had been hidden to me earlier.

A dozen identical cages peeked through the un-dulating vegetation to form a large circle around me.

Dr. Rupert Shaw, the founder and administrator of the Charleston Institute for Parapsychology Studies, had once suggested that my affinity for cemeteries stemmed in part from the unbound energy left be-hind by the dead. According to Dr. Shaw, it was my ability to absorb this lingering force that fueled my gift and enhanced my senses. It was why I could see and hear things that others could not. I didn't dispute Dr. Shaw's theory, although I liked to think and truly believed that my love of old graveyards was far more emotional than the assimilation of unbound energy.

In any case, there was nothing to absorb from the caged graves. It was as if someone or something had been there only moments earlier and sucked out all the oxygen, leaving an eerie, vacuum-like quality to the circle.

My pulse continued to race even as I drew in several calming breaths. I didn't want to be in that circle. I didn't want to be drawn into whatever horror remained hidden beneath the other cages. I wanted to be back in Charleston with nothing more pressing on my mind than my next blog update.

But I didn't retreat because I knew from experience I couldn't run away from my gift. The days of pretending that ghosts didn't exist were long behind me as were the rules that had once protected me. I had entered a new phase of my life, accepting if not embracing who I was and what I was meant to be.

So I emptied my mind to see if anything of the dead woman's last moments drifted in.

Nothing came to me. It was as if a deliberate barrier had been erected to block whatever emotions or memories that might have remained. I'd never felt anything like it. The obstruction was cold and impenetrable. An unscalable wall of darkness.

As I knelt in the weeds, eyes closed in supreme concentration, I began to tremble even harder. The suspicion that a supernatural force had played a role in the young woman's demise terrified me because no normal police officer or investigator would be equipped to track such a culprit. Not even Devlin.

And I very much feared that was why I had been summoned.

Three

Despite the isolation of that forlorn circle, the area surrounding Seven Gates Cemetery was located just inside the city limits and, therefore, fell under the jurisdiction of the Ascension Police Department rather than the Beaufort County Sheriff's Office.

The dispatcher had promised to send a squad car straightaway, and while I waited for the first responders, I busied myself taking photos with my phone. I was careful to tread only where I'd stepped before so as not to further taint what was clearly a crime scene. I wanted to get shots of the other cages, but I didn't think it a good idea to tramp through the weeds before the authorities had conducted a thorough search.

All the while I worked, I remained intensely aware of the watcher in the woods. The sensation of that hidden stare stayed with me even as I immersed myself in the scene, letting my gaze wander over the metal cages, committing to memory details of the devices so that I could later sort through my photographs and research materials for a similar design.

I'd read about a pair of caged graves located in

an old cemetery in Pennsylvania, but those were the only mortsafes I knew of in North America. Their size and weight made them unwieldy to transport so finding them in such a remote location was especially puzzling considering that body snatching was no longer a threat.

How and why had they ended up in this clearing? What other purpose might they have served? Might *still* serve?

The questions droned on as I anxiously waited for the police. The authorities didn't rush to the scene with sirens blaring as I had imagined they would after my descriptive and rather breathless phone call. Instead, a good half hour after I'd reported the find, I heard the slamming of car doors out on Cemetery Road, and then a few minutes later two uniformed officers appeared on the trail, ambling along as if out for an afternoon stroll.

Both stopped short when they spotted me. None of us said a word and the silence stretched until I pointed toward the second mortsafe.

Their gazes followed my finger. They were young officers, perhaps inexperienced in dealing with such a strange and disturbing scene. I detected a collective hesitation before they approached the caged grave. They spent several minutes in quiet conversation as they observed the tiny hands from various angles in much the same way that I had. And then they made phone calls.

After a bit, one of the cops came over and introduced himself as Tom Malloy. He looked to be in his midtwenties, still fresh-faced and earnest with a smattering of freckles across his nose and blue eyes that crinkled appealingly at the corners. He touched a finger to the brim of his hat and gave a slight nod. "Miss."

I nodded back as I folded my arms and then unfolded them because I thought the stance made me look defensive.

"I take it you're the one who called this in," he said. "Amelia Gray?"

"Yes, that's right."

His gaze narrowed as he nodded to the scratch on my face. "What happened there?"

I lifted a hand to the stinging flesh and shrugged. "A thorn caught me."

He glanced back at the hands in the cage and then at me, giving me a thorough scrutiny before taking out his notebook. I could see how the beading blood on a fresh wound might give him pause under the circumstances.

"Let's take care of the busywork first," he said pleasantly enough as he jotted my name on a blank page. "What's the best number to reach you?"

I gave him my cell number and answered a few more rudimentary questions before recounting to him how I'd come upon the cages. I told him everything I could remember except for the part about being summoned by the presence in the woods. I explained that away by saying I'd taken a walk to work out the kinks after hours of bending over the headstones.

"You're from Charleston, you say?" His gaze

flicked over me again and I tried not to flinch at his prolonged appraisal.

"Yes, but I've been staying in Ascension since the end of May. I'm in the process of restoring Seven Gates Cemetery."

He looked surprised. "You've been working here all summer? I don't recall seeing you around."

"I only get into town once or twice a week. The cemetery occupies most of my time. It was in really bad shape when I first started."

"You work alone?"

"Yes. I've put out feelers for local help, but I haven't had much luck. Just a couple of college kids early in the season, but they didn't last long." I bit my lip and turned away with a frown. It wasn't like me to ramble or volunteer more information than was requested. Evidently, the discovery of the mortsafes and the sight of those hands had left me more shaken than I realized.

"Can't say I'm surprised about the lack of local help," the officer said politely. "There's a lot of superstition surrounding that old church and cemetery."

"Such as?"

He shrugged. "The usual stuff. Both have been abandoned for as long as I can remember. Kids used to hang out in the ruins late at night after drinking beer and smoking weed, but I don't think anyone goes there any more. Not after..."

"Not after what?" I prompted.

He glanced down at his notes. "Not after the place got so overgrown. Too many snakes and God knows what else lurking in the bushes. It's too bad, really. The cemetery used to be beautiful."

"It will be again."

He turned back to the circle, his gaze moving around the cages. "I've lived here my whole life. Grew up in a house not five miles from where we're standing. I thought I knew this area like the back of my hand, but I sure never knew these things were here. Have you ever come across anything like them before?"

"Not around here. Mortsafes were mostly used in Europe."

"Mortsafes?" I saw him shiver.

"They kept grave robbers from digging up fresh remains to sell to medical schools."

His expression turned grim as he trained his gaze upon me. "Looks like they were used here to keep something *in*."

I'd thought of that, as well, of course, but I didn't comment.

"Will you be around this afternoon?" he asked. "We may have more questions once we get her out of the ground."

"I'll be working in the cemetery. I never leave before sundown."

He gave a vague nod as he went back to his partner. I hung around watching them. They didn't seem to mind. Maybe they were glad for the company. The place seemed more desolate than ever and the trill of the loon made us all turn anxiously toward the marsh. I couldn't help remembering the officer's broken thought: *Not after...*

Not after what?

The palmettos rustled in a mild breeze. An insect droned in my ear. And from the woods, that presence still watched me.

Who are you? I wondered. *What are you?*

Still no answer.

For the next several minutes, the cops huddled over the second mortsafe, talking in low tones and making a few notes until more personnel arrived on the scene, including a plainclothes detective, a forensic team and the Beaufort County coroner.

A brief discussion ensued about possible ownership of the land and how best to open the cage so the body could be removed. That dilemma brought Officer Malloy back over to me.

"Who hired you to restore the cemetery?"

"It was a joint effort by some of the families and a local historical society," I told him.

"Do you have a contact person?"

"Annalee Nash."

A brow shot up. "Annalee Nash?"

"Yes, why? Do you know her?"

"Everybody knows Annalee. I guess I'm just a little surprised to hear she's involved with that cemetery."

"Why wouldn't she be? She's secretary of the local historical society."

"I don't keep up with that sort of thing. How did the two of you meet?"

"She first contacted me through my website and we've kept in touch ever since. She's the one who made sure all the permits were in order so there wouldn't be any delays once we signed the contract."

He slapped at a mosquito on the side of his neck. "I don't suppose she ever mentioned anything about ownership of the property adjoining the cemetery?"

"This property, you mean? No, she didn't. As I understand it, Seven Gates is located on public land, but nothing I've found in the archives suggests these graves are connected to the cemetery."

"They look like they've been here a long time," he said.

"I'm guessing the mortsafes are only a few decades old, but the dirt underneath the first cage is sunken, which could indicate that the burials are older. If the original graves are over a hundred years old, the state archaeologist would have jurisdiction regardless of property ownership."

The detective came up just then, and after we were introduced, I repeated everything that I'd told Officer Malloy.

Detective Lucien Kendrick looked to be in his early thirties, a man of indeterminate ethnicity with light brown skin and topaz-colored eyes that tilted exotically at the corners. The intensity of his scrutiny took me aback. Not since my first encounter with Devlin had I experienced such an unsettling focus. Even when he addressed Officer Malloy, Kendrick's gaze remained hard upon me until I had to fight the urge to take a step back from him.

He was just shy of six feet, lean and sinewy. By no means a large man, but his bearing gave him an air of toughness and invincibility. I didn't consider him handsome in the traditional sense of the word, but he was one of the most striking men I'd ever met, from the strange color of his eyes to the razor sharpness of his cheekbones.

His attire was casual, but his jacket and boots were of good quality. Not custom like Devlin's wardrobe, but certainly several cuts above what one might expect from a small-town police detective. Sometime in the not too distant past, his left eyebrow had been pierced. I could still see the tiny holes and, once noticed, I started to search for other bits of unconventionality. The tattooed skull on the back of his hand. The raised scar tissue of a brand on the side of his neck. He was an enigmatic man, one who undoubtedly marched to his own drummer, and I found him fascinating in the way one might admire the coil of a cobra or the crouch of a tiger.

Nonconformity aside, my heightened senses warned me that he was no ordinary "cop."

"You say you've been working here since the end of May." His voice was deep and lilting with the barest hint of an accent that I couldn't place. But the nagging familiarity of some of his inflections made me curious about his background. Where had he come from and what had brought him to this part of the world? And how had he ended up as a detective with the Ascension Police Department?

"Miss Gray?"

I started at the sound of my name, dragging my focus from the brand snaking up over his shirt collar to lock gazes with him. "I'm sorry. What was the question?"

His gaze zeroed in on my cheek. "Are you all right?"

"What? Oh, that. It's just a scratch. A hazard of my profession, I'm afraid."

"I know all about those," he murmured. "You should put something on it. You don't want to risk infection."

I lifted my head in a small act of defiance. The detective's caution had sounded strangely like a threat. Which was absurd, of course, and overly defensive. "I'll take care of it later. Right now, I'd rather answer all your questions and be on my way."

He nodded, his gaze cool and assessing. "I understand you've been working in the cemetery since late May."

"Yes, that's right."

"What time do you usually get to work in the morning?"

"Just after sunrise."

"That early every day?"

"I like to get the more strenuous tasks accomplished before the heat of the day sets in."

"That would put your arrival this morning around six-thirty, correct?" Another quirk of his eyebrow, another bold stare.

I swallowed hard. "Thereabouts."

"You didn't notice any suspicious activity? Dogs barking? Strange vehicles parked on the side of the road? Anybody going into or coming out of these woods?" He searched my face. "Anything at all unusual?"

"No, nothing. There's very little traffic on Cemetery Road, especially at that hour. If there had been anyone about, I'm certain I would have noticed. I haven't seen anyone all day except for a group of kids with fishing poles and crab traps heading toward the marsh."

He paused as if carefully evaluating everything I'd told him. "So you worked in the cemetery until around three when you decided to take a walk. I'm surprised. That's generally when the heat of the day sets in," he said, throwing my own words back at me. "Why not rest in the shade?"

"I'd been kneeling and bending for hours cleaning headstones. I needed to work out the kinks." The half-truth slipped out easily because I'd spent a lifetime keeping secrets. Concealment and discretion had become second nature to me.

"And the reason you came all the way back here? The trail from the cemetery is rugged and overgrown. Doesn't look like anyone's been this way in years." His gaze slid to the cages. "Until recently, of course."

I gave another shrug. "No particular reason. I just like exploring new places."

"Well, I guess that was a lucky break for us. What can you tell me about these cages?"

There was an odd note in his voice that set off another alarm. My guard came up instantly and now I did take a step back from him as I turned toward the circle. "They're called mortsafes. As I explained to Officer Malloy, such devices are uncommon in this part of the world. In fact, I've only ever seen similar cages in Edinburgh, Scotland."

"And yet here they are, a dozen of them in Ascension, South Carolina."

"As I said, it's an unusual find."

Our gazes collided once more before he glanced away. He knew something about the mortsafes, I thought. Maybe not the ones in the circle, but he'd seen something like them before, I was certain of it.

I tried to empty my mind again, but before I could absorb any of the detective's thoughts or emotions, he spun back to face me as if sensing my tentative probe. For a split second only, I heard the chanting in the woods. That same indistinguishable word repeated over and over. I cocked my head, trying to decipher the mantra, but the sound was either too far away or buried too deep in Kendrick's memory.

I resisted the urge to try and push past his defenses. For some reason, I felt it important that I not give that particular ability away to him.

"This is a small town so word tends to travel fast," he said. "You can expect a lot of gawkers over the next few days. Since the quickest and easiest way to get a look at those cages is through the cemetery, you'll need to keep the gates locked."

"I will."

Shadows crisscrossed over us as more vultures circled. I didn't glance skyward, but instead put a hand to my eyes as I scanned the treetops where the sun would soon start to slide.

Kendrick handed me a card. "You think of anything else, here's my number. Call any time, day or night. Whatever happened here..." His gaze lifted, tracking the buzzards. "I don't like the feel of it."

"It's disturbing," I agreed. Beyond disturbing. It was the stuff of nightmares. Arms rising up out of a fresh grave. Hands clinging to the locked grid of a mortsafe that was designed to keep grave robbers out, not the dead in.

"We'll begin the excavation once we get the cage opened. It won't be pleasant," he warned as he nodded to the trail behind me. "You may want to head back up to the cemetery before we get started."

"Don't worry about me. I used to work for the state archaeologist's office in Columbia. We were sometimes called in to move whole cemeteries. If there are older remains beneath the victim, it's very important to preserve the integrity of the original grave site."

"Are you offering your services?"

"I wouldn't be so presumptuous," I said, once again startled by the intensity of his focus. I suddenly realized that I could no longer sense the presence in the woods and I had to wonder if Detective Kendrick had somehow scared away the watcher. The notion that he possessed that kind of power was hardly reassuring. "I recommend you call in the state archaeologist," I rushed to add. "Her name is Temple Lee. If she doesn't have time to come herself, she can suggest someone locally to assist you."

"I've heard the name," Kendrick said. "She was on the news during those Charleston excavations sometime back. As I recall, a torture chamber was uncovered beneath a mausoleum in an old cemetery connected to Emerson University."

His expression never wavered but I knew that he

was gauging my response. Either he'd recognized my name or he'd done his research on the way to the scene.

"You're referring to Oak Grove Cemetery," I said easily. "I was involved with that case, as well. I'd just been commissioned to restore the cemetery when the first body was found."

His gaze moved over my features, searching my eyes, my pulse points, the corners of my mouth for a flicker or twitch or some other guilty tell. I didn't so much as flinch. If I could hold myself steady in the presence of ghosts, I could surely keep my cool with Detective Kendrick.

"Seems an odd coincidence. Another body found buried in an old grave near a cemetery you've been hired to restore." His accent had vanished in the cool delivery of what I considered an accusation.

"I can see how you'd think so, but it was pure chance that I decided to take a walk down here to stretch my cramped muscles. And if I'd never left the cemetery, the body and those cages may have remained undiscovered for decades."

"You don't have any immediate plans to leave town." It wasn't a question.

"No, of course not. I have several more weeks of work left in Seven Gates."

"Where are you staying?"

"I've rented a small house near the cemetery. Annalee Nash is my landlady."

"Annalee Nash." A frown flitted across his brow. "I understand she's the one who hired you for the restoration."

"She is. The house I'm renting from her is just down the road a quarter of a mile or so. It's the white one on the right."

"I know the place well. Screened porches, lots of fruit trees. A tire swing in the yard." He hesitated. "Used to be an old storage shed behind the orchard."

"It's still there," I told him.

"If you've been here all summer, I'm guessing you've heard the rumors about that place."

"What rumors?"

Before he could answer, one of the officers called over to him. "Hey, Detective! The locksmith just pulled up. Malloy's headed up there now to show him the way back."

Kendrick nodded and started to return to the grave, but before I could stop myself, I reached out and grasped his arm. "What rumors?" I asked, my voice far more breathless than I would have liked.

Another hesitation. "It's probably just talk. Nothing for you to worry about."

Then why had he brought it up?

I pulled my hand away, embarrassed by the contact.

His eyes glinted darkly. "I'll take your advice and give the state archaeologist a call. But regardless of her schedule, we can't wait to recover the body. I don't know how long the weather will hold and the sooner we get her out of the ground, the sooner we can get an ID. Maybe you'll be able to help us with that."

"I wouldn't count on it. I don't know many people in town. Just Annalee and a couple of college kids I hired early on. As I told Officer Malloy, they didn't last long."

"You fired them?"

"No, they left of their own accord. Cemetery restoration is backbreaking work."

"Nevertheless, I'll need their names and a way to reach them if you have it."

"I'll make sure to get you their information, but I can't imagine they had anything to do with this."

"It's just routine. I'll be in touch," he promised as he strode off to join the others.

I stared after him for a moment, more shaken by our encounter than I could logically explain. Perhaps it was the penetrating quality of those peculiar eyes or the notion that he might know more about me than he'd let on. That he might even know about those cages and the watcher in the woods. Whatever the reason for my disquiet, I had no intention of ignoring my instincts about Detective Lucien Kendrick.

A little while later, the chatter around the graves rose as the locksmith finally arrived. He was a wiry, ponytailed man named Martin Stark. Unlike the young police officers first on the scene, Stark displayed not the slightest hesitation as he strode through the grass toward the graves. I admired his economy of words and motions even as something about his impervious approach tripped an alarm bell. If the hands surprised or repulsed him, he didn't let on. Maybe he'd seen worse during the course of his career, but there was something about him that bothered me. A kind of latent excitement that made me search his face in much the same way that Kendrick had scrutinized mine.

Despite my wariness, I edged closer so that I could hear what Stark had to say about the cages.

"...an owl's head," I heard him explain.

"What's the significance of that?" Kendrick asked.

"Most of the locks with these emblems were manufactured before the turn of the last century, but this one is newer. Back in the late nineties, the company resurrected the design to commemorate their centennial. Someone must have bought up a supply and hung on to them. They're good locks," he added. "Hardened steel body and a tubular key cylinder. Difficult to pick, but I've yet to come across a padlock of any kind that couldn't be opened with bolt cutters or a drill."

"You brought the necessary tools?" Kendrick asked him.

"Of course. Just let me know when you're ready." He was still talking to Kendrick, but suddenly his gaze vectored in on me, as though he'd been aware of my presence the whole time. His unblinking stare seemed oddly hostile and I glanced away, keeping my gaze focused on the caged grave.

By this time, a small army of personnel had gathered. More discussion ensued and a number of phone calls were made. After another half hour of inactivity, I finally gave up and went back to the cemetery to finish my workday.

As I went about the usual chores, I tried not to think about those delicate hands clinging to the grate or that unseen presence watching from the woods. I did my best to tune out the voices drifting up from the clearing.

And hours later as I lay awake in the hammock, my dog, Angus, curled up nearby, I even managed to convince myself the remains inside that caged grave had nothing to do with me. Nor did Detective Kendrick. I would finish my job in Seven Gates Cemetery, return to Charleston to prepare for my next restoration and that would be that.

But any hope I'd had of escaping unscathed vanished the next day when I caught sight of an old nemesis lurking in the shadows of the church ruins.

Four

It was midmorning and I'd already been cleaning headstones for hours. The police had arrived sometime earlier to search the area surrounding the mortsafes. Other than an occasional shout as they scoured the woods, the day had been quiet. I was surprised that the curious hadn't come yet, but maybe word was just now getting out about the murder. In any case, I welcomed the solitude because I had a lot on my mind. I did not welcome Darius Goodwine.

He stood so deeply in the shade of the church ruins that I thought at first I had imagined him. After a restless night, perhaps exhaustion and my subconscious had decided to play a cruel trick on me. The longer I stared, though, the more substantial he became, like a fully manifested ghost.

But Darius Goodwine was no ghost, even though there was a fantastical element to his sudden appearance. He seemed so dreamlike against the backdrop of crumbling brick arches that I found myself biting down hard on my bottom lip to make certain I was fully awake.

Nearly two years had passed since our last

living-world encounter, and in the ensuing months I'd prayed that I would never see him again. I'd hoped he wouldn't come back to collect on the bargain that I'd foolishly and desperately struck with him. At the time, my only concern had been to save Devlin's life, but Darius Goodwine was not the type of man who granted altruistic favors. I'd always known there would be a price to pay for bringing Devlin back from the other side. Now, as I felt Darius's gaze upon me, I shuddered to think what dark compensation he'd come to extract.

A breeze blew across the graves, billowing his loose clothing. Where his shirt parted, I could see an amulet resting in the hollow of his chest and another hanging from a leather cord wound around his wrist. He was a very tall man, nearly six and a half feet. His height alone commanded attention, but it was the magnetic quality of his presence that kept my gaze riveted.

Devlin had once insisted that Darius Goodwine's ability to manipulate and control his followers stemmed from the power of suggestion rather than the magic he claimed to have divined from his time studying with a powerful shaman in Africa. But Devlin was wrong. I'd learned the hard way that Darius Goodwine not only had the ability to cross over to the other side and converse with the dead, but he could also enter the dreams of the living and influence their thoughts.

Once a respected professor of ethnobotony, he'd let his greed and obsession transform him from healer to *tagati*, a dangerous witch doctor who used his knowledge and power to bring harm to others. I knew better than to underestimate him. Unlike Detective Kendrick, whose character I had yet to discern, I was all too aware of Darius Goodwine's treachery and so I steeled myself against his insidious magnetism.

Turning back to the headstone, I continued to scrape away at the layers of moss and lichen while tracking him from my periphery as he wove his way through the headstones. Despite his height, he moved with an uncanny grace. If I hadn't known he was a flesh-and-blood man, I might still have thought him a specter, so ephemeral and floating was his presence.

As he neared, a faint trace of ozone wafted on the breeze, leaving me to wonder if a sudden storm had sprung up or if the scent came from the man himself. A moment earlier, the day had been clear and sunny, but now a shadow fell across the landscape. I shivered in the premature twilight, keeping my gaze averted because I didn't dare look up into those hypnotic eyes.

"Amelia Gray." Despite his cultured manner of speaking, there was something in the low timber of his voice that reminded me of a tribal drumbeat. *Amelia Gray. Amelia Gray. Amelia Gray.* "It's been a while since last we met."

I inclined my head slightly, slanting a glance up through my lashes into those mesmeric eyes for only a split second before shifting my gaze to the talisman that hung around his throat. It was made of some thin metal, intricately engraved with hieroglyphics. I stared at it for a very long time. So long, in fact, that I lost track of the moments ticking by. I suddenly felt very disoriented, as if I had become lost once more in a dream of Darius Goodwine's making.

I didn't try to empty my thoughts to allow his emotions to enter. I was too afraid to trifle with such a cunning mind. So instead I focused on strengthening my defenses and on keeping *him* out of *my* head. I visualized a door slamming shut as I chanced another glance at his arresting visage. His lips curled in amusement, but I saw something that might have been surprise—or annoyance—flicker in his eyes, leaving me with a momentary triumph.

Boldly, I lifted my chin and met his gaze. "The last I heard, you were in Africa. What brings you to Seven Gates Cemetery?"

"I've come to see you, naturally."

There was nothing natural about his presence or his timing, I felt certain. "Why?"

"All in good time. We have some catching up to do first."

I scowled up at him. "How did you know where to find me?"

"Your powers have grown stronger since our last encounter. They leave a trail."

Was that admiration I heard in his voice? A touch of wonder, even?

I drew myself up short as I recognized another of his tactics. I wouldn't allow myself to be seduced into a false sense of security by the likes of Darius Goodwine.

"What kind of trail?" I asked.

"They create a disturbance that might best be compared to the wake of a ship or the contrail of a jet. Easy to follow if one knows how and where to look."

I resisted the urge to glance over my shoulder. The notion that the changes inside me had left an astral pathway that could lead a dangerous witch doctor straight to my door was more than a little troubling. "Do the police know you're back in the country?"

The dark eyes glinted. "If by police you mean John Devlin, does it matter? Now that you're no longer together, he's of no consequence to either of us."

"How did…" I cut myself off before admitting my estrangement from Devlin. The last thing I wanted was to divulge my innermost pain to a predator in search of a weakness. "How did you come to that conclusion?"

"I've known about it ever since it happened. Word travels fast, even in deepest, darkest Africa." Another of those mocking pauses. "Was the separation your idea or his? I'm assuming it was his."

My chin came up once more. "That's none of your concern."

"Isn't it?"

The intensity of his stare drew a deep shiver, and despite my considerable resistance, my own gaze slid back and locked on to his. A breeze drifted across the graves, bringing another draft of ozone and something spicy and exotic, like the perfume of a rare flower. I had a sudden vision of a moonlit garden filled with orchids and songbirds. A seductive oasis where untold dangers lurked in the shadowy recesses. That was what I saw when I looked into Darius Goodwine's eyes.

I quickly glanced away. "I'm not going to discuss Devlin with you, of all people."

He laughed softly. "I admire your loyalty, displaced though it may be."

"Meaning?"

"You don't know the man you've put on a pedestal as well as you think. Few people know the real John Devlin."

"And you're one of them, I suppose."

"I know him better than most. We're far more alike than he would ever dare acknowledge."

"That's not true," I said coolly. "The two of you are nothing alike."

Another flash of those white, white teeth. "To the contrary, I would suggest that the only real difference between us is this—I embrace who I am and what I'm meant to be while John Devlin is still trying to run away from his true nature."

He was goading me and I knew it, yet I found myself asking, "And just what is his true nature, according to you?"

"Have you never wondered why a man who professes nothing but disdain for the unknown was so inexorably drawn to someone as mystical and mysterious as my cousin, Mariama? Her great beauty aside, of course. I'm sure he gave you any number of reasons for the attraction. He enjoyed flaunting her exoticness in the face of his grandfather's rigid conformity. Or perhaps he told you that my influence changed and corrupted her. The woman capable of such dark deeds at the end of her life was not the same woman he fell in love with."

Devlin had, in fact, confided both motivations, but I wasn't about to betray him to a man we both considered an enemy.

Darius continued to study me. He cocked his head slightly, as if something puzzled him. "You must also have wondered about the medallion he wears around his neck. Why would a man who claims to have turned his back on the trappings and privileges of his upbringing cling to an emblem that epitomizes wealth and greed? But then, I suppose it's hardly surprising. Men of his ilk have always had an affinity for secret societies, particularly those that protect and promote the status quo. John Devlin is no exception."

I didn't try to defend Devlin this time because there was an uncomfortable truth in Darius's words. I had wondered about those very things. I'd fretted over Devlin's relationship with Mariama ever since we'd first met and I'd contemplated his affiliation with the nefarious Order of the Coffin and the Claw on many a sleepless night. But I found it hard to admit, even to myself, that the darkness in Devlin and those mysterious gaps in his past still worried me.

Darius Goodwine had wasted no time in homing in on those niggling misgivings.

He knelt and picked up a stick, using the pointed end to trace the shadow of a gravestone in the dirt. I watched, mesmerized by his languid movements. His fingers were long and tapered like those of an artist and his nails were meticulous, bringing to mind the dirt-and-blood-encrusted nails of the victim.

Was that why he had come? I wondered. Did he know something about the dead woman? About her murder? Should I shout for the authorities? They were still combing the woods and the clearing. Too far away to hear anything other than a scream.

"The Order of the Coffin and the Claw." Darius pronounced each word with derisive exaggeration as he drew a snake wrapped around a claw in the dirt.

I hardened my tone. "Why are we talking about the Order of the Coffin and the Claw or even Devlin for that matter? Why don't you just tell me why you're really here? What do you want?"

"You made an important discovery yesterday. You've no idea how important. In order to deal with the consequences, you must understand the deep roots and entangled affiliations of those involved."

"By discovery, you mean the caged graves?" I slid a hand to my chest, tracing the outline of the key resting beneath my shirt. "How do you know about those?"

He smiled. "Have you forgotten that I have eyes and ears everywhere?"

"Even in the Ascension Police Department?"

"Everywhere."

"Even on the other side?"

"*Every*where."

"What do you know about those cages? About the victim?" I demanded.

"I know she won't be the last to die unless you unmask her killer."

I stared at him in shock. "Unmask her killer? How am I supposed to do that?"

"Think back." His voice dropped to a silky murmur, soothing and hypnotic. "In all your years of research and cemetery work, surely you've come across references to other secret societies. Some, perhaps, with close alliances to the Order of the Coffin and the Claw. Have you never heard of a group called the Eternal Brotherhood of Resurrectionists?"

I frowned at the unfamiliar name. "No. But I know that body snatchers for hire in the early nineteenth century were called resurrectionists."

"That was in Europe," he said. "Here in the Lowcountry there was a more literal meaning—those who raise the dead."

A shudder rocked through me. *Those who raise the dead.* What did he mean by that?

He continued to scribble in the dirt with the end of the stick. "For generations, the Order of the Coffin and the Claw provided men of a certain class and breeding—men like Devlin and his forefathers— protection from their indiscretions and unsavory appetites, but the Brotherhood promised them immortality."

"How?" The flesh on the back of my arm crawled and I looked down to find a corpse beetle inching toward my wrist. Repulsed, I tried to flick the insect into the grass, but the pincers dug into my skin and clung. I glanced across the grave where Darius had drawn a likeness of the beetle in the dirt. He wiped away the image with the palm of his hand and the one on my arm disappeared.

For the first time since his arrival, I felt the shock of real fear. Darius Goodwine was up to his old tricks and everything inside me warned of imminent danger. I wanted to rise and put more distance than a grave between us, but my limbs suddenly felt weighted.

He was in control now, I realized. I could protect myself to a certain extent, but he was clever and cunning and knew too many ways around my defenses. I'd insisted that I wouldn't discuss Devlin, and yet that was exactly what we'd done for almost the entirety of his visit. I'd convinced myself that I could keep him out of my head, but he'd slithered underneath the slammed door and manipulated my perception.

No more than a moment had passed since I'd glanced at the ground, but Darius had already etched another symbol. Where he'd wiped clean the rendering of the beetle, he'd drawn three linked spirals. I'd seen a variation of the emblem before, but there was something sinister about his depiction.

"Do you recognize it?" he asked, still in that same numbing voice.

"It's a Celtic triskele. The spiral of life."

"A triskele, yes, but the origin isn't Celtic. The symbol dates all the way back to the Egyptians. Since the beginning of time, the concept of triplism has taken many forms in many different cultures. Maiden, mother, crone. Land, sea, sky. The Trinity. For the Resurrectionists, the interlocking spirals represented birth, death and resurrection. You're familiar with the concept of a dual soul?"

"Yes. According to some beliefs, the soul and spirit divide upon death. The soul leaves the body and transcends its earthly bounds, but the spirit lingers to interfere in the lives of the living. That's why graves in Gullah cemeteries are sprinkled with white sand. Sometimes whole graveyards are covered in order to keep the dead from coming back as *bakulu*."

"You have it partially right." The stick continued to move in the dirt even though Darius's gaze never left me. "When the final breath is drawn, the soul is immediately aware of death and transcends. But the spirit lingers in the body, not to interfere in the lives of the living as you suggest, but because it isn't yet conscious of death. While the spirit still resides inside the deceased, transference may be attained."

"Transference?"

"A powerful spell by which the spirit can be harvested from the dead and transplanted into the body of a living host."

"You mean possession." My voice grew heavy with dread as I flashed back to what I'd witnessed and experienced in Kroll Cemetery.

"It may be easier to think of it this way," Darius said. "Possession is more of a hostile takeover, but transference is a peaceful merger with a willing vessel. The essence of the dead is allowed to exist in the living host, thus attaining immortality."

"This is all very fascinating," I said, with far more bravado than I felt. "But I still don't understand what any of it has to do with me." I drew my hand away from my neck and found another beetle clinging to my flesh. I flicked the insect to the ground where it scurried into one of the spirals. The symbol disappeared, leaving the poor beetle exposed in the dirt. When I looked again, I saw that the insect was nothing more than a pebble.

"Nothing is as it seems," Darius warned. "The Resurrectionists are skilled in deception and trickery, as are their enemy, the *Congé*." He pronounced the word *kän-zhā*.

"Who are they?" I asked.

"Zealots who believe it their mission to stamp out that which they do not understand. Someone with your gift and abilities would be wise to steer clear of them."

The Resurrectionists. The *Congé*. It was all very much Greek to me. But his voice was so honeyed and persuasive, I found myself nodding in agreement even though I hadn't a clue what he meant. I realized that he had once again found a way through my defenses and I tried to summon my resistance as I fought off the seductive lethargy of his hypnosis.

"Do you understand now why you were summoned?" He peered into my eyes, into my soul.

"I don't understand any of this," I said.

"You were summoned because you are the only one with enough power to end this."

My heart thudded in agitation because I instinctively knew that what he said was true. I might not be familiar with the players or the particulars. I might only understand a sliver of his convoluted missive, but I'd known from the moment I entered the caged grave circle and experienced that strange vacuum that I had been called to this place for a purpose. My gift was needed to track an uncanny killer. Yet I continued to resist because a part of me still wanted to believe that I could control my own destiny.

I mustered up a flimsy argument even though my fate was undoubtedly sealed. "You do realize what you're asking of me, don't you? Trying to uncover a murderer could get me killed. At the very least, I could be arrested for interfering in an official investigation. The authorities won't take kindly to me poking my nose into places it doesn't belong. I have to live here until I finish the restoration so I'd rather not get on Detective Kendrick's bad side."

Darius's head came up and I saw a shadow move through his eyes. "*Lucien* Kendrick?"

His reaction startled me. "Yes, do you know him?"

"Our paths have crossed," Darius said darkly as his gaze darted toward the woods. "From what I've heard about him, he is a ruthless and relentless investigator."

"Then why not let him do his job?"

"You're still asking the wrong questions," he said with a rare spark of impatience. "Like your wretched John Devlin, you're still trying to run away from who you are and what you're meant to be."

"Or maybe I just don't trust you," I said with a scowl. "If you know anything about that woman's murder, you should go to the police yourself, no matter your history with Detective Kendrick."

"For any number of reasons, I can't get involved.

It would be better for both of us if no one finds out that we've talked."

"That hardly instills me with confidence," I said, still with that forced bravado. "Give me one compelling reason why I should believe you, let alone help you."

I expected him to remind me of the bargain we'd struck at Devlin's deathbed, but instead he said, "The key you wear around your neck belonged to your great-grandmother, did it not?"

My hand flew again to my chest where the key was still concealed by my shirt. "How did…"

"The key is special," he said. "Blessed by a divine hand. Like hallowed ground, it offers a temporary reprieve from the ghosts. But they're irresistibly drawn to the light inside you so they'll keep coming back, more and more, until you no longer have the means or the fortitude to protect yourself. You'll likely suffer the same fate as your great-grandmother unless…" He trailed away tantalizingly.

"Unless…what?" I held my breath.

"There is another key, a lost key. A key that would lock the door to the dead world forever. Think of what that would mean. No dread of twilight, no fear of ghostly visitations, no riddles of the dead to solve. Eventually, your gift would wither like one of your cemeteries and your calling would become nothing more than a distant memory."

His words drew an irresistible picture, one that I had been painting in my head ever since the night Devlin had stepped out of the mist to confront me. Darius Goodwine had tapped into my innermost dreams, my deepest desires, and I would be a fool to fall for his manipulations.

But he wasn't the only one who had spoken of the lost key. I had known of its possible existence since my visit to Kroll Cemetery. If the key really could lock the door to the dead world forever, how far was I willing to go to find it? What risks would I take to possess it?

"How do I know the key is even real?" I asked. "Or that you can help me find it?"

He said nothing as he continued to scrawl in the dirt. I glanced down to see a series of numbers in the same formation—I could have sworn—as the ones my great-grandmother had painstakingly scribbled on the walls of her sanctuary. I still had no idea what they meant, but I'd wondered for over a year if they were positions on a map. Ethereal coordinates that could lead me to the location of the lost key, either here or on the other side.

My adrenaline surged at the notion, but before I had time to commit the arrangement to memory, Darius erased the numbers with the palm of his hand.

I glanced at him with a gasp. "Why did you do that?"

"Unmask the killer," he said. "And I'll help you find your great-grandmother's key."

He rose gracefully and I followed, lifting my gaze to take in his full height. He towered over me by almost a foot, and for a moment I stood with tilted head, studying his remarkable features—the prominent nose, the magnetic eyes, the full, sensuous lips that parted slightly as he became aware of my survey.

He lifted a hand and beckoned. I took a reluctant step toward him as though I were a marionette responding to a puppeteer's commands. I caught myself and turned away from him. His hold on me diminished, but before I could celebrate another small victory, I realized my freedom hadn't come from my own strength and resolve, but from Darius's lack of focus.

Something in the woods had caught his attention. He knew something lurked in the shadows, hiding among the trees. Like me, like Detective Kendrick, he could sense a presence.

Shifting my gaze to the woods, I emptied my mind once again, trying to detect a hint or a clue of the lurker's true nature. The barrier came up once more. Whatever skulked in those woods was unlike anything I'd ever come up against.

"You feel it, too," I said, but Darius didn't answer. His gaze remained fastened on the trees. He lifted a hand to trace a symbol in the air as he muttered something in a language I didn't understand.

Out over the sea, clouds gathered and I heard a rumble of thunder in the distance. As my eyes adjusted to the aberrant twilight of the woods, I saw something white and nimble darting among the tree trunks.

My breath quickened as I reached for Rose's key. As I lifted the talisman from my shirt, Darius's attention shifted again. He was still looking at the woods, but I could feel a tingle across my scalp, as though one of his beetles had buried itself in my hair.

"What's out there?" I whispered.

He lifted a hand, trailing blue sparks. "Tread carefully," he said. "And trust no one."

Five

"Miss Gray? Amelia? Are you all right?"

The voice had a distant, tinny quality as though someone were calling up to me from the bottom of a very deep well. I wanted to respond, but at the moment I was too busy fighting my way out of a no-man's-land of cobwebs and mist.

I shook myself slightly and the fog thinned. I was still in the cemetery kneeling beside a gravestone, a bucket of water before me and a soft bristle brush in my hand. The inscription carved into the face of the marker was starting to peek through the grime, but for the life of me, I couldn't remember scrubbing the surface.

I glanced skyward where the sun still hovered in virtually the same position as when I'd last checked. Very little time had elapsed, but those lost moments frightened me because I couldn't recall anything beyond my conversation with Darius Goodwine.

Darius!

Quickly, I scanned the graveyard and then peered into the shadowy arches of the ruins. Was he there, hiding behind those ancient brick walls so as not to be discovered by Detective Kendrick?

Or had he even been here at all?

I shivered in the heat as more and more of our conversation came back to me. Whether the discussion had taken place in the cemetery or inside my head, I couldn't be certain, but I had no doubt Darius Goodwine had paid me a visit. I hadn't imagined our encounter. I hadn't made up his proposition. His parting warning still echoed: *tread carefully and trust no one.*

An icy breath blew down my collar as my gaze fastened onto Detective Kendrick's. *It would be better for both of us if no one finds out that we've talked.*

Kendrick canted his head, looking puzzled. "Can you hear me?"

"Yes."

"Why didn't you answer me just now?"

"I'm sorry. I was… I guess I was lost in thought."

He scowled down at me. "Are you all right?"

"Yes, why?"

"You look flushed. Maybe you need to get out of the sun for a while, have something cold to drink." He nodded to the grove of cottonwoods near the entrance. "Is that your cooler?"

"Yes."

"Let's move over there and talk." He offered his hand, but I pretended not to notice as I hurriedly rose and peeled off my work gloves.

His focus was still so intense that I felt as if I had stripped off a good deal more than the gloves.

It wasn't a pleasant sensation, given that he was a complete stranger and I still didn't trust him.

I tried to ignore the unwelcome tingle, assuming a casual tone as I dusted off my jeans. "You didn't happen to see anyone else when you came up just now, did you?"

"Why? Was someone here?" His inquisitive gaze swept the cemetery and the road beyond the gate before snapping back to me.

"I thought I heard something. Probably just voices drifting up from the clearing." I wanted to know if he'd caught sight of Darius Goodwine, but I couldn't come right out and ask. If Kendrick hadn't seen him, how would I explain the question without giving Darius away? It was a strange position I found myself in, protecting Darius Goodwine from the police.

I still couldn't say with any certainty that he had returned from Africa. It was just as likely he'd found a way inside my head, even across all those miles and an ocean, but regardless of his physical location, his presence worried me. Why had he come back into my life now and what was his relationship to the dead woman?

I wondered what Detective Kendrick would say if I told him all that had transpired in the cemetery—or inside my head—before his arrival.

His expression remained neutral despite the gleam of curiosity in his eyes. Before he had a chance to question me further, his phone rang and he put up a finger to pause our conversation. Lifting the unit to his ear, he listened for a moment and then answered in clipped monosyllables. During this brief exchange, his gaze never left me. I found myself growing more and more discomfited by that stare. I wanted to believe it unintentional. Maybe his concentration was so focused on the call that he'd forgotten my presence. But I had a feeling Detective Kendrick knew exactly what he was doing. He was like Devlin, in that respect. He knew how to unsettle.

I dropped my gaze to the gravestone.

"Sorry for the interruption," he said, slipping the phone back in his pocket. "You were saying?"

"It wasn't important."

"Are you sure? There must be a reason you asked if I'd seen anyone else in the cemetery just now."

I shrugged, still trying to retain an air of detachment as I wiped a trickle of sweat from my brow. "Like I said, I thought I heard something, but now that I think back, I'm certain it was just voices carrying up through the woods from the search."

I had no idea if he bought the explanation or not. He looked a little dubious as he waited for me to start down the path. I took my cue, weaving my way along the overgrown trail as the sun poured down hot and bright on the headstones. The cottonwood trees beckoned. As we neared the main gate, the carpet of yellow cosmos and coreopsis gave way to delicate patches of blue forget-me-nots and pools of silvery green moss.

For a moment, time stood still as a wave of longing washed over me. How many summer days had I spent sequestered behind cemetery walls, lost in a daydream or in the pages of one of my favorite books? Those early years with Mama and Papa had seemed like such an innocent time, peaceful and perfect, but my naiveté had withered all too soon. My protected world had come crumbling down long before my gift had evolved into something far more frightening than that of ghost-seer. Long before I had followed my great-grandmother's clues to Kroll Cemetery. Before Devlin had decided that my susceptibility to the unnatural world made me an unsuitable companion for someone like him.

I shook off the smothering melancholia as I moved up under the trees. The shade was deep and cool and I closed my eyes for a moment, dispelling the loneliness left by Devlin's departure and the foreboding that had accompanied Darius Goodwine's arrival.

Kendrick watched me warily. I offered him a bottle of water from the cooler, but he declined. I fished one out for myself and then sat down on top of the chest, lifting the icy bottle to the back of my neck.

"You wanted to talk to me." Twisting off the plastic cap, I drank deeply.

"Yes, but it can wait. Just sit there for a moment until you feel better."

I nodded absently, my gaze moving over the vehicles I could see through the fence. I counted three squad cars and an unmarked SUV that I suspected belonged to Detective Kendrick. A vehicle like that would suit him, I decided. Stealthy, mysterious and more than a little menacing.

As I sat there staring out at the road, a white sedan pulled up alongside the entrance and the elderly driver craned his neck for a look inside the gate. No doubt one of the gawkers Kendrick had warned me about the day before. I was still surprised that more hadn't come. Murder and mayhem were common attractions. People who led otherwise mundane lives often found crime scenes irresistible.

The driver's window lowered as the car inched along. A snowy-haired woman in the passenger seat leaned across the console toward her husband in order to get a better look. When the man spotted us beneath the trees, he stopped the car and got out. Putting up a hand to shade his eyes, he walked through the gate and called out to us. "Hello! We saw the police cars and wondered what happened."

"There's nothing to see here." Kendrick gave a dismissive wave. "Just go on about your business."

"Young man, we have people buried in this cemetery," the woman scolded from the open car window. "If something happened here, it *is* our business."

"Nothing happened in the cemetery," Kendrick said. "Now get back in your car and move along. You're blocking the road."

His harsh admonishment drew twin scowls of disapproval and embarrassment from the couple. The man hustled back to the car and climbed in, grumbling furiously to his wife before shooting Kendrick a contemptuous glare. Then he put the car in gear and drove off.

"Don't you think you were a bit hard on them?" I asked. "You said yourself the curious would come."

"They always do. Predictable as clockwork."

"I would think predictability an asset in your line of work."

"Depends on your perspective," he said with a

shrug. "When you've done what I do long enough, it all starts to seem depressingly the same. Even the victims. Predictability becomes less of an asset and more of an albatross. It's wearing."

"Do you really have that much crime in Ascension?" I asked. "It seems like such a sleepy town."

"I haven't always lived in Ascension. But human nature is basically the same wherever you go."

"I understand your point, but I find it difficult to imagine a world in which a woman buried alive inside a caged grave could be considered predictable."

"As I said, it's all about perspective."

I couldn't tell if his viewpoint was that of a cynic, a sociopath or a little of both.

I set the water bottle aside and leaned back on my hands as I gazed out over the cemetery. I saw nothing among the graves to indicate Darius Goodwine or anyone else had been there only moments earlier. The scent of ozone had faded and the storm clouds that darkened the landscape earlier had now moved back out to sea.

Kendrick kept his distance, standing several feet away in profile, arms at his sides, feet slightly apart. As I studied his silhouette, I became overly aware of the curl of his long lashes, the slight arch of his dark brows. He'd discarded his jacket in the heat so that I couldn't help but take in the definition of his forearms and biceps and the broad expanse of his chest beneath the dark gray of his shirt.

I wasn't attracted to Lucien Kendrick, although I could certainly appreciate his attractions. It took nothing away from my feelings for Devlin to admit this. Not that it mattered now that Devlin had removed himself from my life. I felt a pang at that thought and drew in a breath to dispel it.

Kendrick looked up sharply and I felt my face warm as our gazes connected. His expression was hard to define, but the glint in his eyes made me remember yet again Darius Goodwine's warning to trust no one.

I stirred restlessly on the cooler. "Can I ask you a question?"

He turned once again to watch the road. "What is it?"

I picked up the water bottle, rolling it between my hands. "Your accent. It's hardly discernible except for the way you pronounce certain words. I'm usually pretty good with dialects, but I haven't been able to pinpoint it. You've a bit of the Sea Islands in certain inflections, but sometimes I would almost swear I hear the trace of a French accent in your vowels."

"That's not a question," he said.

"Where are you from?"

I wasn't sure he would answer. There was something very dark and furtive about Lucien Kendrick, but to my surprise, he seemed to relax a bit as he moved in a few steps. "You've a good ear. Not many people pick up on the accent. I thought I'd lost it years ago."

"So you are French?"

"A quarter on my father's side."

"Is that where you grew up? In France?"

"I was born here in Beaufort County. We lived on Port Royal Island until I was nine, and then after my parents split, my father moved us to New Orleans. When I was thirteen he sent me to Paris to live with his mother. Once I turned eighteen…" The slightest hesitation. "I moved around a lot. Prague, Istanbul…" Another hesitation. "Ghazni."

I wondered if he'd been in the service. That would explain the way he carried himself, but the eyebrow piercing and body art was at odds with what seemed to be a military bearing.

"What brought you back here? Do you still have family in the area?"

"I'm told my mother lives around here somewhere." He was silent for a moment. "What about you? Native Charlestonian?"

"I grew up in Trinity. I've only lived in Charleston for a couple of years, but I feel as if I have roots in the city. My mother and aunt were born there."

"Roots are not always good," Kendrick said. "Sometimes all they do is drag you down."

"Yes, I suppose that's true." I gave him another quick study. "How long have you been back here?"

"Apparently, not long enough to lose my accent."

He seemed amused, which emboldened me. "Can I ask you another question?"

"You can always ask."

"You said yesterday that the house I'm renting has a history. What did you mean?"

He lifted a hand to scratch the stubble on his neck. "Are you sure you want to know?"

"Yes, of course. And it must be something you think I should know or you wouldn't have brought it up."

"I only brought it up because I found your choice of living arrangements...odd."

"Why?"

His gaze darted to the church ruins and to the woods beyond. "People say that place is evil."

Six

Kendrick's words faded away, leaving a sinister silence. I thought instantly of that shadow moving through the trees, quick and furtive. Then I thought of the inked skull on Kendrick's hand. The triskele that Darius had drawn in the dirt. The curlicue of a tattoo on the inside of the dead woman's wrist.

A pattern was starting to form. I felt the tiniest prick of a dark premonition.

"It's not haunted," I said, and then realizing he might find my definitive tone curious, I hurriedly added, "At least, I haven't seen or heard anything out of the ordinary in the nearly three months I've been living there. My stay has been quite peaceful, in fact."

"Maybe that has more to do with you than the house," Kendrick suggested.

"So what happened there?"

He seemed to measure his response before answering. "I'll tell you what I've heard on one condition. If you're still curious once we're done, you'll limit your research to the internet."

"Why?"

"It's not a good idea to go around talking about that house. People here don't particularly like it when strangers start asking questions and they get more than a little defensive about the town's past."

"I'll be discreet. You have my word. But now you *have* to tell me."

He turned back to the woods. For the first time since I'd met him, he seemed ill at ease. He twisted a silver ring on his finger, his eyes crinkling at the corners as he scanned the trees. I followed his gaze, peering intently into the deepest part of the shadows, but nothing glided among the tree trunks. Nothing floated up into the branches. Whatever I'd glimpsed earlier had fled with Darius Goodwine's disappearance. Or perhaps Detective Kendrick had once again chased away the watcher.

I glanced up at him, my gaze settling unexpectedly on his mouth, which was not as aesthetically pleasing as Devlin's. But the bloom of his bottom lip cast an intriguing shadow in the hollow of his chin and softened the harsher line of his upper lip and jaw. It was a purposeful mouth and there was sensuality in the resoluteness of its lines.

I tore my gaze away with a shiver. Where on earth had that come from? I didn't like having such thoughts about Lucien Kendrick. They were foreign to me and I didn't trust they were my own rather than another of Darius Goodwine's manipulations. Why he would want to foster an attraction between Detective Kendrick and me, I couldn't imagine, but I put nothing past him. Maybe he wanted to prove how easily he could control me, or more likely, he wanted to drive a deeper wedge between Devlin and me so that I would be more receptive to him. I could be reaching, but it was the only way I knew to explain my feelings.

Unless the manipulation came from Kendrick himself. For all I knew, he was as masterful at head games as Darius. He was certainly no ordinary cop. My instincts had warned me from the start to keep a safe distance, and now that I knew he had a connection or at least an acquaintance with Darius Goodwine, I would be even more careful.

Darius's negative reaction to Kendrick's name should have fostered a kinship with the detective if for no other reason than the old adage *the enemy of my enemy is my friend.* But Kendrick was just a little too slippery, a little too mysterious, and I couldn't shake the notion that he had already known about those cages before he arrived on the scene.

His stillness now was so absolute, his silence so intense, that I couldn't help wondering if he was trying to slip past my defenses. Was he inside my head even now?

It seemed as though the quiet had stretched on forever, but only a few seconds had passed before Kendrick turned back to me. "A couple by the name of George and Mary Willoughby once lived in that house, along with their young daughter, Annie. By all accounts, they were a close family. God-fearing, church-going, salt-of-the-earth types. Then seemingly overnight, George became delusional. He told his neighbors that his wife was not who she seemed to be. She'd gotten involved with some very bad people. Satan-worshippers, he said, but there was never any evidence of the practice in this area. He insisted he'd caught them conducting the devil's business right in his own home."

"What did he mean by the devil's business?"

"Séances. Rituals." Kendrick's gaze darkened. "Who knows what else? He claimed they were trying to raise the dead."

Raise the dead.

I felt the dart of cold apprehension in my veins. I wanted to take all this in calmly, but it was hard to keep a neutral expression in light of my conversation with Darius Goodwine.

"Raise the dead...how?"

"There were ceremonies. Certain spells and incantations. The leader of the group was a root worker named Atticus Pope, who claimed to have descended from a powerful witch doctor. Willoughby swore he saw Pope change forms right before his eyes. From man to beast and back. Like the *loup-garous* my grandmother used to tell me about when I was a boy."

"*Loup-garous?* As in werewolves? Shape-shifters? You don't believe that, surely."

"People see what they want to see," Kendrick said.

Or were persuaded to see by the likes of Darius Goodwine. I thought about how easily and subtly he had planted the notion of corpse beetles in my subconscious so that I'd manifested one on my arm and another on my neck. If the root doctor named Atticus Pope had been half as cunning and powerful as Darius Goodwine, he could have made poor George Willoughby see almost anything.

"I assume there's more to the story," I said as I turned my attention back to Kendrick.

"Willoughby chased away the group with a shotgun, but things were never right with his wife after that. He was convinced something evil had taken over her body."

"He thought she was possessed?"

"Apparently."

According to Darius's simplistic and disturbing explanation, possession was like a hostile takeover, but transference was a peaceful merger between the living and the dead. Had Mary been willing?

"What happened to her?"

"Her husband murdered her in her sleep and buried the body in an unknown location. Or so the story goes. But that's mostly an assumption because all that was ever found of the woman, apart from the blood-soaked bedclothing, was a hank of her hair clutched in George's hand. The police discovered him in the shed behind the orchard where he'd gone after he disposed of her body. He'd put the barrel of the shotgun in his mouth and used his toe to pull the trigger."

"That's quite a gruesome tale," I said with a shiver.

"How much of it's true is anyone's guess. We'll probably never know what really happened." A shadow flickered in Kendrick's eyes. "You said you haven't seen or heard anything out of the ordinary in the house, but I would think that if any place is haunted, it would be that shed."

"Do you really believe a place can be haunted?" I tried to keep any telltale inflection or inference from my voice, but it wasn't easy. "Do you believe in ghosts?"

He didn't scoff at the question as I'd come to expect, but instead he took a long moment to consider his answer. "I've seen a lot of things in my lifetime. Unexplainable things. I learned a long time ago that it's best to keep an open mind."

How different he was from Devlin, who seemed to have an almost pathological need to disavow the supernatural.

"What about you?" he asked.

"Me?" I smiled. "Like you, I try to keep an open mind."

Our gazes held for a moment, and I had the strangest notion that if I told Kendrick about my gift, he wouldn't bat an eye.

The prospect was at once exhilarating and terrifying, and I reminded myself that I knew nothing about him. He was a perfect stranger. For all I knew, a man as dangerously sly and powerful as Darius Goodwine.

"I've often wondered about that old shed," Kendrick said. "And whether or not there's anything still to be found there. Especially when I drive by the Willoughby place at dawn and see patches of the roof peeking through the treetops."

"You've never stopped to explore?" I asked.

"That would be trespassing."

"Just as well. There's a padlock on the door and you can't see much through the windows."

"You've tried, I take it."

"Once or twice. You mentioned a daughter." Very deliberately, I steered the conversation back to the story. "Where was she when all this happened?"

"The police found her huddled on the porch. They figured she must have heard the shotgun blast, got up from bed and went out to the shed to investigate. She may even have tried to resuscitate her father because the police said she was covered in blood. So much so that she looked as if she'd been rolling around in a puddle of gore."

"That poor child. How old was she when it happened?"

"Around ten, I think. As I said, a lot of this is assumption and guesswork. The girl was the only witness and she'd fallen into some sort of catatonic trance or fugue state. She couldn't tell the authorities her name let alone what had transpired between her parents."

"What became of her?"

"She was in a psychiatric hospital for a long time. Then one day she came out of her trance and decided to carry on with her life as though nothing had happened. She claimed to have no memory of that night."

"I suppose that's possible. Trauma-induced amnesia isn't all that rare."

"Anything's possible," he said in a strange tone. "She married and moved away when she was still very young, but after her husband died a few years ago, she came back here. As a matter of fact, you know her. Annalee Nash."

I stared up at him in shock. "Annalee? But she seems so..."

"Normal?" he supplied with a sardonic lift of one brow. "That's a relative term."

Didn't I know it?

"It's just that, on the few occasions we've spoken, I would never have guessed she'd gone through something so harrowing," I tried to explain.

"It's been my experience that people only let you see what they want you to see." He shot me another knowing look and I returned his shrewd appraisal.

"Yes, I'm sure that's true," I said slowly, meaningfully.

He glanced away. "It's also been my experience that the people you would least expect of guile and subterfuge are the most adept at hiding their true nature—at least for a while. But it almost always surfaces sooner or later, sometimes violently."

"I've never sensed anything remotely violent in Annalee Nash. She seems quite gentle."

"I wasn't talking about her specifically. We're all capable of violence under the right circumstances." Kendrick's voice hardened ever so slightly. "Even you, I would imagine."

"Perhaps so." But I didn't like to think about my capabilities in that regard. "They never found Mary's body?"

"Not a trace."

"Where was her husband buried?"

"Here in this cemetery. They put him over by the back gate, facing north."

Kendrick's specificity in the location seemed to

suggest that he knew the significance of such an arrangement. Most bodies were laid to rest from east to west, facing sunrise and the Second Coming. But not those who were compromised.

"At least they allowed him to be buried in the churchyard. There was a time when suicides were treated as outcasts," I told him.

"As you can see, the church has been in ruins for decades and the cemetery has been closed to the public for at least twenty years. So I guess, in a way, George Willoughby was cast out. People tend to hold a lot of superstitions when it comes to old graveyards, but you would know that better than me."

He seemed to know plenty, and at that, he was only letting me see what he wanted me to see. "Thank you for telling me about the house," I said. "It's a fascinating if gruesome story."

"You aren't afraid to stay there now that you know?"

"No, why would I be?"

"Some people would turn tail and run after what I just told you."

"If ghost stories frightened me, would I have chosen my current profession?"

"A good point," he allowed.

"Besides, it all happened a long time ago and the house seems perfectly at peace." Which made me wonder if the key I wore around my neck had chased away the spirits, evil and otherwise. It seemed strange that for all my supposed powers and heightened senses, I hadn't picked up a single discordant vibe from that house. "Anyway, I appreciate your taking the time to tell me about it. But now," I said briskly, eager to leave behind the disturbing plight of George and Mary Willoughby, "we should probably get back to the business at hand. Wasn't there something you wanted to talk to me about?"

"A couple of things," Kendrick said, seamlessly switching back to his detective persona as if he were as willing as I for a change of subject. "First, I thought you'd be interested to know that I was able to get in touch with your friend at the state archaeologist's office. She's agreed to come down and take a look at the graves. She seemed particularly interested in the cages."

"I knew she would be. When is she coming?"

"Not until next week, unfortunately. In the meantime, I've called in a forensic anthropologist from Charleston that can help with the identification of any skeletal remains we uncover. And I'd like you to come into the morgue this afternoon and take a look at the victim. If you've no objection."

"I've no objection. I'm more than willing to help in any way I can, but as I told you yesterday, I know very few people in the area. The odds that I'll be able to make a positive identification are slim."

"I understand that. But the victim was alive for a period of time after she was buried. Which means there's a chance she got to that clearing under her own steam. Maybe she was coerced or lured there or maybe she came of her own free will. In any case, unless she was taken there by way of the swamp, she would have likely come through or at least near the cemetery, perhaps in the company of her killer."

I felt a chill go through me. I hadn't considered that possibility.

"Even with so little traffic, it's still possible you saw something and don't remember it," he said. "A face in a car window or someone in the woods. All I ask is that you view the remains with an open mind."

I nodded. "When do you want me to come in?"

"Let's say one o'clock. I'll meet you there and walk you through it."

"Thanks."

"No need to thank me. I would never expect you to do this alone. Although…" His gaze swept over me, deep and fathomless. "You strike me as someone who is more than capable of taking care of herself."

For some reason, I didn't think he meant it as a compliment.

I left the cemetery in time to stop by the house for a quick shower and change of clothes before I drove into town. The silence of the place bothered me now that I knew the grisly history, but I didn't allow myself to dwell on the story Kendrick had told me. There would be time enough later to explore the rooms with a new eye and perhaps even take a stroll through the orchard to the shed.

For now, I busied myself with the mundane tasks of drying my hair and refilling Angus's water bowl on the back porch and then propping open the screen door so that he could come and go as he pleased. But I couldn't resist glancing over my shoulder now and then. I couldn't help thinking that the vibe of the house had been subtly altered by my newfound knowledge.

I chalked it all up to imagination as I drove into town and followed Kendrick's directions to the hospital morgue. I didn't relish the task that lay before me. The last time I'd been near a morgue, the voices of the dead had filled my head, making me aware of another terrifying aspect of my gift. I'd later come to believe that the recently deceased had somehow opened a door, allowing the trapped and restless souls of Kroll Cemetery to make contact with me. Once the ghosts had been released, the voices had faded, though I didn't expect the silence to last for much longer. Not after my discovery of those mortsafes.

Kendrick waited for me at the front desk. After we signed in, an attendant showed us back to a room where the body had been placed on a stainless steel table, awaiting autopsy. He went around to the far side of the table and I stepped up to the near side. He gave a nod and the attendant peeled back the sheet that covered the body.

I braced myself for the possibility of seeing a familiar face staring up at me, but I didn't recognize the dead woman and I was thankful for that.

The first thing that struck me was the condition of the body. She hadn't been prepped for the postmortem, which surprised me. She was still fully dressed in jeans and a band T-shirt, her face and arms streaked with grave dirt and her long, dark hair matted with leaves and twigs. A silver cross glinted in the hollow of her throat and a series of ruby studs ran from her lobes all the way up into her cartilage. One of the studs was missing, I noted.

She looked to be my age, late twenties or perhaps a year or two younger. She was slim, almost petite, but even in death, she appeared strangely dauntless. She wouldn't have gone down without a fight, I thought, though I saw no evidence of a struggle on her body.

"Do you recognize her?" Kendrick asked.

I could feel his gaze on me across the table. I shook my head as my hand crept to the key around my neck. "I've never seen her before."

"You're sure? Take a closer look."

"I am looking. I don't remember ever having seen her before." But even as the words slipped out, something tugged at the corner of my memory. *Had* I seen her before?

And just like that, an image came back to me. The flash of those ruby earrings as a dark head tossed. The glimpse of a tattoo as a hand lifted to open a glass door.

Whether the memory was real or imagined, I had no idea. It was there one moment and gone the next.

"Can I see her left arm?" I asked.

Kendrick gave me a quizzical look, but he said nothing as he nodded to the attendant and she lowered the sheet.

"Can you turn it so that I can see her wrist?"

The woman complied and I leaned in to get a better look at the tattooed words on the pale flesh as I muttered the phrase aloud, *"Memento mori."*

I jerked back in shock as the import of the message sank in.

"What is it?" Kendrick asked.

"Her tattoo…"

"It's Latin, right? What does it mean?"

I lifted my gaze to his. "Remember to die."

Seven

I had only a few moments to speak with Detective Kendrick before he was called away on another case. I didn't mention the memory of those flashing rubies. Until I knew if the image was real and what it might mean, I saw no need to draw more attention to myself. A stranger in town was an easy target for suspicion so I needed to be careful in my dealings with the police. My discovery of the body had already elicited a certain amount of curiosity, if not outright distrust, and I certainly didn't want the killer to cast an eye in my direction. For now, it was in my best interest to remain on the periphery of Kendrick's investigation.

I had intended on returning to the cemetery to finish the section of headstones I'd started that morning, but as I drove through town, the enticing aromas drifting out from the restaurants along Main Street reminded me that I hadn't eaten since breakfast. Normally, I would have stopped by the house for a quick bite or taken something back to the cemetery with me, but today I felt compelled to dine among the living. I parked the car, got out and walked over to the café where I'd eaten a few times since my arrival in Ascension.

As I paused to study the lunch menu taped to the plate-glass window, the reflection of the building across the street caught my eye. A large skeleton key had been painted on the window in gold leaf. I'd noticed it before and had always meant to stop in because the gilded key reminded me of the one I wore around my neck. I had no idea of the nature of the business. There was no other adornment on the window, no name or street number on the door.

As I returned my attention to the menu, a memory fluttered at the back of my mind. I saw again the flash of those ruby earrings as the sunlight caught them. I glimpsed the curlicue of that tattooed message as a slender hand lifted to open the glass door. And now something else came to me—behind that gilded key, a lurking silhouette inside the shop.

The memory...the image...whatever it was wavered for a moment and then vanished. I turned slowly toward the building, heart tripping at the implication. If those vague flickers could be trusted, then sometime before her death, the victim had visited that shop. She might even have gone there to meet the person who had waited inside. I tried to remember when I might have seen her. My last trip into town had been at least a week ago.

I stared long and hard at that gold key, hoping something else would stir, but the memory remained elusive. On impulse, I crossed the street and tried the door of the shop. It was locked and I could see very little of the interior when I peered through the window.

A narrow alley ran alongside the building and I followed it back to a wooden gate that stood wide open—an invitation. If the gate had been closed, I would never have entered. At least that's what I told myself as I peered through the opening into a tiny courtyard.

A fountain splashed against colorful mosaics and a dozen or more pinwheels clicked in the hot breeze. There were any number of sculptures and yard decorations cluttering the small space, but what caught my attention, what brought a gasp to my lips, were the dozens of padlocks hanging from pegs hammered into the wooden fence. They instantly brought to mind my great-grandmother's key collection, which had hung from the ceiling of her sanctuary for decades, waiting for me to come along and find them.

This couldn't be a coincidence, I felt certain. Once again, I had been brought to a particular spot for a reason. I was meant to find this courtyard. I was meant to see all those locks. The sight so intrigued and puzzled me that I failed to register the sound of voices until it was almost too late. Someone was coming.

I backed into the alley and slipped behind the wooden gate. I had a perfect view of the courtyard between the fence pickets and it disturbed me more than a little that I no longer even tried to justify my eavesdropping. I could have easily scurried down the alleyway and out to the street, but I didn't.

Instead, I waited breathlessly as a man and woman came out of the building and paused near the fountain to speak. I recognized the man at once. He was Martin Stark, the locksmith that Detective Kendrick had summoned to open the mortsafe. Now the locks on the fence and the painted key on the plate-glass window made sense. This was undoubtedly his place of business.

I could only see the woman's profile, but I knew her, too. I'd met with Annalee Nash enough times now to be familiar with her features. She was tall and fit, but where an air of grit had lingered over the petite dead woman, Annalee's wide eyes and heart-shaped face gave her a delicate, almost frail appearance. She wore jeans and a striped T-shirt that made her seem very young even though I knew her to be a few years older than me. As she stood there in dappled sunlight with the breeze tousling her short locks, I could easily imagine her as that ten-year-old catatonic girl covered in blood. *As if she'd been rolling around in a puddle of gore.*

I couldn't make out anything of their conversation, but as Stark turned to go inside, Annalee caught his arm. When he whirled back around, I could have sworn I glimpsed fear in his eyes. He tugged his arm free and hurried away from her.

Something unpleasant prickled at the base of my spine as Annalee headed toward the gate. She seemed very different at that moment. The illusion of frailty and innocence vanished as a satisfied smile tugged at her lips.

As she neared the entrance, I tried to shrink more

deeply into my hiding place. If she closed the gate, I would be exposed and I had no good reason for being there.

But she didn't close the gate. She breezed through the opening and strode down the alley. I thought I was home free, but before she got to the street, she whirled back around. I couldn't tell if she was trying to peer between the gate pickets or if she was looking for something inside the courtyard. For a split second, her gaze was so focused and intense I worried that she had spotted me.

I felt the crawl of something unpleasant at the back of my neck and the scutter of insect feet across my scalp. I imagined an infestation of Darius Goodwine's corpse beetles in my hair and it was all I could do to remain still. I wanted nothing more than to run screaming into the sunlight, but I stood frozen, my gaze fixed on Annalee Nash.

She lifted a hand, fingering the curls at her nape, and the spidery sensation crept down my collar. I could feel those scurrying feet all up and down my spine now and inside the legs of my jeans. I told myself it wasn't real. The bugs were merely a manifestation conjured by my own fear. But real or imagined, I couldn't stay still for much longer. I had to get out of there. I had to...

Annalee's fingers slid up into her hair and I could have sworn I saw her shudder before she turned and headed back to the street. I waited until she disappeared around the corner before leaving my hiding place. I shook out my hair and batted my clothing, but already the sensation had faded. There were no beetles, no scurrying feet, nothing but deepening dread that perhaps I had stumbled into something far beyond even my capabilities.

By the time I came out on the street, Annalee was gone. Which was just as well. I'd already taken too many risks. It was time to regain my perspective.

For all I knew, the meeting between Annalee and Stark had been perfectly innocent, but I couldn't forget the fear in his eyes when she'd caught his arm. Or the way her lips had curled as she strode through the gate. I hoped I was reading too much into her demeanor. What I now knew about Annalee's past had undoubtedly colored my perception, just as it had with the Willoughby house.

But the image of that sly smile lingered all afternoon as I cleaned headstones in Seven Gates Cemetery.

Eight

I didn't return to the Willoughby place until well after sunset. I justified the late hour by telling myself I needed to play catch-up for all the time I'd lost since discovering those mortsafes, but in truth, I'd been avoiding the house for as long as I could. Which was silly. It was still the same house.

Pulling into the driveway, I rolled down my window, letting the cooling air chase away the lingering cloud of the day's events. Tantalizing scents drifted in—four-o'clocks, ginger lily and the darker, dreamier perfume of the angel trumpets.

For the longest time, I sat staring at the house. My stay there had been as peaceful and harmonious as I could have ever hoped, but a sinister pall had been cast. I'd noticed it earlier when I stopped by to change, but I hadn't wanted to dwell on it then. Now as evening approached and the dark hours stretched before me, I couldn't help but recall Kendrick's disturbing story.

He'd wanted me to know about the gruesome history of the house and the shed, but why? Did he think George's and Mary's deaths were somehow connected to those caged graves? Did he suspect that Annalee was somehow involved in the young woman's murder?

A childhood trauma leading to a permanent psychosis might well be within the realm of possibility, but I wasn't prepared to jump to that conclusion, even after witnessing her encounter with Martin Stark. Yet as I sat there gazing at the quaint facade, the image came back to me of a ten-year-old girl huddled on the porch covered in blood. When I peered into the darkened front windows, I pictured her cowering under the covers as her father dragged her mother's body down the hallway.

What did that old tragedy have to do with the present-day murder of the woman I'd found in the mortsafe? And how was any of this the business of Darius Goodwine?

I remained motionless, pondering question after question as the engine ticked down and the shadows across the lawn grew longer. The day was coming to an end and the house seemed to be waiting.

Which was ridiculous. Nothing had changed about that place except for my perception.

Shivering in the late-afternoon heat, I climbed out of the vehicle and locked the door. But instead of going inside, I headed for the backyard where I could hear Angus pawing at the wooden gate in excitement. The fenced property gave him ample room to safely roam while I worked, which was a nice change from our tiny backyard in the city.

The moment I opened the gate, he bounded through, but then drew up short, as if he'd momentarily forgotten his wariness. His continued reticence tore at my heart and I wished, as I always did when he seemed so guarded around me, that I knew some easy way to earn back his affection.

There was a time when Angus had trusted me completely, but his canine senses were even more attuned to the supernatural than mine and the progression of my gift unnerved him. He was all too aware of the changes inside me and sometimes still I would catch him watching me with those dark, soulful eyes as if to say, *I know who you are but I don't know what you are and that worries me.*

We'd made some headway during the past year, but he wasn't yet ready to accept me wholeheartedly. Until such time, I could do nothing but give him his space. The same as I had done for Devlin.

Kneeling, I put out a hand so that he could catch my scent. He eyed me from a safe distance. When he finally ambled over, he didn't relax as he once would have done, but instead held himself in rigid acquiescence as I stroked his scarred head and scratched behind his ear nubs.

"I know," I murmured, smoothing the fur on his back. "I know you don't like the changes inside me. I don't like them, either. But there's nothing I can do about them."

Unless I located Rose's long-lost key. Unless everything I'd heard about it was true. That still seemed a remote possibility, an improbable fairy tale, but if the key I wore around my neck could hold the ghosts at bay temporarily, who was to say another key couldn't lock them out forever?

Angus put up with my attention for as long as he could stand before trotting off to explore the front yard. He wouldn't go beyond the ditch. No matter his reservations, he still felt protective of me and for that I was both humbled and grateful.

I let him nose around for a bit and then called to him to follow me into the backyard. As I closed the gate and turned, my gaze lifted to the flat roof of the shed jutting up through the treetops. The outbuilding was located at the back of the property, separated from the marsh by a salt-tolerant forest of loblolly pines and from the backyard and house by a small grove of orange trees.

As best I could tell from the windows and roofline, the shed was divided into three distinct rooms, one leading back into the other in the shotgun fashion of an old farmhouse. The structure looked to be in decent condition so I assumed someone had taken care of it over the years. It was painted white like the house with a high window on either side of the front room to allow in light. On a few occasions, I'd stood on tiptoes and taken a peek through the glass, but other than a jumble of old furniture, boxes and garden tools, I hadn't been able to tell much about the interior.

I sat down on the back porch steps, my gaze still fixed on the roof. As the horizon deepened, the moths came out, flitting among the bee balm and catmint that grew at the side of the porch. The breeze blowing in from the sea was cool and fragrant, and I could hear music somewhere in the distance. Closer in, cicadas and bullfrogs serenaded from the marsh as the bats flew out of their houses. It was a lovely time, a lonely time, with the last rays of the sunset valiantly staving off twilight.

Angus and I sat there until the shadows thickened at the edge of the yard and dusk crept over the orchard. I felt nothing unnatural in the breeze, but there was a sense of wrongness about the house and yard that I had not experienced before.

Perhaps it really was nothing more than my imagination fueled by Kendrick's story. Or perhaps my finding those caged graves had somehow stirred a dormant evil. Whatever the reason, I found myself lingering on the steps and then on the screened porch because I didn't want to enter the house.

"Oh, just get it over with," I muttered as I pushed open the back door and stepped across the threshold. Fumbling for the light switch, I paused just inside the doorway as my gaze darted about the kitchen.

Most of the fixtures and cabinets were original to the house and created a vivid sense of time and place. I had a sudden vision of a woman in a black dress standing at the old farmhouse sink washing dishes. She wasn't a ghost or a mirage or even one of Darius Goodwine's illusions, but rather another product of my imagination. My gaze drifted to the table where a man with wire-rimmed glasses sat reading the Bible. What had driven a gentle, God-fearing man to murder his wife in her sleep and hide her body so well she'd yet to be found?

I watched the Willoughbys for a moment longer before allowing them to fade back into the past.

For the next few minutes, I busied myself attending to Angus's dinner needs and then left him to his food as I walked slowly from room to room, searching for cold spots, listening for inexplicable sounds and sniffing the slightly musty air for peculiar scents.

Nothing seemed amiss even in the large front bedroom, which I assumed had belonged to George and Mary. I'd chosen the space for myself because of the southern exposure, but I'd spent very little time in the room. On most nights, the summer heat chased me out to the back porch where I would lie in the hammock watching the stars until I grew drowsy.

I wondered now if I had avoided the room because I'd subconsciously picked up on a disturbing feel—that sense of wrongness I'd experienced on the back steps. My gaze traveled over the room, searching every corner and crevice. If I peeled back the area rug at the end of the bed, would I find bloodstains on the floorboards? If I emptied my mind, would I feel the reverberation from Mary Willoughby's screams?

There was nothing here, I told myself. No ghosts. No evil presence. Just that slight fusty odor that came from aging places. The house remained at peace.

Even so, I quickly packed up all my belongings and hauled my suitcase down the hallway to one of the smaller bedrooms at the rear of house. After I stored my things, I took a long, cool shower and put on a fresh nightgown before wandering back out to the kitchen.

Angus had finished his dinner by this time. He seemed content to curl up in a corner and watch drowsily as I ate a bowl of cereal standing at the sink. Then fetching my laptop, I settled down at the table for an evening of research.

So much had happened I hardly knew where to start. As on edge as I already was about the house, I decided to leave the topic of the Willoughbys for another day, concentrating instead on *memento mori* symbolism and the concept of triplism. I found a wealth of information on the transmigration of souls, but nothing at all on the Eternal Brotherhood of Resurrectionists or their enemy, the *Congé*. Finally putting all that aside, I searched through dozens of mortsafe images trying to find a duplicate or similar design to the cages in the clearing.

I had hoped once I began my research, a pattern would emerge that would help define my investigation, but by the time I finally closed my laptop for the night, enlightenment still eluded me.

Angus followed me out to the porch and I stood at the screen door, gazing into the darkness while he took care of business. I saw no ghosts hovering at the edge of the yard, no in-betweens skulking through the shadows, but the dead world seemed closer than it had in months.

Little wonder I felt so unnerved. It wasn't every day Darius Goodwine came to me with a dangerous proposition. I half expected to catch a glimpse of him lurking in the shadows, but nothing stirred. The night was calm and yet my heart continued to race.

As if sensing my unease, Angus came trotting over to the door, whimpering to be let in. I placed a hand on his back and felt the bristle of his fur.

"What's out there?" I murmured.

If only he had been able to warn me.

That night I dreamed about Devlin. He appeared to me in the cemetery in much the same way as Darius Goodwine had. I looked up from cleaning headstones and there he was, standing so deeply in the shadows of the old church ruins that I thought at first he must be a mirage. When I tried to speak to him, he lifted a finger to his lips to silence me. And when I would have gone to him, he shook his head as if to warn me away. The dream seemed so real and I felt his presence so strongly that, when I awakened, I almost expected to find him standing over me. Instead, I saw Annalee Nash peering down at me in the dark.

I bolted upright in bed. The moonlight streaming in through the windows was so bright I didn't bother with the lamp. Clutching the covers to my chest, I glanced around, certain I would find Annalee hiding in one of the corners, but no one was there. I must have still been dreaming when I saw her.

Angus was nowhere to be found so I climbed out of bed and padded down the hallway to look for him. He stood on the back porch peering through the screen into the yard. He didn't seem alarmed or frightened, but when I opened the door to let him out, he wouldn't go.

I rested my hand on his head, gently scratching behind his ear nubs as I searched the yard. The night was still and quiet, perfumed by the lemony scent of the catmint. Moonlight spilled across the yard, cool and silvery, but the shadows along the orchard were impenetrable. I scanned the tree line once, twice, at least three times before I noticed a slight movement. When the outline of a crouching form took shape, my heart leaped to my throat and I reached for the hook on the screen door to make certain that I'd latched it.

Even in the dark, I recognized her at once, and for a moment, I could have sworn she was the ten-year-old Annalee from Lucien Kendrick's story.

I started to call out to her and then thought better of it. She stared up at the house, but I didn't think she'd seen me. I wasn't even sure she was cognizant of her whereabouts. Whatever caused her to hunker in the shadows was something from her past. Something that only she could see.

She watched the house for a moment longer and then rose tentatively as she glanced over her shoulder. Still half crouching, she backed deeper into the shadows and disappeared into the trees.

I wondered if I should follow her, make sure she was all right, but the memory of that sly smile stopped me. I went back inside the stifling house, calling softly for Angus to come. With the doors and windows closed, the musty odor seemed stronger tonight and I detected a cloying under note that turned my stomach.

Walking slowly through the darkened rooms, I opened closet doors and peered into murky corners. I didn't know what I expected to find. I doubted that Annalee had actually been inside the house. Somehow, I must have picked up on her nearness in my sleep and manifested her face in a waking dream. Still, the very fact that she had come creeping around the property so late at night bothered me.

The moldy odor was stronger in the front bedroom. The windows were closed here, too, and the closet was empty. There was nothing under the bed or behind the headboard. Nothing lurked in the corners. No one had been in that room since I'd moved out all my things earlier, but I sensed a presence as strongly as I'd felt Devlin's in my sleep.

"Show yourself," I whispered.

I heard something then that reminded me of a mewling kitten. The sound was so soft and distant I couldn't be sure I'd heard anything at all. I held myself perfectly still, listening to the silence of that bedroom. The house didn't creak and moan as would be expected in such an old structure. To the contrary, the quiet seemed uncanny.

I'd had some experience with an entity that could scurry and scrabble through walls, but I didn't think the sound had come from inside the house. Rather, the tinny, echoing quality made me think of a well or a tomb. Something deep underground. Something buried alive.

My heart pounded as I turned to the doorway where Angus hovered. He wouldn't come inside the room and his reluctance, even more than the sound, sent a warning thrill down my spine. I might have succumbed to my earlier curiosity and thrown back the rug to search for bloodstains, but my cell phone rang just then and I left the room in relief to hurry down the hallway to answer.

A phone call in the middle of the night was never a good omen, but since I didn't recognize the number, I expected it was just a misdial.

"Hello?"

Silence.

"Hello?" I said, a trifle impatiently.

Nothing. Not even so much as a hitched breath. But someone was there. Someone who knew that I was in the house alone.

Nine

I didn't sleep much after that phone call. I returned briefly to the front bedroom, but I didn't hear, smell or see anything untoward. Whatever I'd sensed earlier had faded with the interruption. I was glad for that. Still, I made another round through the house before going back to bed. When the alarm went off at dawn, I was tempted to burrow under the covers, but I dragged myself out of bed, showered and headed for the cemetery at my usual time.

I was alone for the early part of the morning and the quiet gave me time to think. About those caged graves. About Darius Goodwine's proposal. About the tattoo on the dead woman's arm, the anonymous phone call in the middle of the night and Annalee Nash's strange behavior at the edge of the orchard. So much for a peaceful summer.

A little after midmorning, Malloy and another officer showed up to resume searching the woods and the area surrounding the circle. One of the officers the day before had found another route to the clearing without having to pass through the cemetery and I was grateful for that. They'd been respectful and mindful of the graves, but the constant disruptions left me unsettled. Now it was easier to pretend they weren't there.

I'd been working steadily for hours with only a brief break for lunch when I heard a shout erupt from the direction of the circle. The broken silence startled me and I lifted my head, momentarily struck by the unmistakable note of excitement in the officer's voice. Then I returned resolutely to my work, reminding myself that I needed to keep a low profile. The less attention I drew to myself, the better, especially if I intended to conduct my own discreet investigation.

A few minutes after I heard the shout, two police cars careered down the gravel road and crunched to a halt. Then came the coroner's van. These new arrivals and the scurry of activity I sensed from the circle threatened my resolution. Curiosity and dread niggled but still I kept my head down and continued to scrape away at the layers of moss and lichen.

Detective Kendrick arrived next with a man I recognized as James Rushing, a forensic anthropologist from Charleston. We'd never met, but I'd seen Rushing around town at various functions and Temple had spoken highly of him and his credentials when he'd replaced Ethan Shaw as consultant to the county coroner's office. And Temple being Temple, she'd also noted how easy he was on the eyes. I'd never given James Rushing more than a passing thought, but his presence today, along with that of the coroner's, could only mean one thing—human remains had been discovered, presumably in the caged grave where the body had been removed.

Still, I kept myself in check until the sun hovered just above the treetops and then I could resist no longer. I tossed down the brush, peeled off my gloves and left the cemetery by way of the back gate. I told myself that a quick peek from a distance would do no harm. After all, it was only natural that I'd be curious. It might even seem more suspicious if I acted disinterested.

The closer I got to the clearing, the more anxious I became. As I rounded the first bend, I could see the uniformed cops milling about the circle. I put a hand to my eyes as my gaze went around the cages, resting briefly on the second mortsafe, which remained open from the excavation. But the officers' focus was no longer on the caged graves. Instead, Kendrick and the coroner stood in the center of the clearing staring down at something I couldn't yet see.

As if sensing my presence, Kendrick turned and nodded when he saw me. Then he motioned for me to join them. I hesitated for a moment before making my way through the tall weeds to his side.

"Are you sure it's okay for me to be here?" I asked reluctantly.

"I wouldn't have asked you over if it wasn't." He shifted his position to make room for me. Again, I braced myself for the possibility of recognizing the deceased, but I needn't have worried. The remains were skeletal.

The unmarked grave site had been carefully staked and gridded and now the skeleton lay completely exposed in a shallow grave. A tattered cloth had fallen away from the torso and I could see bits of old leather that might once have been shoes. I wasn't particularly squeamish about bones, but these remains bothered me. My hand lifted automatically to the key at my neck as I realized why.

"The skull is missing," I said under my breath.

I didn't think I'd muttered it loud enough for even Kendrick to hear, but I felt him tense beside me and Rushing glanced up from his work.

His dark eyes took me in for a moment before he said, "I know you. Amelia Gray, right? The cemetery restorer. Temple Lee speaks very highly of you."

I murmured a polite response, trying to make myself as inconspicuous as I possibly could.

Kendrick turned back to Rushing. "You were saying?"

"You asked about scavengers. Always a likelihood, but the rest of the skeleton is in remarkably good shape for such a shallow burial and there isn't as much evidence of predation as I would have expected."

"Can you tell how long it's been here?"

"A decade at least, probably closer to two, although the proximity to the marsh can speed up decomposition. I'll have a better idea when I get him back to the lab."

"Him?"

"The remains are definitely male," Rushing said.

Kendrick hunkered in the grass, putting himself closer to the skeleton. "Any chance the skull was removed before burial?"

Rushing shifted his position so that he could point to the upper vertebrae. "Decapitation, either post- or perimortem, would leave deep cuts. Skulls have a natural tendency to disarticulate from the body. While I don't rule out scavengers, there is evidence of a prior excavation, which leads me to believe the skull was intentionally removed after decomposition."

"What's the evidence?" Kendrick asked.

Rushing nodded toward the cloth that had fallen away from the torso. "As you might expect after all this time and in this environment, very little of the clothing remains. There's some bits of leather and not much else. But this swath of linen is still mostly intact. My guess is, the shroud was added after the exhumation. Once the skull was removed from the grave, the remains were wrapped and re-buried, which suggests a certain amount of respect, if not reverence, for the deceased."

I didn't feel the absence of air in the clearing today, but suddenly I found it difficult to breathe. Something was going on here. Something frightening and perverted. I couldn't help but remember Darius Goodwine's warning that there would be more deaths unless I, and I alone, unmasked the killer.

"Was there a marker or any identification in the grave?" I heard myself ask.

"Not a marker," Kendrick said. "But we did find a partially buried medallion, which is how Malloy discovered the grave. I'm glad you showed up when you did. Maybe you can help us identify the symbol."

He removed an evidence bag from the collection beside the grave and handed it to me.

Given my conversation with Darius, I almost expected to see a claw entwined with a snake like the one Devlin wore around his neck, but no. The symbol on the medallion was even more disturbing.

"Do you know what it is?" Kendrick asked. I could feel his gaze on me as I turned the evidence bag over to study the back of the medallion.

"It's a triskele."

"Celtic, isn't it?" Rushing said.

"I've been told this particular symbol dates back to the Egyptians. Some believe it represents the cycle of life. Birth, death and resurrection."

"Resurrection." I heard a note in Kendrick's voice and glanced down. His gaze was still on me and I again felt those icy prickles at the base of my spine. "An odd symbol to be placed in the grave of a man missing his skull."

Almost as strange as a *memento mori* tattoo on the wrist of a woman who had been buried alive.

As our gazes locked, I heard chanting, distant and dreamlike. It was all I could do to tear my gaze away to glance at the mortsafes. Twelve caged graves and an unmarked grave in the center. A young woman buried alive and a skeleton with a missing skull. What on earth had I gotten myself into this time?

"What about the other graves?" I asked, striving for a disaffected tone. It wasn't easy. Not with that phantom chant echoing in my ears. Not with Kendrick's compelling eyes measuring my every move.

"Did you find any evidence of exhumations or fresh burials?"

"The ground is so overgrown with weeds and vines, we wouldn't be able to tell unless we remove the mortsafes," he said.

"Will you remove them?"

He hesitated. "We plan to start with the one that's already open and see what we find. The one thing we know for certain is that the victim didn't lock herself in that cage, nor did the skull vanish of its own accord. Someone has been using this place for a long time. Decades, most likely. To what end…" He trailed off as he rose and glanced around the circle. "That's what we have to figure out."

A little while later, we left the burial site and made our way back to the cemetery. Kendrick and I brought up the rear of the procession. As we trudged along the path, I kept thinking how badly I wanted the day to be over, but I knew, in the same way that I knew other unknowable things, that this was just the beginning of many dark days to come. I would need to be constantly on my guard if I accepted Darius Goodwine's proposal, because insinuating myself in the search for a killer, human or otherwise, was no small matter. I would be deliberately placing myself in harm's way on the very slim chance that my great-grandmother's lost key actually existed and could be found.

A part of me—the sensible part—wanted to distance myself from anything involving Darius Goodwine. I was sorry that a young woman's life had been taken and genuinely horrified at the circumstances surrounding her death and burial. But I didn't know her. This was not my business.

Someone or something seemed intent on making it my business, though. Why else had I been summoned to that clearing by the watcher in the woods? Why else had I stumbled upon that meeting between Annalee Nash and Martin Stark? According to Darius Goodwine, only I could end this. But how? And at what price?

My heart started to pound in earnest at the prospect because no matter how suspicious I found Darius Goodwine's proposal, no matter how many times I resolved to keep my distance, a fascination was starting to grow. Already I could feel myself getting caught up in the intrigue and I knew how things would go from here on out. All too soon I would become absorbed in the secret societies that Darius Goodwine had spoken of and I would obsess over their deep roots and entangled alliances as I tried to painstakingly piece together a connection. I would become engrossed in *memento mori* art and the placement of those cages and the identities of the remains inside. I would study the triskele and its convoluted meanings and then I would delve as deeply as I dared into the concepts of soul transference and raising the dead.

And all the while I conducted my stealth investigation, I would spend many a sleepless night worrying about Devlin's involvement even though I knew that Darius had purposely planted that seed of doubt to torment me.

I was so deeply contemplative that I didn't see the tree root snaking across the path in front of me. I tripped, half expecting Kendrick to grab my elbow to balance me, but he seemed not to notice. I supposed that, like me, he was lost in his own churning thoughts. After a bit, though, I could sense his attention.

When I glanced at him, he said, "What do you make of all this?"

"You're asking me?" I gave an uneasy shrug. "I'm not a detective. What I think hardly matters."

"If your opinion didn't matter, I wouldn't have asked for it. And I would have sent you on your way the moment you turned up at that grave site. I'm asking because you know about burials and symbols. You're the closest thing I have to an expert on those cages."

I took a moment to consider his question. "The presence of the mortsafes in such a remote location still puzzles me. I can't imagine where one would go to buy such a device in this day and age, let alone a dozen of them. They must have been custom-made. But how they were transported into the clearing without being seen, I have no idea. There's a sense of isolation out here, but we're still within the city limits."

"This area wasn't incorporated until a few years ago and it hasn't changed much," Kendrick said. "The cages could have been hauled out here by cover of darkness, maybe over the course of several nights or even weeks."

"But why?"

"That's the million-dollar question, isn't it?"

I swatted a mosquito from my face. "Something else has been bothering me. I told you yesterday that the original purpose of mortsafes was to protect fresh remains from body snatchers known as resurrectionists. The symbol on the medallion you found in the center grave represents birth, death and resurrection. It's probably a loose connection at best, but the word *resurrection* keeps cropping up." I wanted to ask him if he knew of a group that called themselves the Eternal Brotherhood of Resurrectionists, but I didn't want to explain where I'd heard the name. Something about Kendrick still niggled and I didn't think it a good idea to reveal what I knew of the Brotherhood, especially considering the source. For now, I wanted him to continue thinking of me as nothing more than a cemetery restorer who had been in the wrong place at the wrong time.

"It does seem a loose connection," he agreed. "But the skull in that grave was certainly resurrected."

"And what do you make of *that*?" I asked.

He shrugged. "I agree with Rushing. The grave was exhumed, the skull removed after decomposition and the remains wrapped and reburied."

"But why?"

"Maybe someone wanted a trophy."

I glanced at him sharply. "Trophies are usually associated with serial killers, aren't they? Is that what you think you're dealing with here? Do you think the circle is his burial ground?"

"Serial killer in the way that you mean is a reach.

But like I said, someone's obviously been using that place for decades. As to the purpose…" He trailed off again on the same question, as if reluctant to take the speculation any further. "For now, let's concentrate on the victim. The woman in the cage. How did you know to look at her arm when you viewed the body?"

Was that a note of suspicion I heard in his voice? "When I first came upon the grave, I glimpsed part of the tattoo on her wrist through the cage."

He nodded. "And the tattoo itself—*memento mori*. That phrase means something to you, doesn't it? I saw your face as you translated."

"It doesn't mean anything to me personally, but I was startled to find such a message on the arm of a woman who had been buried alive. Weren't you?"

He didn't answer. "What else can you tell me about that phrase?"

"I'm hardly an expert, except perhaps when it comes to cemetery *memento mori*, but I suppose it can best be described as a reflection on mortality."

"Remember to die." He repeated the words to himself as if he were trying to work something out.

"Sometimes translated as 'remember death' or 'remember that you must die.'" I pushed back the damp tendrils at my temples. "*Memento mori* was both a philosophy and an art movement that sprang up in Europe around the time of the Black Death. Poems were written about the fleeting nature of earthly pursuits and portraits were often painted with the subject holding a human skull."

We exchanged a glance and I resisted the urge to

look over my shoulder. We were approaching day's end and the elongated shadows that fell across our path seemed menacing.

"Go on," he said.

"The depictions can seem a little gruesome nowadays, but in the context of the time, it was a reminder that life on earth is just the beginning of our journey and that one's thoughts and deeds are best focused on the afterlife. As you might imagine, death images were especially prevalent in religious-themed art. Other than museums and cathedrals, the most common places to find examples in this country are old churchyards, particularly the Puritan cemeteries on the Eastern seaboard. The symbols etched into seventeenth-century gravestones—death's-heads, skeletons in coffins, scythes, winged hourglasses—are all examples of *memento mori* art. As is the skull tattoo on the back of your hand."

"And here I thought it was just a memento of an unfortunate night in Amsterdam." Kendrick kept his gaze focused straight ahead, but a smile flashed so brief I almost didn't catch it. The teasing glimpse made me wonder why he didn't do it more often. That smile made him seem more approachable. More human.

But maybe that wasn't such a good thing.

I studied his profile from the corner of my eye. "You mentioned earlier that you'd been to the Czech Republic. An example of *memento mori* on a very grand scale is the Sedlec Ossuary."

"The Church of Bones," he said. "I've been there."

Somehow I wasn't surprised. "I've always wanted to visit."

"It's quite a sight if you aren't too squeamish. I was particularly impressed by the bone chandelier and the garlands of skulls in the nave."

"I've seen pictures. They're really very beautiful in their own way."

He paused, giving me another glance. "You seem to know a lot about all this."

"I obviously don't know as much as you as I've never seen the chapel in person."

"I don't mean the ossuary. I'm talking about *memento mori* in general."

"Given my profession, it's only natural I'd be drawn to gravestone art and symbolism. It's a passion of mine. I've done a lot of research over the years."

"Which is precisely why I asked for your opinion," he said.

By this time we were back inside Seven Gates Cemetery walking side by side through the headstones and monuments and then pausing when we came to the cottonwood grove where we'd talked before. We stood watching the procession pass through the main gate to the coroner's van parked at the side of the road.

As the vehicles pulled away one by one, Kendrick's gaze came back to rest on me, causing little tingles of unease at the back of my neck.

"Thank you for coming into the morgue," he said. "I know that wasn't easy for you."

"I'm just sorry I wasn't more help, but we knew positive identification would be a long shot."

"It's possible you may yet remember something."

I thought of those flashing rubies and that waiting silhouette in the shop window, but still I held my silence.

"If you do remember something, you have my number," he said.

I nodded.

"It's getting late." We turned as one to glance at the horizon where the sun had started to sink beneath the treetops. "Not a good idea for you to be out here alone. There aren't any streetlights along the road and it'll get dark fast once the sun goes down."

"I appreciate your concern, but working alone in remote locations comes with the territory."

A scowl flickered across his brow. "Yes, but you did just stumble across a woman's body and her killer is still on the loose. He might start to wonder at some point if you caught a glimpse of him."

"I didn't see anything," I insisted.

"He can't be sure of that."

"Then I'll be careful. I'll lock all the gates until I'm ready to leave and I'll keep my phone handy. Please don't concern yourself with my safety. As I said, I'm accustomed to working alone in remote places. I know how to take precautions. I'll be fine."

He leaned in a little closer and lifted his hand. My instinct was to recoil, but something kept me rooted to the spot as my breath caught unexpectedly.

"You have something in your hair." He plucked

a leaf from the tangled strands and let it float to the ground.

"Thanks." I didn't outwardly react to the contact, but a pulse jumped in my throat. I knew that I should pull away at that moment, step back and take a breath. But I didn't and neither did Kendrick. Instead, we remained so close I could feel his breath against my face. He smelled surprisingly of mint, a fresh scent that seemed at odds with the direness of his warning. I had the strangest urge to cup my hands around my nose and mouth and draw that cleansing scent deep into my lungs.

I didn't understand my fascination for Detective Kendrick. What I felt wasn't physical attraction or a fleeting infatuation and it certainly wasn't love at first sight. I was still very much in love with Devlin. I would never want any man as deeply as I desired John Devlin.

But there was an undeniable pull to Kendrick. He was a curiosity, an enigma. A rebound that I instinctively knew could be my downfall.

Tread carefully and trust no one.

I could see the sun reflected in his eyes. Like his scent, the glow belied the darkness that I knew must thrive inside him. Those eyes were enticing and so mesmerizing it took me another moment before I managed to glance away.

Kendrick stirred restlessly at my side, but he made no move to leave. It was as if something had rooted him to the spot, as well.

We were all alone in the cemetery and the situation affected me on a surprisingly emotional level.

Lucien Kendrick was the first man I'd been alone with since the last time Devlin and I had been together. Unless, of course, I counted Darius Goodwine's visit, but I wouldn't allow Darius to intrude upon the moment because I couldn't afford a diversion. I needed to maintain my focus on Lucien Kendrick. I had to keep up my guard around him. Not because I thought he would try anything untoward. His behavior had been nothing but professional. It wasn't even about my suspicions. I needed to stay alert and on guard because I suddenly found myself wondering what it would be like to be kissed by him.

"Not a good idea," Kendrick said.

His response startled me. "What?" My hand flew to my neck as if the supernatural properties of Rose's key could chase away my embarrassment. "What isn't a good idea?"

"Being out here by yourself." Those scintillating eyes took me in. I could feel the stroke of his gaze at my throat, on my shoulders and all down the length of my bare arms, making my fingertips tingle.

His voice lowered, quickening my breath and triggering a dangerous response. "Like I said, you shouldn't linger once the sun goes down. That's when the monsters come out."

I knew about monsters. I knew about the dark, inhuman things that came calling once twilight fell.

But I didn't know if Lucien Kendrick was one of them.

Ten

After Kendrick left, I locked all the gates and made sure my phone and pepper spray were well within reach. I wasn't afraid, but I couldn't deny a growing sense of unease. What if Kendrick was right? What if the killer thought that I had caught a glimpse of him?

For all I knew, he could be watching me from the woods at that very moment, waiting for the chance to tie up a pesky loose end. What better time to strike than now, while I was alone in the cemetery? The nearest house was a quarter of a mile away and the road was completely deserted. No one would hear me scream.

Not afraid, huh?

I forced myself to take a deep breath as I picked up the scrub brush and ran a hand over the soft bristles. I had no reason to believe that I was a target. I hadn't seen or heard anything to indicate that I was in danger, and despite Detective Kendrick's supposition to the contrary, the killer wouldn't have dared bring his victim through the cemetery in front of a witness. More than likely, the crime had been committed at night while I lay sleeping peacefully in my hammock. I had nothing to fear. The killer was long gone by now. Why would he hang around the cemetery when the police had only just left?

But try as I might to calm my prickly nerves, I kept glancing up to check my surroundings. The sun was barely visible above the horizon. Soon the light would fade and dusk would fall. The ghosts would come out. So far I'd been able to keep the manifestations at bay with Rose's key, but how long until Darius Goodwine's prophecy came true? How long until I no longer had the means or the fortitude to protect myself? *You'll likely suffer the same fate as your great-grandmother unless...*

Unless I found her long-lost key. Darius had vowed to help me if I unmasked the killer, but it was a little too easy for him to make such a promise. He didn't even want anyone to know that we'd spoken. He couldn't get involved, he'd said. Because he wasn't physically present or because he knew more than he wanted to reveal?

I sensed with every fiber of my being that he was up to something. That he hadn't yet told me the whole story. I would be a fool to consider his scheme for even a moment except for two very important reasons. He knew about Rose's lost key and he'd shown me the arrangement of her numbers. How he'd acquired that knowledge, I couldn't imagine unless he truly did have eyes and ears on the other side.

The light grew steadily thinner and the silence in the cemetery became so profound that I could hear nothing beyond my own breathing as I worked. It was time to call it a day and head home before twilight. Angus would want his dinner soon, and besides, it was the smart thing to do. I could turn in early and get a fresh start in the morning.

For some reason, though, I didn't want to leave that section of the headstones unfinished. Why I felt such a compulsion to complete the task I really couldn't say except that I wasn't anxious to return to the house. But even more than that, my job was the only thing in my life I had any control over. My work ethic was the last bit of normalcy I could cling to and so I scrubbed and scrubbed at the delicate stone as if I could somehow wash away all the bad things that had happened.

I bent my back to the chore, letting time and daylight slip away as my mind wandered back to the confrontation with Darius Goodwine. Back to the conversation with Lucien Kendrick. Back to Annalee Nash's crouching form, to the corpse's tattoo and to the watcher in the woods.

Suddenly my mouth went dry as a premonition skirted along the curvature of my spine. My head came up and I once again scanned the woods, peering into the shadows cast by the church ruins, searching along the shady tree line before focusing my gaze upon the north entrance.

Someone was there.

I could feel the penetration of an uncanny stare through the gate, but unlike the day before, I wasn't coerced from my work to follow a silent command. This was a different scrutiny. A cold and calculating surveillance. Like a hunter stalking its prey.

Goose bumps popped on my arms as a thrill of panic raced across my scalp. I drew a deep breath and steadied my nerves as I reached for the pepper spray in my pocket. Thumbing off the top, I stared unblinking at the gate. Nothing moved. Nothing stirred. Not so much as a squirrel foraged in the underbrush.

But someone was there.

I could feel a presence. Could almost hear the shallow breaths and thudding heartbeat of excitement.

Turning my head slightly, I listened and observed with my heightened senses. Sniffing the air for a telltale fragrance and peering into the shadows for a deeper silhouette. Then opening my mind to try and pick up a stray thought or even slip into the watcher's memory.

The wall was still there, an impenetrable fortress. I shivered and withdrew, concentrating instead on my own defenses as I took a quick assessment of my setting.

Seven Gates had once been a churchyard, presumably built on hallowed ground. Between that and my great-grandmother's key, I'd been safe here from ghosts and those strange beings I called in-betweens. But a human monster was a different matter. In some ways a deeper terror.

I reminded myself yet again that no one could enter the cemetery without difficulty. I'd locked all the gates and scaling the fence would be no easy feat. By the time someone crawled over, I could be up and through the front gate, in my car and long gone.

But why was I so determined to tempt fate? What did I really hope to accomplish by remaining here alone with dusk fast approaching? Was I really that desperate to prove to myself and to Detective Kendrick that I was unafraid and untouched by recent events? That with the evolution of my dark gift, I was more capable than ever of taking care of myself? I didn't need Kendrick, I didn't need Devlin and I certainly didn't need the likes of Darius Goodwine.

Even so, I was being reckless and I knew it.

Sliding the pepper spray back into my pocket, I dumped the water bucket, and then gathered up all my tools and brushes, trying not to panic but all the while keeping a wary eye on the north gate. *Where George Willoughby had been buried.*

With everything in hand, I headed for the main entrance, stooping to grab the handle of the cooler on my way out. Quickly, I loaded everything into my vehicle and then went back to relock the main gate. As I fumbled with the key, I glanced out over the cemetery.

The north gate hung open and swung ever so slightly on its hinges as if someone had just entered the cemetery.

I'd secured all the entrances earlier. No mistake about that.

Which meant that someone with a key had unfastened the gate and slipped through while I had been busy with the tools. The same someone who still watched me from the shadows. Possibly the same someone who had buried that poor woman alive in a caged grave, insuring there would be no escape.

Blood pounded at my temples as I stood there clutching the gate. I saw nothing out of the ordinary, but I had the strongest sensation that someone— something—moved steadily toward me through the headstones, using the crumbling statuary for cover. Whatever was out there had no fear of hallowed ground.

I held my breath, searching and searching.

And then I caught sight of her. The dead woman I'd last seen in the morgue.

She stood in the deep shade of an ivy-covered obelisk. So still, so silent, I hadn't even noticed her at first.

Her appearance…

She looked as if…

A wave of revulsion rolled over me. I wanted to believe that I was seeing things, that I was trapped in another lucid dream or a waking nightmare. But I was wide awake and there she was.

Risen from the dead.

Immortal.

I tried to swallow past the knot of fear in my throat as I peered at her through the shadows. She didn't present herself in the way of a ghost. Most of the spirits I encountered manifested as they'd looked in life, even the ones who'd met with a violent demise.

Not this one. She appeared exactly as I'd seen her in the morgue—pale, bluish, filthy from the grave, dark hair matted with twigs and rolled leaves. Nor was she transparent. There was nothing airy or ethereal about her form. Instead, she looked solid and fleshy. Earthbound.

I blinked to see if I could make her go away. No such luck. She was still there, half a graveyard between us but near enough that I could detect a faint smell emanating from her body. Not jasmine, not lavender, not any of the scents I'd come to associate with certain ghosts, but rather a sickly sweet putrescence that brought to mind the premature decay of a terminal patient. Someone more dead than alive.

Or someone recently dead and brought back to life.

If not a ghost, what are you?

I didn't want to ponder that question at length, didn't dare put a name to her presence. It couldn't be. But the truth stood right there before me.

Panic swelled in my chest as I watched her, watched *it*. And *it* watched me back, head slightly cocked, mouth agape.

At last I tore my gaze away, glancing past the wretched manifestation to the woods that loomed over the cemetery. The shadows near the north gate were deeper than those along the fence. Someone was out there just beyond my field of vision. Someone with intelligence and cunning. Someone with a purpose.

My gaze shot back to the dead woman. To my horror, she'd moved out of the shadow of the monument so that I could see her more clearly now. As I stood frozen in place, she took a halting step toward me. And then another and another.

Her movements were heavy and uncertain. I

didn't worry that I'd be unable to outrun her. I worried that she existed at all.

She put up a hand, not in supplication, but as if she needed to push something out of her way. I saw the tattoo on her wrist and the glint of those ruby studs in her ears. The knees of her jeans were caked with dried dirt as if she had fallen or been shoved to the ground before her death.

Slowly but surely she plodded toward the gate. Toward me. A thousand images from a thousand horror movies rose to mind and it was all I could do to stifle a scream.

You're not real. You can't be real. I see ghosts, yes, and sometimes in-betweens, but I've never seen anything like you.

The putrid smell grew stronger as did the sound of buzzing flies. Maybe it was my imagination because she was still some distance away, but I thought I saw the bluish-green iridescence of a corpse beetle clinging to a strand of hair that had fallen across her face.

I reacted then, twisting the key in the gate lock until I heard the tumblers click. With no semblance of calm or bravado, I turned and sprinted to my vehicle, stumbling over a rock in my haste as I pushed the unlock button on the remote and the lights flashed. I didn't dare look back, but I could have sworn I heard her footsteps. Still heavy, still lumbering, but steady and determined. And getting closer.

A twig snapped behind me and I spun to face the horror that had come after me.

There was nothing, of course. Nothing but shadows and fading sunlight. Nothing but the distant hoot of an owl, the haunting wail of a loon. No one was there. I was alone.

I forced myself to take a deep breath as my fingers clutched the remote. Scrambling into the vehicle, I slammed the door, pressed the auto lock button and started the engine, but I didn't pull away. I sat staring through the gate into the cemetery as I gripped the steering wheel with both hands.

Even if the dead woman somehow managed to get through the locked entrance, all I had to do was put the car in gear and drive away. I wasn't quite sure why I didn't do so at that very moment. Maybe I still wanted to prove I was unafraid. Maybe I wanted to tempt the watcher in the woods out into the open so that I could get a sense of what or whom I was really up against. Or maybe I was just plain crazy.

No matter the reason, I sat there trying to control my fear as a little voice goaded me to leave. *Only an idiot would sit here with that thing in the cemetery.*

But I still didn't drive away because as my heart began to settle and my pulse slowed, I realized that the dead woman didn't really exist, after all. At least, not in any ambulatory form. She wasn't an ungainly apparition or a waking dream or even a figment of my imagination, but instead one of Darius Goodwine's illusions.

Relief washed over me even as I felt the chill of a fresh apprehension.

"Darius Goodwine." I whispered the name under my breath with the same exaggerated derision I'd heard him use.

I didn't know why he'd come back into my life,

but I had no doubt he was up to something illegal, immoral and quite possibly unnatural.

He wanted something from me and I suspected his motivation had very little to do with finding a killer. He'd yet to reveal his true agenda, and until such time, he meant to keep me off guard and vulnerable with these visions. By making me see what he wanted me to see.

Like the corpse beetles he'd conjured on my skin. Like the beast persona conjured by a root doctor named Atticus Pope.

Nothing is as it seems.

Not even the zombie in Seven Gates Cemetery.

Eleven

After another long and mostly sleepless night, I took the next morning off and drove up to Charleston to confer with Rupert Shaw.

We'd come a long way since the early days of our friendship when I'd presented mostly hypothetical situations because I couldn't bring myself to fully confide in him. Keeping the secret of my gift had been too deeply ingrained for far too long and unburdening myself hadn't come easy, even with Dr. Shaw. If he suspected the truth about my inquiries, he'd never let on, but instead seemed content to savor the tidbits that I'd felt comfortable sharing.

As the director and founder of the Charleston Institute for Parapsychology Studies, he was as close to an expert in matters involving the unknown as I'd ever come across and, more important to me, he had an open mind and boundless curiosity. Given everything that had happened in the past two days, it was only natural that I should seek him out.

His assistant welcomed me with a curious smile as I entered the restored antebellum. She showed me back to Dr. Shaw's office and he rose from his

cluttered desk to offer a warm greeting. The scent
of aged leather and old books enveloped me and I
found his careworn features and threadbare clothing as comforting as a mother's embrace. His presence never failed to soothe me and I was happy to
see him looking so robust after everything he'd been
through in recent years.

He waved me to the seat opposite his desk and
we both settled in for a long conversation. I spent a
couple of minutes catching him up and then we got
right down to business.

"Ever since I read your email last night, I've buried myself in research," he said, with what I could
only interpret as reluctant excitement. "You've presented some very interesting situations over the
years, but none more so than the one you've come
here about today. Those caged graves will keep me
occupied for weeks."

"Considering what I found inside one of those
cages, I'd say the situation is not only interesting,
but deeply disturbing."

His smile vanished. "The young woman buried
alive. Yes. Very disturbing. I certainly didn't mean
to make light."

"I know you didn't."

"Has she been identified yet?"

"Not that I've been told." I stirred in my chair,
finding myself anxious and jittery. So many things
had happened in such a short amount of time I hardly
knew where to begin. At any other time, the sight
of the dead woman lumbering through the graveyard would have been uppermost on my mind and

I would have grilled Dr. Shaw on the possibility, no matter how remote, of a corpse being brought back to life. But I'd already written off the incident as one of Darius Goodwine's tricks and today I was more occupied with historical matters. Namely, the deep roots and entangled affiliations of the secret societies he'd mentioned. I felt certain one or more of those stealth groups were at the heart of the circle of graves, I just didn't yet know how.

"We can talk about the mortsafes later," I said. "I would really love to hear your thoughts. But first I need to know what you've been able to find out about the Eternal Brotherhood of Resurrectionists and the *Congé*. I know you haven't had a lot of time to research, but I'm hoping you'll be able to help shed some light."

"I hope so, too," he said. "You mentioned an affiliation with the Order of the Coffin and the Claw. As you know, I'm well versed in the history and the workings of the Order. I won't go into the details of my relationship, but suffice to say I can speak with some authority on the topic."

Spoken like a true Claw, I thought. Artifice and stratagem had always been their discipline. It went against the nature of the group to disclose anything pertaining to the privileged membership and inner workings.

"As a matter of fact, I've always been interested in secret societies in general," he went on. "The South, particularly our own fair state, has always had an affinity for cloak-and-dagger clubs going back to the Revolutionary War days. But the Eternal Brotherhood of Resurrectionists and the *Congé*..." His snowy brows furrowed as a shadow flitted across his features. "May I ask where you heard about these groups?"

"From Darius Goodwine."

His lips thinned in disapproval as he observed me over steepled fingers. "So he's made a return, has he?"

"We've been in touch," I replied vaguely. No need to burden Dr. Shaw with Darius's extraordinary proposition or my continued susceptibility to his trickery. Given Dr. Shaw's history with the Goodwines, he might be so concerned for my safety that he'd feel compelled to call Devlin. The last thing I wanted was to drag him into my latest intrigue. If he were to finally make contact after all these months, I wanted it to be out of his desire for my company and not because he felt an obligation to protect me from an old enemy.

I flicked my ponytail over my shoulder as I sat forward. "According to Darius Goodwine, the Eternal Brotherhood of Resurrectionists was involved in something he called soul transference. Another group known as the *Congé* was their mortal enemy. Both groups may have been affiliated with the Order of the Coffin and the Claw, but I have no idea how. To use your own description, it's all very cloak and dagger."

"Indeed," Dr. Shaw agreed with a brief nod. He picked up a fountain pen, toying with the cap as though he needed to occupy his hands. "The Order has always taken great pains to keep their ceremonies and initiations hush-hush. The clandestine nature of the group is a large part of their mystique and mythology. But anyone who has ever spent any time at Emerson University knows of them. On campus—in fact, all around Charleston—the Order of the Coffin and the Claw is an open secret. But the Eternal Brotherhood of Resurrectionists and the *Congé* seem to be true shadow organizations. So ambiguous as to only be spoken of in whispers."

"And the connection between the three groups?" I pressed.

He hesitated, as if weighing how much he should tell me. He capped and uncapped the fountain pen so many times that I found myself on the verge of snatching it away from him. "There have been rumors over the years. Vague suppositions at best. I'd forgotten all about those old stories until I read your email last night. Then I began to wonder."

I leaned in, my attention riveted. "Wonder about what? What are the rumors?"

"As I said, this is all supposition at best."

"I understand."

"Nothing of what I say must leave this room."

"Dr. Shaw…"

He put up a hand to silence me. "Indulge an old man his precautions."

I drew a breath and tried to tamp down my impatience as I nodded. "Of course. You know you can trust me. I won't say a word."

He shot a glance toward the doorway as if to make certain no one listened in. "According to these rumors, every so often a Claw is recruited by an organization that is buried so deeply underground no one seems to know its name."

"Recruited for what purpose?"

Again he silenced me as he got up to slide the pocket doors closed. His precautions were starting to make me nervous and I found my own gaze darting to the French doors to see if anyone lurked among the roses.

"Membership is legacy and goes back for generations," he said as he resettled himself behind his desk. "A new recruit is only brought in upon the death of an old one. The most powerful and influential are selected from the ranks of the most powerful and influential. The elite chosen from the elite, if you get my meaning."

I got it, but I was hard-pressed to imagine a group even more powerful and secret than the Order of the Coffin and the Claw.

I gave him a doubtful glance. "You think this supersecret organization is either the Eternal Brotherhood of Resurrectionists or the *Congé*?"

"Not the Brotherhood. I've found no reason to believe they're affiliated in any way with the Order." He paused thoughtfully. "But the *Congé*…yes, I think it's certainly possible."

I stared out at the sunny garden, idly probing the shadows along the wall as I tried to recall everything Darius Goodwine had told me about the *Congé*. They were as devious and cunning as their enemy and every bit as dangerous. It all sounded like pure fantasy, but some would think the same about my ability to see ghosts. After all this time and after so many extraordinary sightings and experiences, I knew better than to dismiss anything as far-fetched. There was no such thing in my world.

But a secret organization called the *Congé*—that was something new and I felt a surge of excitement and trepidation over what might be another life-changing revelation.

"The word itself is of French origin," Dr. Shaw said, and I looked up with a start. "It means quite literally a ceremonious sendoff. A bit of humor or irony, considering the purpose of the group."

"Which is?"

"I suppose one might call them restorers."

I lifted a brow without comment.

He set the pen aside as he coupled his hands on the desk. I thought I detected a slight tremor but that may have been my imagination.

"I can see how the *Congé* would be considered the mortal enemy of these so-called resurrectionists," he said. "Everything about the Brotherhood would be anathema to them."

"How so?"

"If the Eternal Brother of Resurrectionists sought to bring the dead back to life, the *Congé* believed it their mission to stamp out the unnatural in any shape or form. To restore and maintain order in the living world by eradicating anything or anyone that threatened the balance." He paused. "A sort of special forces team for the supernatural, if you will."

Twelve

"There cannot possibly be such a group!" Surely he was toying with me. Having a bit of fun at my expense until he told me what he'd really learned.

But Dr. Shaw merely shrugged. "Not as an official or sanctioned body. Of course not. But as a private organization existing on the fringes… Who knows? The rich and powerful have always been drawn to the occult and the work I do here is not really so different. It may well be nothing more than folklore, but it's not the most extraordinary thing I've ever heard."

I wasn't so sure about that. Even by my measure, the concept of a supernatural special forces team was fairly extreme.

By this time, I was bolted to my chair, utterly enthralled by Dr. Shaw's revelation and not a little unsettled by the implication. I wanted to believe it a coincidence that we were discussing an underground organization with a French name the day after I'd met a mysterious police detective who had once lived in Paris, but I didn't see how any of this could be happenstance.

Which meant my instincts about Kendrick had

been right all along. There was a good chance he'd known about those cages before I ever stumbled upon the body and an even greater chance that he'd been aware of the watcher in the woods. I couldn't help asking myself again how a man with his background and edge had ended up on a small-town police force. What had brought a world-weary traveler such as he back to the bracken waters of the Lowcountry?

"The *Congé*." I said the word aloud, testing it on my tongue. Could such an organization really exist? Could the influences from the dead world be so strong as to require a specialized team to combat it?

For so many years, Papa had been the only other person I knew who saw ghosts. I'd grown up believing that our gift was unique to the Gray side of the family, to *us*, but I now knew that my ignorance was a testament to how sequestered and protected I'd been, how insular my worldview. Little by little, the truth about my birth and my legacy had been revealed. Doors to the dead world had been thrown open and I'd encountered all manner of supernatural entities.

So why couldn't I accept the possibility—even the probability—that others like me existed? That some had even banded together to rid the living world of the forces that refused to be constrained by the boundaries of death?

Such a group would be a good thing, wouldn't it? After all, I was in search of a lost key that could conceivably close my door to the dead world forever.

So why did the notion of the *Congé* and their mission bother me so much?

I wiped suddenly clammy hands down the sides of my jeans. "If this group is so secret, how is it you even know about them?"

Dr. Shaw looked a little rattled by the question. "My dear, I don't *know* anything. As I said, everything I've heard is mostly conjecture and gossip. Please don't mistake my ramblings as any kind of factual information. My knowledge of either organization is extremely limited."

"I understand." But his adamant denial made me even more curious. I studied him furtively, wondering how much he still kept from me. Despite the excitement of a new discovery, he seemed agitated by our discussion and getting more so as we progressed.

"I have no way of knowing if any of these things are true," he stressed. "But a person in my position hears things. Over the years, my investigations have led me to any number of unlikely places, and I dare say, many of the friendships I've cultivated would surprise you. From the rumors I remember and the sources I've contacted since reading your email, I've come to believe that the *Congé* was formed by some of the oldest and most powerful families in the state. Do you see now why I must insist on keeping this conversation between the two of us?" he asked worriedly. "And why I don't wish to speak as though I have any authority on the matter? At the very least, reputations are at stake and I would hate for anyone to make trouble for the institute."

"Could they do that?" I asked in alarm.

"Why take the chance? I've always found it better to fly under the radar than into the fray."

"I'm sure you're right." But I still didn't think he was being altogether forthcoming and fear of repercussions had little to do with his reticence. He was a Claw, after all, and that pedigree came with its own influence and privilege. He wasn't worried about the institute or even his own personal safety. Something else held him back.

We both fell silent as he turned to stare out at the garden, his attention so rapt that I couldn't help following his gaze. I saw nothing but a butterfly flitting among the roses. Nothing more sinister than a tabby stalking the shadows. But like the Willoughby house, a pall had been cast over the garden and our visit.

"Dr. Shaw?"

He roused himself. "Yes, my dear. You were saying?"

"You've explained a possible relationship between the Order and the *Congé*, but what about the Eternal Brotherhood of Resurrectionists?"

"The Brotherhood?" He scowled down at his desk, refusing to meet my gaze. "I'm afraid that may be a dead end. My sources had nothing of consequence to impart and the internet has proven no help at all. Although my assistant tells me there is something called the Darknet, which might yield more fruitful results if one knew where to look."

I recognized an evasive answer when I heard one. Dr. Shaw had uncovered something he didn't want to share and my mission now became one of how best to relieve him of that information.

"What aren't you telling me?" I asked gently.

He glanced up in surprise. "My dear, I've told you all I know."

I leaned toward him. "Have you forgotten what I confided in you about my gift? I've become very sensitive to emotions. I can tell when someone is stressed. If I concentrate hard enough, I can sometimes even interpret their thoughts or enter their memories."

His gaze turned reproachful. "My dear Amelia, have you forgotten how well I know you? You would never violate my privacy. Of that, I'm certain."

I sighed and offered an apologetic shrug. "You're right. I wouldn't. Not intentionally. But if emotions are strong enough, I sometimes can't help it. It just happens. So maybe it would be best if you tell me what you found out about the Brotherhood."

He picked up the pen, fingering the barrel like a worry bead. "I'd rather not speak of such unseemly things."

I blinked at his sudden propriety. "Please don't be concerned on my account. I've dealt with a lot of unpleasantness these past few years and my eyes have been thoroughly opened."

"You haven't dealt with this," he said grimly. "In all my years of investigating the paranormal, I've never come across anything half so disturbing."

"That sounds ominous."

His eyes snapped with sudden emotion. "It is ominous and I would urge that you proceed with the utmost caution. From what I've been able to ascertain, the Eternal Brotherhood of Resurrectionists was a very sinister organization. One best left in the deepest, darkest shadows of the underworld."

How sinister? I wondered. Raising-the-dead type of sinister? Soul-transference type of sinister?

I thought of the young woman in the caged grave. Buried-alive type of sinister?

"Were they ever involved in murder?"

I saw a shudder go through him. "My dear, murder was the very least of their transgressions."

My breath caught. "What do you mean?"

"Young women held captive, tortured and abused. Orgies and human sacrifices." His gaze darted back to the garden. "Sexual deviancy of the most twisted variety."

Icy needles pricked. "But that was a long time ago. The Brotherhood no longer exists, surely. Even if they did, they couldn't get away with holding people captive in this day and age." But, of course, young women were taken all the time by murderers and sexual predators. One only had to watch the news to know that such horrors still existed.

I glanced at Dr. Shaw. "I feel as though you're still keeping something from me. Please don't. I need to know everything you've found out about these organizations, no matter how horrific or indelicate you deem the information to be. I know you tend to worry about me, but the best defense I have is knowledge. I can't protect myself if I don't know who and what I'm up against."

He sighed. "You're right, of course."

"Then please continue."

He didn't look at all robust now. I could trace every one of his years along the deep furrows of his brow. "As I said earlier, I've heard rumors about the *Congé* for years. Legends and folklore passed down through the generations. But in all my time of studying the unknowable and the unexplainable, I've only ever come across one written reference to the Eternal Brotherhood of Resurrectionists, and that in a book that was published in the early 1800s. A book about witchcraft and black magic."

My eyes widened. "Do you still have the book?"

He removed a leather-bound volume from a locked drawer and flipped to a section that he'd marked with a scrap of paper. Turning the book to face me, he slid the fragile tome across the desk so that I could view the accompanying illustration of robed and hooded figures clasping hands in a circle around a dead man. A gossamer likeness floated over the body. The deceased's soul or spirit, no doubt, rising to take refuge in a living vessel.

In the background, men and women in various stages of undress danced and copulated while caged young women looked on in terror.

There were other indecencies in the drawing. Pornographic depictions of the basest nature.

My stomach churned unexpectedly. Despite my veneer of sophistication, I was still at heart the girl that had spent a large part of her life sequestered behind cemetery walls.

"The text is in Latin," I said, turning the tissue-thin pages with the utmost care. "I can only pick out a word here and there, but am I correct in assuming from the illustration that this is a soul transference ceremony?"

Dr. Shaw nodded. "Conceivably, the same spirit could change vessels any number of times, thus attaining immortality."

I looked up. "Immortality?"

"Just think of it," he said. "The spirit of a man born centuries ago residing in the body of someone alive today. The concept boggles the mind, does it not?" He seemed to catch himself then and his excitement dwindled as his smile thinned. "Of course, those worthy of immortality—the Madame Curies, the Albert Einsteins, the Da Vincis—would likely not be the ones to seek it."

"What purpose did the captives serve in the ceremony?" I asked. "Were they sacrificed?"

"Not in the way you mean. Are you familiar with the African term *muti*? It means *medicine* and it usually consists of a mixture of roots, herbs and body parts that aid in magic rituals."

"Body parts?" My hand crept to my throat.

"It gets worse," he warned. "The most desirable *muti* is made from the limbs and organs of the living. It's believed that the terror and agony of the victims make the spell more potent. Consequently, medicine murders are extremely brutal, usually committed with machetes and hatchets. Sometimes even shards of glass."

I stared at him in horror. "You said the murders *are* brutal. Present tense."

"It's still a fairly common practice in certain parts

of Africa. While the preference is always for parts from the living, I've read that there's been a recent uptick in grave robbing."

"Could that explain the mortsafes?"

"I suppose it's possible. African roots run deep in the Lowcountry." He pulled the book from my hands and closed the cover. When he glanced back at me, his blue eyes had deepened. "Are you sure you wish to continue? If either the Brotherhood or the *Congé* are still active, even the most superficial meddling could put you in danger."

"I don't think I have a choice. I can't run away or hide from any of this. You know as well as I do that the unresolved matters of the dead tend to follow me wherever I go."

"Yes," he said. "In that way, you are a very gifted and extraordinary young woman."

I didn't want to get into a lengthy discussion about my mission or the purpose of my abilities. Dr. Shaw and I had differing views. He saw my gift as a noble calling, but I wanted no part in helping the ghosts move on. I solved the mysteries of the dead so the dead would leave me alone.

"What else did the book say?" I asked.

"It tells the story of a witch doctor named Tuma, who was brought over on one of the slave ships in the late 1600s. Charismatic and mesmeric, he used his black magic to ingratiate himself with the most powerful men in Charleston. In exchange for his freedom, he cast dark and sinister spells to insure their continued good health and fortune. The rituals were held in secluded locations and no one dared speak of them in public. But behind closed doors, there were whispered accounts of bondage, torture and mutilations. Of young girls gone missing and their families too terrified to look for them. As the wealth and power of the witch doctor's benefactors grew stronger, their enemies and rivals became weaker. Tuma was held in such high esteem within this secret group that when he fell ill, he taught his devotees a powerful spell so that the alliance could continue even after his death."

"His spirit was transferred into the body of one of the benefactors?"

"If the story is to be believed."

"Do you believe it?"

"As I said, I've only ever run across one written reference to the Eternal Brotherhood of Resurrectionists, but I've heard a verbal account by someone who claimed to have intimate knowledge of a similar group. A kind of offshoot of the original Brotherhood."

"Who did you hear this from?"

"You'll recall my friendship with Essie Goodwine."

My brows shot up in surprise. Essie Goodwine was a root doctor of no small repute who also happened to be the grandmother of Darius Goodwine and Devlin's late wife, Mariama. She was a sage and wizened woman, powerful in her own right, and despite her relationship to Darius, I was stunned to hear her name brought into such a lurid tale.

"I know that you studied root work with her some

years back and that you were the one who brought Mariama to the institute."

"A decision I will regret to my dying day," Dr. Shaw said, and glanced away for a moment as if having to battle a sudden wave of emotion. I knew what he was thinking but would not say. If he'd never brought Mariama Goodwine to live at the institute, his son, Ethan, might still be alive today. But that was all in the past and it did no one any good to dwell.

"What does Essie know about the Brotherhood?" I asked.

Dr. Shaw kept his gaze fixed on the garden for a moment longer before turning back to me, his features perfectly composed. But his eyes were still shadowed and the furrows in his brow had deepened. "She told me about a group she referred to as Resurrection Men. They were disciples of a root doctor turned dark. A man by the name of Atticus Pope."

"Atticus Pope."

He gave me a strange look. "You've heard of him?"

"Yes, from the detective in charge of the investigation. It involves the house I've rented for the summer. It's a long story and I'll fill you in later, but right now I don't want to get sidetracked from Essie."

I could tell he was curious and wanted to question me further, but he merely nodded. "Yes, well, according to Essie, Atticus Pope claimed that the spirit of a powerful witch doctor resided within him. A dangerous *tagati* who was over three hundred years old."

"Tuma?"

"Possibly, if one assumes that Pope knew of the legend. Pope, himself, was charismatic and hypnotic and his devotees flocked to him in droves, including Essie's younger brother. These sycophants were only too willing to follow his every move and carry out his every order."

I wondered if this might account for Darius's interest in the case. His family's connection to a man like Pope could explain a lot of things about Darius Goodwine.

"Pope became the target of a police investigation," Dr. Shaw went on. "The authorities were closing in on him, and in order to escape arrest and imprisonment, he convinced his followers to perform the transference ceremony. Out of his twelve most trusted disciples, the one chosen to host his spirit remained a secret even from the others. They all disappeared one night and were never heard from again."

"Before or after the ceremony?"

"No one seems to know. Most thought they'd gone into hiding, but Essie believed they were murdered by a group even more powerful than Atticus Pope."

"The *Congé*," I said.

"A faction so ruthless and single-minded they were willing to kill a dozen men in order to destroy one evil spirit. Whether or not you believe in the mystical aspects of Essie's story, the murders may well have been real. That could explain the circle of graves you found."

My mind reeled with all that Dr. Shaw had told me. Twelve disciples, twelve caged graves and a desecrated grave in the center. And one young woman who had been buried alive.

"How is it that no one stumbled upon those graves before now?" I asked. "How could so many people vanish without the authorities and their people looking for them? Surely the marshes and swamps were combed at the time."

"Perhaps no one looked for them because no one wanted to find them," he suggested.

"Is that what Essie told you?"

"Not in so many words, but I was given the impression."

"Even her own brother?"

"So it would seem."

The apparent ease with which the families and the police had accepted the disappearances struck me as odd, but I knew nothing of the havoc that had been wreaked by the likes of Atticus Pope and his disciples. Torture. Bondage. Mutilations. *Murder was the least of their transgressions.*

I said with a shudder, "You realize that if anyone were to overhear our conversation…"

"They would think us quite mad, but that's nothing new for me. I know what people say behind my back. However, I find that as I grow older, eccentricity has become a virtue rather than a burden."

"You wear it well," I said.

He smiled. "And now that I've imparted all the information I've been able to dig up, what do you plan to do with it?"

"I wish I knew."

Thanks to Dr. Shaw, I now had some knowledge

of the Eternal Brotherhood of Resurrectionists and their horrifying rituals. I'd learned about the *Congé* and their deadly mission. I understood better the deep roots and entangled alliances that Darius Goodwine had warned me about, but I was no closer to solving that poor woman's murder than I had been before my visit to the institute.

Thirteen

After I left Dr. Shaw, I drove over to Rutledge Avenue to check on my place. I had been gone for nearly three months and the musty odor of neglect assailed me as I let myself in the front door. Wrinkling my nose at the accumulation of dust, I went from room to room, checking windows and doors and assuring myself that everything was exactly as I'd left it.

Despite the heat, I put on the teakettle while I tidied up, and then carried a cup of chamomile out to the backyard where I could sit in the shade and think. The scent of oleander drifted over the fence and a mild breeze stirred the late roses. I was happy to see that the garden had flourished during my absence and I hated to sully the splendor with the ugly specter of bondage, body parts and murder.

My skin crawled at the images that my mind insisted upon conjuring. I wanted no part of any of this madness, and if I hadn't left Angus in Ascension, I might have been tempted to abandon the restoration and disregard Darius Goodwine's proposition.

But as I'd reminded Dr. Shaw, running away was never an option. Not for me. The watcher in the woods would follow me wherever I went and Darius Goodwine could track me through my dreams. I couldn't escape the mystery of those caged graves any more than I could free myself of the ghosts.

As I sat there with the comforting warmth of the teacup between my hands and the breeze cool upon my face, my thoughts turned even blacker. I couldn't stop visualizing what the victim's last moments had been like as she'd frantically clawed her way up through the dirt only to realize the cage still imprisoned her. Why had she been placed there in the first place? Had the killer planned to return for her? For her organs and limbs?

The notion was too horrible to contemplate and I tried to turn my thoughts elsewhere, but I kept coming back to Darius Goodwine's claim that I was the only who could end this. End what? More killings? The spirit of an ancient witch doctor? The age-old battle between the Brotherhood and the *Congé*?

And what of the Willoughbys? How were their deaths connected to the woman in the caged grave?

According to Detective Kendrick's account, George Willoughby had caught his wife with Atticus Pope and his disciples doing "the devil's work" in their home. Séances and spells, Kendrick had said. But who really knew what they'd been up to?

George Willoughby had been so convinced that something or someone had taken over his wife, he'd killed her in her sleep and hid the body so well that no trace of her had ever been found.

As I rolled all of this around in my head, a thought

came to me. An improbable theory that made my hand tremble and my heart start to race.

What if George Willoughby hadn't killed his wife?

What if the twelve murdered disciples had been decoys? What if the transference ceremony had ended before the *Congé* arrived on the scene? What if the living host, the *willing* host, had been Mary Willoughby all along?

With the cunning spirit of Atticus Pope inside her, she could have staged her own death, murdered her own husband and then vanished, leaving behind a ten-year-old girl who remembered nothing of that night.

What had Annalee Nash seen before her father's death? What atrocities had she witnessed because of her mother's affiliation with Atticus Pope?

With an effort, I reined in my imagination as I sipped the cooling tea. After a few moments, the chamomile helped calm me and I released a long breath as I let my head fall back against the chair.

The warmth of the sun on my face soothed me and the movement of the clouds was so hypnotic I found myself drifting off. Which wasn't at all like me. I rarely slept in the daytime. Even in my drowsy state, I wondered if I'd once again fallen prey to Darius Goodwine's mind games. For all I knew, he could be inside my head at that very moment, but I was too tired to force him out.

The cup slipped from my hand and shattered against the patio. I barely stirred, barely registered the sound. Darius was there, all right, and he'd brought the dead woman with him. Even as I slid deeper under his spell, I could sense her presence in the darkest corner of the garden. I could smell the decay of her rotting flesh, could feel those milky eyes upon me. Slowly, I lifted my head and gazed around. She was there in the shadows, staring across the plumbago to where I sat transfixed.

Her flesh had turned a putrid greenish gray and the smell was stronger today, her movements more labored as if the passage of time had further constrained her mobility. She tried to move toward me but could manage no more than a shaky half step.

Strangely, I was no longer afraid of her. Still shackled by that strange inertia, I took my time studying her, once again drawn to the flash of those ruby earrings and to the curlicue of the tattoo that wrapped around her wrist to the back of her hand. I noted the band T-shirt she wore, the quality of her jeans and jewelry and that missing stud in her left earlobe…

What was she trying to tell me?

I saw the oily patina of the corpse beetles as they crawled up and down her arms, heard the buzz of nearby blowflies. The progression of her putrefaction momentarily distracted me and it took some effort to refocus. I was missing something vital, something she wanted me to see. Something I knew would torment me once I awakened.

I searched and searched, but the clue eluded me. And when consciousness tugged at me, I resisted because I knew the sign was *right there*, like a memory that remained out of grasp.

A songbird pulled me up from Darius Goodwine's shadow land. The trill seemed to taunt me as I remained motionless, still trapped in the steely vise of lethargy before summoning the strength to break free. Then I sat up, my gaze probing into the farthest corners of the garden.

No one was there, dead, living or in between. Nothing lurked or lumbered in the shady recesses.

I had only been out a moment or two judging by the ooze of tea down into the cracks of the patio pavers. The sun was still shining and I could still smell flowers on the breeze that gently stirred the wind chimes.

Everything remained so peaceful and static I might have wondered if I'd been under at all except for the shards of porcelain at my feet and the hint of ozone that lingered. Not the scent from an approaching storm, but the crisp, lightning-strike odor of Darius Goodwine's magic.

Fourteen

Leaving Charleston, I headed south on the Coastal Highway, but I didn't return to Ascension. Instead, I drove to the tiny community near Hammond where Essie Goodwine lived. I hoped she wouldn't mind my dropping by unannounced, but I was more concerned about my reception from her great-granddaughter.

The last time our paths had crossed, Rhapsody Goodwine seemed to be following Darius over to the dark side rather than in Essie's benevolent footsteps. I told myself she was young yet and could easily be influenced either way. I hoped her great-grandmother would win out, but I didn't discount her father's powerful caché.

When she opened the door at my knock, I searched her face for hints of his slyness, but her demeanor remained passive.

Even so, my smile was tentative. "Hello, Rhapsody. Remember me?"

Her gaze darkened as she observed me through the screen door. "Yes. If you've come to see Granny, she's not here right now."

"Oh." I bit my lip in disappointment. "Do you know when she'll be back?"

"Soon, I reckon." She toed open the door with a slender barefoot. "You can come inside and wait for her if you like."

"Thanks, but I wouldn't want to intrude. Would it be all right if I wait for her on the porch?"

"It's hot out there," she warned.

"That's okay. I'm used to the heat."

"Then suit yourself." Opening the door wider, she stepped out on the porch to join me. She was tall for her age, which was not unexpected in Darius Goodwine's offspring, nor was the graceful way she carried herself. There was an unaffected sensuality in her litheness, in the sway of dark curls down her back.

The Rhapsody I knew had always been a bit full of herself, boasting upon our first meeting that as the only remaining Goodwine daughter, she would be taught all of Essie's secrets, all of her spells and incantations. I hadn't given that claim proper weight back then, but I'd since learned not to underestimate any of the Goodwines. I suspected Rhapsody was still a prideful girl, but now her confidence was quieter and more regal. In that way, she reminded me of Mariama.

She cocked her head slightly. "He said you would come."

"Who?"

"Darius." Not Father, not Dad or Papa, but Darius. "He really is back, then?"

She lifted a thin shoulder. "I don't know where he

is. He came to me in a dream. He said I should trust you because you're the only one who can save me."

My heart jolted painfully. "Save you from who? From what?"

"The man with two souls."

I opened my mouth to question her further, but she put a finger to her lips. "Granny's here," she whispered, a split second before she turned toward the yard.

I followed her gaze to where Essie had paused at the edge of the road to watch us. She stood there for a moment, hand shading her eyes before crossing the yard in a gentle flurry of flapping skirts and sandals. Despite her age and girth, she was as graceful in her own way as Rhapsody. When she got to the porch, Rhapsody ran down the steps and took her arm, but Essie shook her off.

"The day I need help to climb dem steps is the day you kin lay me six feet under," she declared stoutly. She spoke in a mixture of English and Gullah, the lovely, rolling rhythm conjuring an image of wind rippling through Spanish moss. I wondered if she'd adjusted her speech for my benefit or if I'd simply grown more accustomed to the Sea Island cadence during my summer in Beaufort County. In any case, I had no trouble understanding her where once I might have struggled.

"We've got company," Rhapsody said at her side.

"I kin see dat, chil'. I still got eyes, don't I? Now run inside and pour her some sweet tea before she passes out in dis heat."

The first time I'd come to Essie's house, I'd blacked

out on the porch, only to awaken sometime later to find her hovering over me, muttering even then about the darkness headed my way.

"I don't want to trouble you," I said quickly. "I'm sorry for dropping by like this."

"You're always welcome." Essie took a moment to settle herself in her rocker. She motioned for me to sit, too, and I sank down on the porch, leaning back against a newel post to face her.

Rhapsody had already disappeared inside by this time. I could hear the slamming of cupboard doors and the rattle of glasses through the screen.

"How have you been, Essie?"

"I'm well, girl. And you?"

"I don't know. Some strange things have been happening lately. That's actually why I'm here. I've just come from a visit with Dr. Shaw. Rupert Shaw," I clarified.

"I know who you mean." She picked up a batch of quilt blocks from the sweetgrass basket at her side and smoothed the colorful fabric across her lap. She didn't take out her needle, though, and I suspected she just needed to occupy her hands.

I tucked a strand of damp hair behind my ear. "Dr. Shaw told me a story that you once told him about a group you called Resurrection Men. The leader was a man named Atticus Pope and his followers included your brother. Is that true?"

"Ezekiel always did have a nose for trouble, God rest him."

The screen door opened and she fell silent as Rhapsody carried out a tray of sweating glasses and a plate of sesame seed cookies. I took a cookie and a glass of tea and thanked her. In return, she gave me a knowing smile before turning to serve Essie.

"Granny," she said, bending to place the tray on a small table near Essie's chair. "I'm walking over to CeCe's now."

"What you walking over dere for?" Essie grumbled.

"We're going swimming. Remember? I told you about it this morning. Don't worry," Rhapsody said as she grabbed a cookie from the tray. "I'll be home early."

Essie shook a finger at the girl. "By daa'k, you hear me?"

"Yes, ma'am."

"Go fetch my picture box before you go. The one I keep in the cedar chest in my bedroom. Hurry now."

Rhapsody scurried inside and came back out a few minutes later with an old cigar box, which she placed on Essie's lap as she leaned down to kiss her cheek. "See you later, Granny." She threw a glance in my direction and then she was gone, running down the steps and across the yard so lightly it seemed as though she were floating.

Essie watched her with narrowed eyes.

"She's a beautiful girl," I said.

"She a han'ful, dat one."

I could well imagine.

I finished my cookie and set the half-empty tea glass on the porch. "You were telling me about Ezekiel. He was your brother?"

"My baby brother. He came along after I was

already married with children of my own. Our da spoiled him rotten, him being the youngest, so he never left home 'til she passed on. Then he came here to stay one summer. Just 'til he find work, he say. My boys were already gone by den, but I was raising Mariama and Darius, and dem two…" She shook her head. "Dey more than a han'ful."

I had no doubt.

"Ezekiel, he fall in with a bad bunch. Staying out 'til all hours. Dragging his sorry hide home at daybruk with bloodshot eyes and clothes reeking of something no living body should smell like. He started bringing dat man around here, too."

"Atticus Pope?"

"First time I see him, I say to myself, dat one done sold his soul to the devil." She rocked back and forth, hands folded in her lap. "Den I start hearing talk. People whispering about bad goings-on in the swamp. Black magic ceremonies and rituals. I never pay mind to gossip so I turn a deef ear. None of my business, I say. But den I see the way dat man look at my Mariama, and her little more dan a chil'. I tell Ezekiel if he bring him around here agin, I fill dem both with buckshot."

"Did he stay away?"

"He did and he didn't. I never saw him agin, but I could feel him out dere in the woods watching us. Watching her." Essie shuddered. "Next t'ing I hear, two girls gone missing over in the next town. No older than Mariama. Dey walking home from school on the railroad tracks and somebody nab 'em day-clean. In broad daylight," she amended so I would know what she meant.

"Were they ever found?"

"A fisherman came upon the bodies in the swamp. Police say gators been at 'em so long even dey own mothers couldn't recognize them."

"Did they find out who took them?"

"Atticus Pope took 'em," she said grimly. "And he did terrible t'ings to dem babies. *Terrible* t'ings."

She didn't need to elaborate. It wasn't hard to imagine the nature of those terrible things.

Essie said, "I worried myself sick after dat. Couldn't eat or sleep. Afraid Ezekiel got himself in a mess of trouble. Afraid dat man would come and take my Mariama while I lay sleeping."

I drew my legs up and wrapped my arms around my knees. "What did you do?"

"I tell Darius we need to go to the police, but he say the police already know about Pope. Dey know he's guilty, but nuthin' can be done without evidence. He say he hear tell of some people in Chaa'stun. Men with money and power who kin take care of monsters like Pope. Make sure he never hurt nobody else. Con-gee, he called dem." She pronounced the word with the emphasis on the first syllable.

"Darius was the one who brought in the *Congé*?" Now I understood why he couldn't get involved and why he'd said it was better if no one knew we'd talked. He wouldn't want his whereabouts known.

"Darius say, 'Granny, somet'ing bad about to happen.' He say, 'You need to watch Mariama like a hawk and keep Ezekiel home any way you kin.' But

Ezekiel wouldn't listen. He slipped out his window dat night with me sitting here in dis rocker wide awake." Essie sighed and kept rocking. "I never saw him agin. Police say he and the others left town, but I reckon dey all dead."

"You didn't tell the police about the *Congé*?"

"I didn't tell no one except Rupert Shaw and now you. And I only tell you because you wouldn't be here if you didn't need to know."

She looked at me expectantly and I nodded. "I found some graves near the cemetery where I've been working in Ascension. Twelve of them in a circle with another grave in the center. I'm wondering if that circle is where the *Congé* buried Pope and…the others."

She didn't answer, but her unblinking regard made me uneasy. "Essie, do you believe it's possible for a soul or spirit to be transferred from one body to another?"

"I've seen it with my own two eyes," she said. "A body leave home one night and come back the next day a different person."

"Do you think that could have happened with Atticus Pope? Do you think he could have transferred his soul into another body before the *Congé* found him? Into someone no one would ever suspect? And now he's come back. Or maybe he's been here all along, biding his time."

"God help us if dat be true." She opened the cigar box and sorted through the photographs until she found the one she wanted. "I found dis picture in Ezekiel's room after he gone." She held out the snapshot to me and I scrambled across the porch to examine it.

I stared down at all the faces, doing a mental headcount as I studied their features. Twelve men of varying ages and ethnicity all lined up in a row. With a start, I realized the snapshot had been taken in the backyard of the Willoughby house. I could see the roof of the old shed peeking up through the orchard.

Two children, a boy and a girl, played at the edge of the yard. Annalee Nash looked much the same as she did now even though she couldn't have been more than nine or ten when the photo was taken. The boy was a few years younger, a scrawny towhead who seemed more interested in digging in the dirt than in the adult goings-on around him. Not so, Annalee. She stared straight into the camera lens, the same sly smile playing at her lips that I'd seen yesterday after her confrontation with Martin Stark.

My gaze traveled over all those faces again, pausing with another start. One of the men looked a bit like Stark, but I knew it wasn't him. The man was about Stark's age now. His father or an older brother, perhaps? Or maybe my mind had fabricated the resemblance now that his meeting with Annalee was once again fresh on my mind.

I pointed him out to Essie. "Did you know this man?"

"I only know Ezekiel." She tapped her finger on the face of a young man with exquisite bone structure.

"He was very handsome," I said.

She sighed without comment.

"Why isn't Pope in this picture?" I asked.

"Look close," she advised.

I peered into the shadows, seeing nothing at first and then gasping aloud when I caught sight of a man lurking underneath an oak tree. I couldn't tell if he'd donned a mask or if he had managed to contort his features, but he had the appearance of something bestial, something primal and inhuman. I thought of George Willoughby's claim that he'd witnessed Pope change from man to beast right before his eyes. Now I understood.

I looked up. "Has Rhapsody ever seen this photograph?"

"Might have. Why?"

"She told me earlier that Darius had come to her in a dream. He said that I was the only one who could save her from the man with two souls."

Essie gave me the strangest look. "Darius come to her in a dream?"

"That's what she said. Essie…there's something I didn't tell you yet. Something you need to know. The body of a young woman was found in one of those cages. She'd been buried alive."

Essie didn't answer. Her gaze had gone vacant and I wondered if she was even listening to me or if she'd slipped into some sort of trance.

"Essie?"

"I hear you, girl."

I hesitated before plunging on. "The dead woman hasn't been identified yet, but she had two tattooed words on the inside of her wrist. *Memento mori*. It means 'remember to die' in Latin. Do you have any idea who she might be? Or why someone would have buried her alive?"

"She Con-gee," Essie said, and then muttered something under her breath that I couldn't understand.

"What?" I stared at her in shock. "How do you know that?"

"Some t'ings I know, some t'ings I don't." Her dark eyes bore into mine. "If Pope is here, you best watch yourself, girl."

"Why?"

"He likely mean to fill dem cages with anyone who try to stop him." She took my hand and pressed a charm into my palm. "Keep dis close. In your pocket and under your pillow."

"Thank you, but what about Rhapsody? Do you think she could be in danger from Pope?"

"You protect Rhapsody, I protect you."

"But I don't know how to protect Rhapsody," I said helplessly. What did the Goodwines expect of me? First Darius and now Essie.

"You'll know how when the time come. For now, you keep dat mojo bag close, you hear?"

I couldn't help but shiver at her ominous tone. "I will."

"You got power. Maybe even more than Pope. If I kin see it, den so kin he. He'll come for you, girl. Make no mistake about dat. He'll come for you when you least expect it."

Fifteen

I arrived back in Ascension just after noon and stopped by the house to collect Angus before heading to the cemetery. I didn't want to dwell any longer on what I'd learned from Essie and Dr. Shaw. There would be time enough later to obsess over both conversations. For the rest of the day, I just wanted to immerse myself in Seven Gates. Work had always been my salvation and never more so than now with the specter of Atticus Pope hovering in the shadows.

Two adolescent boys on bicycles milled about the main entrance and the black SUV with the tinted windows was parked on the opposite side of the road, along with another vehicle I didn't recognize. I suspected the second SUV belonged to James Rushing. I saw no sign of him or Kendrick, but I assumed they were down at the circle.

I got out of the car and motioned for Angus to follow. He bounded out of the vehicle and then drew up short when he spotted the boys. He didn't growl or bare his teeth, but his tail shot up and he stood at rigid attention until I coaxed him through the gate.

It took a couple of trips to get everything inside

the fence and Angus stayed right at my heels. I was glad to have his company. It was broad daylight and a police detective was only a shout away. As always, a part of me welcomed the solitude, but having Angus nearby was never a bad thing.

At some point Kendrick came out of the woods and took the long way around to his vehicle. As he strode near enough to the cemetery fence for me to catch a glimpse of him, I saw that his head was bowed as if he were in deep concentration. I didn't call out to him and he seemed unaware of my presence. He must have known I was there, though, because my vehicle was parked across the road from his.

Rushing left a little while later by the same route. When he saw me in the cemetery, he waved and then continued on to his car. Like Kendrick, he seemed preoccupied and I wondered what they might have found in the circle.

As I watched the dust settle on the road from Rushing's departure, I couldn't help but remember Essie's warning that Pope—in whatever body he now resided—meant to fill the cages with anyone who tried to stop him.

An icy shiver seized me as I glanced around. I didn't want to be alone even though daylight lingered. Solitude was no longer a comfort. The silence of the countryside had become deep and weighty and I found myself tensing at the slightest sound.

I continued to work for another half hour and then gave up. I was too jumpy to get much accomplished. As I gathered my tools, I turned once more toward the north gate. Was Pope out there somewhere? Did the watcher in the woods still lurk? Were they one and the same?

I canted my head, listening for the snap of a twig or the whiff of an odd scent. From deep within the forest I thought I heard chanting. That elusive one-word mantra that repeated over and over. I could smell a bonfire, too, and it took no effort at all to imagine a scenario straight from Dr. Shaw's book about witchcraft and black magic.

Quickly, I scanned my surroundings, assuring myself that I was in no immediate danger. It was a reflexive precaution because Angus would have surely alerted me if anyone had come through the main entrance or any of the side gates. He stood at sharp attention, head cocked, tail up. He seemed alarmed, but not yet frightened. His restrained demeanor should have reassured me, but in that breathless moment as we both stood listening, I could think of nothing beyond those dark rituals, nothing beyond those whispered rumors of mutilation, torture and bondage. And then I thought once more about the woman who had been buried alive less than half a mile from where I stood.

That first sight of her lumbering form had kept me rooted to the spot, but now the sound of a faraway chant had me rushing toward the entrance without bothering to collect the cooler.

Angus didn't follow me. He remained frozen, his attention riveted on the woods. I paused outside the entrance, turning my head to listen once again. Over the chanting, I could have sworn I heard the rasp of

labored breathing and the muted thud of heavy footsteps hurrying along the path toward the back gate.

My heart leaped to my throat. Pope was coming for me!

Essie had been right. He knew about me, knew
that I was a unique threat to him. I was the only one
who could end this and now he was coming for me.

A gust of wind sharpened the scent of smoke and
deepened my panic. "Angus, come!" I rasped.

The edge of hysteria in my voice startled him into
action. Whirling, he closed the distance between us
and lunged through the entrance. I slammed the gate
and then snapped the padlock.

The smoke followed us. Not in a wispy cloud as I
would have expected, but in one serpentine stream
that slithered beneath the back fence and undulated
over statues and monuments as it crept ever closer.

The caustic smell grew stronger and I staggered
back from the gate, pulling my shirt over my nose
and mouth. Angus had no such shield. The only way
I could protect him was to get him inside the car.

The SUV was only a few yards away, just across
the ditch, but the distance seemed to stretch as the
vapor seeped through the flimsy fabric of my shirt,
oozing up my nostrils and down my windpipe, fill-
ing my lungs with a fiery pollutant. Angus whimpered at my side, but I had no time to soothe him. I
scrambled across the ditch, tripping as I scaled the
shallow embankment. By the time we reached the
safety of the vehicle, my eyes were inflamed. Tears
streamed down my face, but when I tried to palm
them away, the contact deepened the burn. I gasped,

resisting the urge to claw at my eyeballs so great was the agony.

Beside me, Angus began to howl as he rubbed his face against the seat in desperation. In the throes of panic, I tried to think what to do. I couldn't see to drive, and if I called for help, the responders might be too late.

Water! We needed to flush out the toxins, but I'd left the cooler in the cemetery.

I braced myself, knowing I would have to leave the safety of the locked vehicle to go back and get it. The smoke was still out there. *He* was still out there. Like Essie, I could feel him skulking in the trees, watching us. Taunting and toying with us.

No matter. I had to get to that water. If I waited any longer, the damage to our vision could be permanent.

Climbing out of the car, I stood for a moment with my hand resting on the door as I tried to get my bearings. The only way I could stand the pain was to keep my eyes squeezed shut, which meant I would have to rely on my other senses to guide me.

I slid my hand along the car until I reached the front fender and then once again paused as I turned my head toward the cemetery, listening for danger. Leaving the vehicle behind, I inched down the ditch, arms outstretched until I came up on the other side and made contact with the fence.

Unfastening the lock, I felt my way through the gate and then followed the sound of rippling leaves to the cottonwood grove. The shade was cool upon my burning face. I shuffled in ever-growing circles until I felt the ice chest with my foot. Dropping to my knees, I flung off the top and scooped up handfuls of slush to douse my eyes.

The cold was an instant balm. I took one of the bottles and poured water directly onto my upturned face. The burning subsided, but my vision remained blurry. I could just make out the silhouettes of the headstones and monuments and the line of the fence. Grabbing the handle of the cooler, I rushed back to the car. If footsteps followed me, I didn't hear them. If eyes tracked me through the gate, I didn't feel them.

I cradled Angus in my arms as I poured water over his face and into his eyes. He didn't once try to break free. The icy liquid had the same effect on him. His whimpers eased, and after a few moments, he climbed back into the car to curl up on the front seat, snout on paws as he watched me through teary eyes.

During all this frantic activity, I hadn't let myself think about the threat that lay beyond the back gate. Now as the pain and panic faded, I turned an ear to the woods but the chanting had stopped. No sound at all came from the trees. Even the breeze had died away.

I might have convinced myself that the chant had been nothing more than the shouts of children down at the swamp, but I hadn't imagined that creeping smoke. I only had to look at Angus's red and swollen eyes to know the danger had been real.

Hurrying around the vehicle, I climbed behind the wheel and wiped tears from my eyes as I started the engine. Peering through the windshield, I glimpsed a figure at the edge of the woods. I couldn't see him well. His form wavered like a mirage.

I blinked several times to clear my vision. When I looked again, I thought he had vanished, but he'd moved into the deeper shadows along the tree line.

He stood very still now, head slightly bowed, shoulders hunched and hands clenched in front of him as if grasping the hilt of a sword.

Not a sword, I realized in horror. A machete.

I remembered then what Dr. Shaw had said that morning about the most desirable *muti* being made from the limbs and organs of the living. The agonized screams of the victim made the spell more potent.

From what I could see, the person appeared to be hooded, but he blended so well with the looming trees that he seemed to be weaving in and out of existence. As I sat there watching him, his head came up and I caught a glimpse of his bestial visage.

The man with two souls.

The coldest chill went through me as I took in his animalistic features. Even his arms appeared elongated and I could have sworn I saw him bare his teeth. Beside me, Angus rose up on the seat and growled a warning. I heard an answering growl from the woods and then an ear-piercing howl that died away as he turned to lunge back into the trees, leaving me to wonder if I'd really seen him at all.

I didn't wait to find out. I tromped the gas and the vehicle shot forward in a shower of gravel. I very

nearly lost control and poor Angus had to hunker
on the seat to keep his balance.

Once I had the wheel straightened, we sped down
the road toward home. Only when I could no longer
see the graveyard in my mirror did I slow the car to
a more manageable speed. Angus rose up again to
gaze out the rear window.

"Who was that?" I muttered. "*What* was it?"

Angus's whimper told me all I needed to know.

Sixteen

While I waited for the police to arrive at the house, I gave Angus a quick bath in the backyard to rid his coat of any lingering pollutants and then I showered, washed my hair and changed my clothes. By this time, the redness around my eyes had diminished and neither Angus nor I seemed to be suffering from any residual effects. Still, I knew I would need to keep a lookout for any new symptoms.

When the authorities finally arrived in two separate squad cars, I recognized Malloy and the officer that had first accompanied him to the caged graves. I remembered thinking of them as young and untested, an observation prompted by a fleeting moment of reluctance to approach the mortsafe and those grasping hands. As I watched them get out of their cars now and confer in the driveway, I tried to ignore an unreasonable twinge of impatience. Why hadn't a more seasoned officer been sent? A detective, even?

As they started across the yard toward the porch, Angus got up and placed himself in front of me.

"It's okay," I murmured as I slipped my fingers

under his collar and coaxed him into the house. "He's normally not aggressive unless he feels threatened," I said to the officers. "But we're both a little on edge right now."

"Understandable and no need to apologize," Malloy said with a quick smile. "A good guard dog is worth his weight in gold."

"Angus is certainly priceless," I said.

He took a quick survey of the property. "No one else has been by yet?"

"You're the first."

He frowned as he exchanged a look with the other officer. "The dispatcher must have gotten her wires crossed," he muttered. "Someone should have already been by."

The second cop had been standing apart from us, but he turned and swept his gaze over the porch and then into the side yard. I hadn't paid much attention to him at the mortsafes, but now I could see that both he and Malloy were a few years older than I'd first thought.

"This is Officer Reeves," Malloy said.

Reeves gave a brief nod, which I returned.

"Mind if I have a look around?" he asked.

I lifted a brow at his request. "I don't mind, but I'm not sure what good it would do. The incident happened at the cemetery."

"It's always helpful to get the lay of the land, so to speak." He and Officer Malloy exchanged another glance before he took off around the corner of the house.

"What's he looking for?" I asked in alarm.

"Routine check of the premises," Malloy said.

"It just seems a little strange. Wouldn't it be better to search the area around the cemetery? The person I saw earlier could still be skulking about."

"Don't worry about the cemetery. That's already covered," Malloy said as he put a foot on the bottom step.

"You've already been there?"

"Not me. But someone's there now checking out the scene." He nodded toward the porch steps. "Have a seat if you'd feel more comfortable. You still look a little shaken up."

I sat down on the porch while Malloy remained at the bottom of the steps gazing beyond me to the front door as if trying to get a peek through the side windows. I glanced over my shoulder to see what had captured his attention. I could see Angus's vague form through the glass where he stood watching us.

"What is it?" I asked as I turned back to Malloy. "If you're worried about Angus, he can't get out."

"What? No. I was just thinking about this place. I came here with my uncle a few times when I was a little kid. He and the people who lived here were friends. I couldn't have been more than four or five at the time, but I seem to recall a blue parlor and a yellow kitchen."

"Nothing's changed," I said. "You have a good memory. Was that when the Willoughbys still lived here?"

He seemed surprised that I knew about them. "Yes, that was their name. I don't remember the adults very well, but I sure remember Annie. You know her as Annalee. She was a very strange girl even back then."

"Strange how?"

"My uncle would ask her to watch me while he and the other grown-ups visited inside. I remember once we sneaked off down through the orange grove to an old shed where her grandparents kept a bunch of antique furniture and stuff. That was before..." He trailed away. "Anyway, she called it her playhouse. I don't think she was supposed to be down there, but she'd come across the key somehow. She lured me inside and then fastened me up in an old wardrobe. It took hours before anyone came to let me out."

"That must have been scary for a child."

He gave an uncomfortable laugh. "I had night-mares about it for weeks. When they finally found me, Annalee claimed I'd run off from her and gone down to the shed on my own. Just straight-up lied about it."

"That's not so unusual for a kid."

"No, but that girl had the face of an angel. She could make you believe what she wanted you to be-lieve. But I guess her mother knew her well enough by then not to trust her. She lit into her good. My uncle never took me back and neither of us ever told my folks. I'd forgotten all about that incident until I drove up here just now."

"It's interesting how things can come back to you." I'd been observing him closely as we talked and I saw something flicker in his eyes as if he'd re-membered something more troubling than a child-hood prank. I was remembering something, too. The image of Annalee and a little boy playing in the dirt while someone—her mother, perhaps—snapped a photo of Atticus Pope's twelve disciples in the backyard. I wondered if Malloy's uncle had been one of them.

His gaze was still fixed on the front door and I could have sworn I saw him shiver. Then he seemed to shake himself and gave another laugh. "Sorry. I didn't mean to get sidetracked. Here I am rambling on about something that happened twenty years ago when I should be taking your statement."

Only moments earlier, I'd been annoyed by the police's slow response time. Now I found myself wanting to question Malloy further about his visits to the Willoughby house and the time he'd spent with Annalee Nash.

But he'd already taken out his notebook and flipped to a blank page. Without looking up he said, "Tell me what happened."

"I will, but what did you mean earlier when you said the cemetery was covered?"

"It's my understanding that Detective Kendrick is canvassing the area himself. If there's anything to be found, he'll find it. Right now, I need you to start at the beginning and walk me though what happened."

I did as he asked, describing in as much detail as I could recall the chanting, the pungent smoke and the hooded man at the edge of the woods. With a little time and distance, the story sounded wildly fantastical even to me, but to his credit, Malloy seemed willing to suspend his disbelief. Or at least he pretended to.

"Anything else?"

I shrugged. "That's all I can remember."

"We'll file a report and keep an eye out for anyone hanging around the cemetery, but I honestly don't think there's much call for alarm. My guess is, those boys you saw earlier on bicycles are the culprits. They probably heard about the body that was found, saw that you were alone in the cemetery and decided to have a little fun at your expense."

I would have liked nothing better than to believe that I was the victim of a harmless if cruel practical joke, but that didn't explain the diabolical properties of that strange smoke.

Malloy had an answer for that, too. "Believe it or not, folk magic is still practiced around in these parts, especially on some of the islands. Root work, they call it. Mostly superstitious nonsense, but people like to cling to their beliefs. They chant a lot and use certain medicinal botanicals in their practices. Harmless enough, but when they light fire to some of those leaves and roots, the smell can be pretty potent."

"It wasn't just the smell," I said. "There was some kind of poison or irritant in the smoke."

"You ever been around a campfire when someone decides to burn poison ivy? If you're allergic, that smoke is lethal. Lesson learned the hard way," he said with a grin. The minuscule gap between his front teeth gave him a boyish charm that wasn't altogether lost on me. But as pleasant and disarming as I found Officer Malloy, I couldn't quite dismiss the look I'd seen in his eyes as he recalled his time at the Willoughby house.

"I'm not allergic to poison ivy," I told him. "And believe me, I've been around plenty of it in my line of work. Whatever was in that smoke was nothing I've ever experienced before."

He searched my face. "You don't appear to have suffered any side effects."

I wasn't comfortable with his lingering scrutiny and glanced away. "No, thank goodness."

He tapped the notebook against his thigh. "How much longer before you'll be finished in the cemetery?"

The question surprised me. "As I told you the other day, I still have several more weeks of work. Why?"

"You're a material witness in a murder investigation so we'd like to make sure you plan to stick around for a while."

"And as I also told you, I'm not going anywhere."

I couldn't tell if my answer satisfied him or not. His gaze had strayed back to the front door and I saw a frown fleet across his brow as if he'd sensed something inside that even Angus couldn't detect. "I'll talk to Kendrick about having someone drive by here every so often. We'll try to keep an eye on the cemetery, too."

"Thanks."

By this time the other officer had returned to the driveway. He leaned against the front of his squad car, cell phone to his ear as he waited for Malloy to wrap things up.

But Malloy seemed in no hurry to leave, taking his time to scribble in his notebook before he tucked it away in his pocket. He cast a glance at the waiting officer before returning his attention to me. His eyes were very blue in the fading light, but the smattering of freckles across the bridge of his nose kept them from being too intense, unlike Kendrick's gold eyes, which made me feel as if he could peer into the very depths of my soul.

What a disturbing notion. How was it that in the course of a few short days, Lucien Kendrick had come to occupy so many of my thoughts?

I felt the creep of a blush and was glad when an impatient prod from the other officer momentarily diverted Malloy's attention.

He continued to loiter at the bottom of the steps, hands in his pockets as he gazed up at me. "What happens when you finish your work in Seven Gates?"

"You mean for good? I'll go back home and prepare for my next job."

"A cemetery restorer," he said with a slight shake of his head. "I've never met one before."

"There aren't many of us around."

"You don't get lonely working by yourself the way you do? You never get spooked?"

"I was spooked just this afternoon," I reminded him.

He flashed another grin. "I mean *spooked* spooked. As in ghosts."

"I've yet to meet a machete-wielding ghost," I said. "Or one that buries his victims alive."

"We'll find him, you know. The killer. It's just a matter of time. Kendrick won't rest until he does."

I heard something in Malloy's voice that might have been respect or resentment or a little of both. I wondered about Kendrick's position in the department and whether or not he'd displaced someone local upon his return to Beaufort County.

"Have you known Detective Kendrick long?" I asked.

"I don't think anyone really knows Lucien Kendrick."

"But you seem confident in his abilities to find the killer."

"Put it this way. There's dedicated and there's obsessed. Kendrick can be both."

"You think he's obsessed with this case?"

"I think he's…" Malloy checked himself abruptly and gave me a shrewd appraisal as he straightened. "Kendrick is an odd duck. Maybe we should leave it at that."

"Maybe we should." I rose and dusted off my jeans. "I won't keep you. Thank you for your help."

"All part of the job. Just to be on the safe side, keep your doors locked when you're home and take your dog with you when you go back to Seven Gates."

I felt the weight of Essie's mojo bag in my pocket and nodded. "I'll take the necessary precautions, don't worry."

He fished a card from his pocket and handed it up the steps to me. "I saw Kendrick give you his number the other day, but in case you can't reach him or…for any other reason, you can always call me. Day or night."

"Thank you."

I thought he would surely take his leave then, but instead he came up a couple of steps so that he could speak without being overheard by his partner. I was so surprised by the action that I didn't have time to move away.

"You don't know me," he said in low voice. "And you've no reason to trust me. But I've lived in Ascension my whole life. You can ask anyone in town and they'll vouch for me."

"Vouch for you for what?"

His gaze on me deepened. "Be careful with certain people."

"Like who?"

"I think you know who I mean." He cast a quick glance over his shoulder. "It's a feeling I've had for a while now. Certain things don't add up."

"What things?"

"I can't say anything more right now. I've probably said too much. But if you ever feel threatened or even just need to talk, call that number. No one else has to know."

So much for his disarming grin, I thought as I watched him stride across the yard and climb into his squad car. So much for his boyish charm. Officer Malloy was a far cry from the untested rookie I'd judged him to be. He was shrewd and wary and cunning. And unless I missed my guess, he had it in for Lucien Kendrick.

Seventeen

The two officers hadn't been gone long when the sound of a car engine drew my attention back to the road. I was still sitting on the front porch reflecting on all that had happened when a black SUV pulled into the driveway.

My heart skipped a beat, but whether in excitement or apprehension, I wasn't certain, nor did I care to examine my reaction too closely. Given Malloy's vague warning and my own suspicions regarding Lucien Kendrick, it was only natural that I should have a few palpitations at the unexpected sight of him.

As I watched him get out of his vehicle and walk toward me, I told myself those tiny flutters were the result of trepidation and nothing more. It was foreboding, not anticipation, that tingled down my spine and pulsed at my throat. It couldn't be anything else because I wasn't ready for it to be anything else.

But Malloy had touched upon an uncomfortable truth, one that I didn't like to dwell on. I did get lonely. I enjoyed the solitude of my cemeteries and the tranquility of my own company, but there were moments in the middle of the night when the bed seemed too big and the house too quiet. Moments when the weight of my aloneness became almost more than I could bear. It was during those times when sleep remained elusive and daylight seemed a distant memory that I wondered if it might be time to let go. If it might be time to move on.

No easy thing, letting go. The pain I carried in my heart was constant and at times served as a comfort and a touchstone, the only thing I had left of Devlin. Once the pain went away, he might be lost to me forever.

In all the time we'd been apart, my feelings for him had never wavered, may even have grown stronger. But I couldn't wait forever. I couldn't trust that he would eventually resolve the issues that had torn him from my side. Carrying a torch for too long could easily turn into bitterness, or worse, an unhealthy obsession.

But Lucien Kendrick wasn't the man to help me get over a broken heart. In some ways, he was too much like Devlin. Too intense, too driven, too secretive. There was a difference, though. An important distinction between the two men that had been encapsulated in a single moment of understanding. *I've seen a lot of things in my lifetime,* he'd said to me in the cemetery. *Unexplainable things. I learned a long time ago that it's best to keep an open mind.*

Such a pronouncement might seem a small thing to most people, but not to someone like me. Not to someone with my gift. With the exception of Papa and Dr. Shaw, I'd never known anyone with whom I could share my experiences. Certainly not Devlin.

I shivered as Kendrick paused at the bottom of the steps. My gaze went to that mysterious raised skin at the side of his neck, to the skull tattoo on the back of his hand and then to those tiny telltale marks where his eyebrow had once been pierced. His adornments intrigued me and yet I found his nonconformity a little unsettling, which undoubtedly said more about me than it did about him.

The silence stretched for an uncomfortably long time. I began to worry that he'd picked up on my thoughts, but when he spoke, his voice sounded briskly professional. "Someone came by to take your statement?"

"Officers Malloy and Reeves were here a few minutes ago. You just missed them. Malloy said you'd gone to the cemetery to have a look around." I leaned forward anxiously. "Did you find anything? Or see anyone?"

He propped a foot on the bottom step, gazing up at me. "The place was deserted. He probably fled the scene knowing you'd call the police."

"He?"

"I'm using your pronoun. You told the dispatcher you saw a man lurking in the woods, right? This was after you'd smelled smoke."

"Yes."

"You also said he wore a mask over his face. Can you describe it?"

"I think it must have been a mask. I don't know

how else to explain what I saw. He looked…" I trailed away. "Animalistic."

A brow lifted. "Can you be more specific?"

"Not really. He was some distance away and my eyes were still burning from the smoke."

If my observation struck him as peculiar, he didn't let on. "What about the rest of him? Was he tall, short, thin, heavyset?"

"He was thin. Not short, but not really tall, either. I would say less than six feet." I paused, lifting my hand helplessly from my knee. "I'm sorry. I'm not being very helpful, but it was hard to tell about his height. He stood hunched over, gripping a machete."

"A machete." Kendrick's gaze on me seemed to deepen. "You sometimes use a machete in the cemetery, don't you?"

"Yes, why?"

"Is it accounted for?"

"It's in the back of my vehicle with the rest of my tools."

"Did you check to make sure it's still there?"

"Yes, as soon as I got home. Do you want to see it?"

"That's not necessary."

He came up the steps then and sat down beside me on the porch. I scooted over to make room for him, but our arms brushed, making my pulse jump.

"You think I'm making this up, don't you?"

"No, I'm sure you saw someone," he said. "But you just admitted that you're an unreliable witness. Even if you'd been close enough to get a good look at his face, your vision was blurred by smoke. And about that smoke…" He paused. "I didn't smell any in the cemetery or even in the woods. Not a whiff."

I glanced at him in alarm. "How far into the woods did you go?"

"All the way to the swamp. It's possible the wind shifted by the time I got there so the scent was carried downstream. But if there'd been a recent fire in those woods, I would have found some evidence."

"What about footprints?"

"I saw plenty of prints in the woods and along the side of the road, but that's hardly surprising, considering the recent activity." He hesitated again as if trying to calculate how best to proceed. "Let's go back to the physical description. You say the person wore a hood and possibly a mask. Is it possible he was a she?"

"A woman?" An image of Annalee Nash hunkered at the edge of the orchard flashed in my head. "Why? Do you have someone in mind?"

"I'm just trying to get a clear picture of what you actually saw. What about the two boys you said were hanging around the gate earlier? Would either of them match the description?"

I gave him a long look. "I know where you're going with this. Officer Malloy is convinced those boys pulled a prank on me. Sounds like you think so, too."

"It's not out of the realm of possibility with everything that's happened lately. That's probably why they were there in the first place. They heard about the body and were trying to find a way down to the clearing. That would also explain why you weren't actually threatened, let alone attacked. You said you were blinded for a time by the smoke. Surely it's occurred to you that if this person meant to harm you, he or she had ample opportunity to do so."

It had also occurred to me that the smoke might have been another of Darius Goodwine's tricks, but I couldn't dispel that bestial facade so easily. Not after everything I'd learned about Atticus Pope.

"I wouldn't be surprised if those boys had also heard about the recovery of the skeleton," Kendrick said.

"How would they know about that? The information hasn't been released to the public, has it?"

"We try to keep a close rein on the flow of information, but this is a small town and word gets out. And our activities in and around the cemetery haven't exactly been discreet."

I gave him another look. "I saw you and James Rushing out there again today. Has he already begun the excavations?"

"I'm not sure this is the best time to get into that."

I felt a chill of excitement along my nerve endings. "You found something else, didn't you?"

"I didn't say that. Most of the afternoon was spent photographing the mortsafes. Rushing is bringing in a couple of his colleagues to help with the excavations so the actual work may not begin until the end of the week. But just so you won't be alarmed if you see him coming and going, I've asked Martin Stark to begin removing the locks in a way that will cause the least amount of damage to the cages."

"So you're planning to exhume all the graves regardless of what you find in the first one?"

"Let's just say, we plan to be prepared for any contingency."

I took that as a yes. "Have you used Stark before on other cases?" I asked carefully.

Kendrick seemed surprised by the question. "Once or twice. Why?"

"I'm just a little curious about him."

"Curious about a locksmith?"

"More specifically about his shop. I've been drawn to the key painted on the front window ever since I arrived in town. The work is beautifully detailed. Not the kind of artistry one normally sees on a commercial building."

"I can see why that key would catch your attention." Kendrick's gaze dropped subtly to my throat. "It's a lot like the one you wear around your neck."

I resisted the urge to grasp Rose's key in protection against his scrutiny and my reaction to it. "You're very perceptive."

"I wouldn't be worth much as a detective if I didn't notice things. You have a tendency to reach for that key when you're nervous or preoccupied. It must mean a lot to you."

"It belonged to my great-grandmother."

"More of your roots?" His smile was cynical.

"Yes. Unlike you, however, I don't consider having roots as a bad thing. But that's neither here nor there. We were talking about Martin Stark."

He looked amused. "Surely we've exhausted that topic."

"Not quite. At the risk of sounding like a gossip, I'd like to ask you something. Do you know of any connection between Martin Stark and Annalee Nash?"

He thought for a moment. "The only connection I'm aware of is a vague one. Stark sells old locks and keys in his shop and the Willoughbys were in the antique business. I've heard that the two families had a professional arrangement at one time, but anything beyond that…" He shrugged. "Why all the interest in Martin Stark?"

"It's not just about Stark," I evaded. "I saw him in town with Annalee and I can't stop thinking about the story you told me. About what happened here." I still wondered why he had decided it necessary to inform me of the house's gruesome history, but there were a lot of things about Lucien Kendrick I had yet to figure out. I found the prospect of delving into his motives, let alone his psyche, more than a little daunting. "I followed your suggestion and searched the internet, but there's not a lot of information available. I did find one interesting tidbit. Mary Willoughby wasn't the only one who disappeared back then. Atticus Pope and twelve of his closest followers vanished at around the same time. But I'm sure you already knew that." I eyed him closely.

He didn't seem too impressed with my findings. "I've heard a lot of stories about Atticus Pope. I doubt very many of them are true."

"Twelve missing disciples, twelve caged graves? You don't find that at all suspicious?"

"Disciples?"

"That's how they were referred to in the article. The skeletal remains recovered from the center grave may well be Pope's."

"And you came to all these conclusions after reading one article online?"

I frowned. "The conclusions are logical, aren't they? At the very least, it's a starting place once the graves are exhumed. There must be dental and medical records still available. DNA if any relatives remain in the area."

"Slow down," he said with a flash of annoyance. "I'd rather not have that kind of talk getting out. We've got enough of a circus on our hands as it is. Even if we do find evidence that Pope and his followers are buried in those graves, my priority is still to the victim."

"Of course. But don't you think it could all be related? You said yourself that someone has been using that circle for years. Maybe the killer was close to Pope. Another of his followers." Or the spirit of Pope operating inside another body. "Removing the skull from the grave may have been ceremonial or ritual, like the wrapping of the remains in linen before reburial. As Rushing said, the shroud indicates respect, if not reverence, for the deceased."

Kendrick didn't say anything for the longest moment. Then suddenly he leaned in and my heart lurched. He was so close I could see shadows in his eyes, could trace the sharp curve of his cheekbones. I could smell the mint on his breath and a dark, heady scent that seemed to emanate from his skin. It was dangerous, that scent. It lured me in when I knew that I should run away. It dared me to throw caution to the wind when I needed my defenses more than ever. I was wounded and human and Lucien Kendrick was right there.

He moved closer still and I thought for a moment he meant to kiss me. A fleeting and foolish notion because his eyes had gone very cold save for a spark of something that might have been suspicion. Whatever attraction I'd entertained a moment ago fled as my pulse pounded in agitation. I wanted to scramble away or at the very least put my hands up and shove him back to a safe distance. But I remained motionless, my gaze fixed on his pupils.

In that moment I knew that Lucien Kendrick wouldn't be as forgettable as I'd wanted to believe. I had a feeling if I let him in, my life would never be the same.

His hands were at his sides and yet I felt as though he held me in a death lock. His expression never changed, but there was an underlying menace hanging between us.

"Why do I get the feeling you know a lot more about all this than you're saying?" he asked softly.

I tried to glance away, but I felt myself sinking more deeply into his gaze. "I don't know what you mean. I did some research as you suggested and I found a reference to what happened in this house. To Atticus Pope and his followers. I formed an opinion, which you seem to think is inconsequential to your current case. Fair enough. I'm not a detective, obviously. I'm just a cemetery restorer who happened to be at the wrong place at the wrong time."

He searched my face, something tugging at the corners of his mouth. A smile? A grimace? I really couldn't say. "I don't think you're *just* anything," he said. "There's a lot going on inside your head. You see things, don't you? You know how to probe into the deepest shadows. You know how to read between the lines. You may not be a detective, but my guess is, there's not a lot that gets by you. And to certain people, that makes you a very dangerous woman."

Eighteen

After Kendrick left the house that evening, I remained on the porch for the longest time, trying to sort through my feelings and make sense of my reaction to him. No matter how many times I resolved to keep my distance, no matter how strongly my internal alarms sounded, I couldn't subdue a growing fascination.

The way he'd looked at me in the fading light... that dangerous edge in his voice. *"You may not be a detective, but my guess is, there's not a lot that gets by you. And to certain people, that makes you a very dangerous woman."*

To him? I wondered.

Dancing so close to a flame could be thrilling, I had to admit, but I could easily get burned if I wasn't careful. Maybe I was wrong and Kendrick really was nothing more than a small-town police detective, but I couldn't bring myself to buy that. I couldn't help wondering if he'd come to Ascension for the same purpose as the woman in the caged grave. Maybe he, too, was *Congé*. That would explain his return to the

Lowcountry after years of being away. It might even explain the undeniable pull I felt for him.

But there was something else that worried me, a burrowing suspicion that kept me awake long after I'd turned in that night. How could I be certain that any of my experiences in Ascension were real? If the smoke had been conjured by Darius Goodwine and if the dead woman lumbering through the cemetery had been nothing more than one of his tricks, then how could I know if my attraction to Kendrick was anything more than a malicious manipulation?

Despite my instincts and the heightened senses that came with my gift, I could still be fooled by the likes of Darius Goodwine or a resurrected Atticus Pope or even by Lucien Kendrick himself. I felt certain none of these men had my best interest at heart and all of them had their own secret agenda.

As I lay there in the sweltering darkness with the covers pulled to my chin and Essie's charm tucked underneath my pillow, I had never felt more confused or more alone. And Devlin had never seemed farther away.

Days went by and I saw Detective Kendrick only in passing. No one from the Ascension Police Department came to follow up on my complaint, nor did I call into the station. If there had been news or another sighting of the man in the mask, someone would have surely notified me.

Occasionally, I would see Kendrick's vehicle parked at the edge of the road near the cemetery, along with James Rushing's, but neither man approached me and I kept my distance from the circle. I spent my time cleaning headstones and cutting away brush and vines until my arms and shoulders ached and perspiration soaked through my clothing.

The heat remained relentless. Every afternoon, dark clouds gathered in the distance, and sometimes at night I could see flickers of dry lightning on the horizon, but the rain never came. The air grew heavy with waiting. I began to wish fervently for a thunderstorm to break the tension, but I knew the weather was the least of my worries. I was on pins and needles because of everything that had happened and for what I feared was still to come.

At night I would lie in bed listening for furtive footsteps or strange sounds coming from the front bedroom. By day, I searched the shadows at the edge of the woods for the watcher, but if he still lurked in the trees, I never sensed him. The days and nights passed uneventfully and this, too, made me nervous. Beneath the tranquility, I sensed the restless stir of something evil.

Every morning before I left the house, I scoured the online edition of the local paper for any mention of the murder investigation or the remains that had been found in the center circle, but little was to be gleaned from the articles. Evidently, Detective Kendrick had clamped down on the flow of information, so much so that I didn't even know if the victim had been identified.

I thought about her a lot, that nameless woman from the caged grave. It seemed wrong that no one had come forward to claim her. Surely, she'd had a family, friends, someone who missed her. But if she were *Congé* as Essie had said, then maybe she'd been working undercover. Maybe no one knew of her whereabouts.

I still had a hard time accepting that such a group existed—a stealth faction with a mission to stamp out the unnatural in whatever form it assumed. *"Someone with your gift and abilities would do well to steer clear,"* Darius had warned me. It seemed impossible to fathom that I should find myself in the crosshairs of two old and opposing alliances when all I wanted was to restore Seven Gates Cemetery in peace. When all I'd ever wanted was to live a quiet and normal life.

But that was not to be and I had every right to be on edge. By all indications, I'd been dragged into something larger and darker, something far more sinister than anything I'd yet encountered. Forces were gathering and I didn't feel at all prepared for what would be expected of me. For what I might have to do in order to survive.

As the week progressed, however, things gradually returned to normal and my worries abated, as they tended to do during the quiet times. I was able to enjoy my days in the cemetery without glancing over my shoulder every few minutes or tensing at the slightest sound. I even managed to get a good night's sleep now and then.

But I wasn't so lulled by the calm as to remain unfazed by the sight of Darius Goodwine lurking near the church ruins one afternoon. I put up a hand to shade my eyes as the blood in my veins turned to ice. Even as I braced myself against his magnetism and trickery, I found myself rising and abandoning my work to move across the cemetery toward him.

It was late in the day and I could hear voices drifting up from the clearing as Kendrick and Rushing continued their exploration of the circle. Angus hunkered in the shade of the cottonwoods watching a squirrel. His presence should have been reassuring, but I felt the tug of an ominous premonition as I wove my way through the headstones. Why had Darius come back? And what would he require of me this time?

He stood silhouetted in one of the openings— waiting for me, I assumed. But as I neared the structure, he disappeared inside. I glanced over my shoulder. Angus hadn't moved from his spot in the shade. He was so focused on the scurry of feet across the tree branches that he didn't seem to notice me at all.

I turned back to the ruins. Very little remained of the church beyond the brick facade. The roof had long since collapsed and the back walls had crumbled almost to the ground. Through the arches, I could see the woods beyond the fence and the spangle of sunlight down through the branches.

I told myself there was nothing to be afraid of inside those ruins, and yet as I followed Darius through the arch, the premonition deepened and a smothering claustrophobia threatened to bring me to my knees. I stood just inside the doorway for several long minutes, breathing deeply as I tried to fight off a panicky tightness in my throat and chest.

Despite the open roof, much of the interior lay in deep shade. Vines from the forest crept over the walls and snaked across the stone floor. Weeds grew in profusion. The air smelled dank and fishy, not unlike the bait shop I'd gone to as a child with Papa. I hadn't much cared for that place. The buckets of earthworms and night crawlers in damp earth had turned my stomach. A strange reaction, perhaps, since I found the smell of a cemetery soothing.

I searched the tenebrous recesses for Darius Goodwine. "Where are you?" I called softly.

"Here," he said from the shadows. "Can't you see me?" His voice was low and resonant. Otherworldly.

Wrapping my arms around my middle, I took another few steps inside. I spotted him then, or thought I did. Maybe my eyes were still dazzled from the sunlight, but like the man in the mask, his form seemed to waver in and out of reality. I had no doubt that he was there, though. In one form or another.

A breeze rippled his loose clothing, and when he moved, a trail of blue sparks followed him. I could smell the ozone of his presence, could hear a faint tinkle from the metal charms he wore around his neck and wrist. I wondered how I could take in all these details if he only existed in my head.

"Are you real?" I murmured.

His white teeth flashed in the gloom. "I'm as real as you need or want me to be."

"I don't need or want you at all," I said. "You're the one who keeps seeking me out."

"But there was a time when you came to me and

now we have unfinished business. A score to settle, as it were."

I sighed. I had always known it would eventually come back to the debt that I owed him for bringing Devlin back from the other side. "What is it you want from me this time?"

"Our bargain remains the same. Expose the killer and I'll help you find your great-grandmother's key."

"You make it sound so easy."

"Not easy, but necessary. I told you before, he'll kill again if you don't stop him."

"Atticus Pope, you mean." The very mention of the witch doctor's name seemed to have a chilling effect on both of us. My heart started to hammer in trepidation and I couldn't help glancing over my shoulder. No one was about. The cemetery remained sun-drenched and empty, yet I felt we were being watched.

As for Darius, he'd moved back so deeply into the shadows that I thought for a moment he'd disappeared altogether. Even the scent of ozone had faded.

I took a few more steps inside the ruins. I was well away from the arches now. Too far to make a dash back into the sunlight if I felt threatened. "If you know Atticus Pope is responsible for that woman's death, then why not tell the police? You could do it anonymously if you don't want to get involved."

"And tell them what? That a man who died twenty years ago now hides in the body of another? What do you think their response would be?"

He was right, of course. Even if Kendrick remained open-minded, that would be a hard pill to swallow. "Do you know who Pope is now?"

"Only you can unmask him."

"Then how can you be sure it's him? How do you know he's come back?"

"The signs are all there," Darius said. "You just have to know where to look."

He pointed to a place on the wall between two of the arches and I turned to follow his direction. The vines and foliage had been recently chopped away to reveal a large triskele that had been etched into the surface of the brick.

I glanced at Darius. "I don't understand. What does that prove?"

"This was his place. He's come back to claim it."

I scoured the ruins anxiously. "I never noticed before how unsettling it is to be inside here."

"You're only now opening yourself up to the vibrations," Darius said. "To the dark emotions that reside here. During all the months that you've worked near these ruins, the key you wear around your neck has protected you. It allowed you to deny your true nature by blocking their screams, but you can't keep them silenced forever. Just like the ghosts of Kroll Cemetery, they demand to be heard."

"How do you know about the ghosts of Kroll Cemetery?" I asked with a frown.

"I know everything about you. Your whole life is right there in your head, right there in your dreams. Buried deep, some of it, but not too difficult to find if one knows where to look."

The notion of him having access to my private

dreams and buried memories terrified me, but I didn't bother trying to shut him out because I was no match for his cunning. Not yet, anyway. "Is that why you brought me here? To show me that symbol?"

He put a finger to his lips to silence me as he lifted his head, listening. I did the same, but I heard nothing beyond the sawing of the breeze through the trees.

"What is it?" I asked, but I wasn't sure I wanted to know. I wished fervently to go back to the peace and quiet of early summer before I'd stumbled upon those mortsafes. I wanted to end my day with the lull of a sea breeze and the sway of the hammock and the satisfying exhaustion of hard work. I wanted to hide behind the protection of Rose's key until everything went back to the way it had been before Darius Goodwine's arrival, but I knew in my heart there was no turning back. I'd passed the point of no return the moment I followed him into the ruins. I had no choice but to do his bidding because he wouldn't leave me alone now that my defenses had tumbled.

"Listen," he said. "Just listen to them."

I had the urge to press my hands to my ears and block out whatever had endured inside that abandoned place, but instead I forced my gaze to move slowly over the symbol. The linking spirals were oddly hypnotic. I felt myself weave as a cold sweat broke out on my forehead.

"Don't fight it," Darius said, his lyrical cadence deceptively mesmeric. "Let them in."

My hands clenched into fists at my sides as if

I could somehow defy his witchery. But I felt an all too familiar tightness in my chest as my stomach began to churn. "I'm not well," I said. "I need some air."

"Let them in."

My ears began to roar. The day was still and silent and yet suddenly I felt as if I'd been caught in a powerful vortex, one that might sweep me off my feet and carry me into the next world if I let it. I tried to move back toward the arches, but a terrible vertigo seized me. I fell to the floor on hands and knees as the world tilted and the arches, the cemetery and all the trees in the forest began to spin around me.

Over the howl of that rushing wind, I heard their screams. I could even catch a glimpse of their wavering forms in a twilight corner of the ruins. Two young girls chained and terrified, their agonized wails echoing for eternity inside those fragmented walls.

I dropped all the way to the floor, curling myself in a ball as I reached for Rose's key, clutching it tightly until the dizziness began to pass. I heard Angus whimper as if from a great distance, but he didn't come into the ruins and I didn't call to him. I lay there until my world finally settled and then I sat up, hugging my knees to my chest as I sought Darius Goodwine in the half-light.

"You heard them?" he asked.

"Yes. Who were they?"

His gaze seemed to burn into mine. "You've spoken with my grandmother. You already know the answer."

I gave a vague nod as I searched my memory for everything Essie had told me about the two missing girls. "She said they were taken in broad daylight from the railroad tracks on their way home from school. Weeks later, they were found in the swamp, their bodies so mutilated by alligators their own mothers couldn't recognize them."

"Alligators did not desecrate them," Darius said. "*He* did that to them."

"Pope?" I whispered his name fearfully now, afraid that I might somehow summon him.

"Night after night, he brought them here in chains, forcing them to witness his depravity and the atrocities he committed for the sake of his magic. First he took their blood and then their hands, their eyes, their tongues. By the time he removed their hearts, they were beyond fear and suffering in the living world, but from the dead world, they still cry out for justice."

The picture he painted sickened and devastated me. My first instinct was to flee through the arches and get as far away as I could from those ruins, from Darius Goodwine and his dangerous proposal. From Atticus Pope and his grisly alchemy. I did not. I remained frozen, not from fear of the truth or the aftermath of vertigo, but from a sudden and unholy thirst for vengeance.

"There were others before them," Darius said. "Runaways and the homeless that no one knew or cared about. But to attain the kind of power Pope sought through his spells, he needed the blood and innocence of the very young."

Darius came toward me then and I didn't try to scramble away. I wasn't afraid of him now. Our unified quest had dissolved some of his mystique, but I knew I would be a fool to trust him completely. He was who he was, after all. A scorpion with a treacherous nature.

"Essie told me you were the one who brought in the *Congé* to stop him. That's why you remain in the shadows, isn't it? Why it's better if no one knows that we've spoken. You're afraid of him." My voice held a note of wonder because there was a time when Darius Goodwine had seemed like the ultimate nemesis. But his crimes involving black magic and gray dust paled in comparison to what I'd learned about Atticus Pope.

"I don't fear for my own safety," Darius said. "There are things more precious than one's life."

I nodded in understanding. "You're worried he'll come for Rhapsody."

His eyes flashed fire, a manifestation of his strong emotions. "She's little more than a child, headstrong and foolish and only now realizing the full potential of our bloodline. It will be a difficult task to save her from herself, let alone from Atticus Pope."

And from her father's influences, I thought. "She said you'd come to her in a dream. You told her that she should trust me because I'm the only one who can protect her."

"And protect her you must. Not only for her sake and mine, but because there is more at stake than you realize." I heard a strange element in his voice, one that I didn't dare try to decipher. "If the blood and energy of the very young empower Pope's spells, the heart of a Goodwine could make him invincible."

My fingers sought the key around my neck as I shivered. "Surely you'd be more equipped to deal with him than I am. You also have powers. I've witnessed your magic."

"But you're the only one who can see inside his soul."

"Yet you seem to see so clearly into my thoughts and dreams."

"Not for much longer, I fear."

I closed my eyes, toying with the notion of trying to peer into Darius's soul, but I didn't want that connection. It wasn't a good idea to be linked psychically or otherwise to a man such as he.

"I think you give me too much credit," I said. "If you can enter my head so easily, who's to say Pope can't do the same? What if he's already been inside my thoughts and dreams? What if he already knows about me?"

"If he had an inkling of your capabilities, he would have dealt with you long ago."

"Like he dealt with the woman in the caged grave?" I got slowly to my feet. "Essie said she was *Congé*, but how could she know that?"

"They mark themselves with symbols and creeds, some more discreetly than others."

"Like the *memento mori* tattoo on the victim's wrist?"

"A fitting precept, wouldn't you say? *Remember to die.*"

I stared at him with open suspicion. "Did you bring her here?"

He shook his head. "She was an initiate. Young, inexperienced and out to make a name for herself. She was undoubtedly lured here by Pope so that he could send a message to the others. And for his own perverted enjoyment. It was the *Congé*, you see, that buried his twelve disciples alive."

"They were buried alive? Why?"

"To trap Pope's soul. Make no mistake. The *Congé* were as cold-blooded and ruthless in their mission as Atticus Pope was in his."

Darius came all the way out of the shadows then so that I could see him more clearly. So that I could take in the menacing set of his mouth and jaw and the warning glint in his eyes. "You have a common enemy in Atticus Pope, but the *Congé* are not your friends. If they knew about you, about your abilities, they would hunt you down for no other reason than their abhorrence of those whom they perceive as unnatural."

I trembled at his warning, at that terrible gleam in his eyes. He towered over me, ethereal and omniscient, his clothes billowing in a nonexistent wind. I could hear the rumble of thunder in the distance as the scent of ozone deepened inside the ruins.

"I can see that you're afraid," he said. "You should be. Someone close to you has been assimilated into the ranks of the *Congé*. Someone you think you know well. Someone you think you can trust. But don't be fooled." His voice faded as he moved back into the shadows. "If they learn of your gift, not even your great-grandmother's key can protect you."

Nineteen

"Who is it?" I asked on a breath. "Tell me!"

But he'd already vanished in the same way that he had appeared, leaving nothing behind but a distant thunder and the lingering chill of his presence.

I wasn't alone, though. Someone was calling to me. Someone I thought I knew. Someone I thought I could trust.

"Amelia? Can you hear me?"

The familiar voice pulled me out of the spell Darius had cast over me. When the haze of his magic began to clear, I found myself kneeling beside a headstone, a brush in my hand and a water bucket beside me. Angus watched me from the shade. Neither of us had moved from our original positions and very little time had passed. But once again, I didn't doubt the encounter with Darius had been real.

"Amelia!"

For a moment, I remained so lost in the swirling haze of his hypnosis that I wondered if the sight of Temple Lee walking toward me through the headstones was another of his illusions or tricks. Why else would she be here when Detective Kendrick had said she wouldn't be free until the following week?

Strange that she should show up at this very moment with Darius's warning still echoing in my head.

I had once wondered about Temple's affiliation with the Order of the Coffin and the Claw. I'd even entertained the notion that she could have been one of the first women inducted into the secret society. She'd never sufficiently debunked my suspicion and, if she were a Claw, would it be that much of a leap to consider the *Congé* may also have recruited her?

Stop it! I told myself firmly as I pressed fingertips to my temples. *This is not your thought.*

Darius was still there in my head, toying with my emotions and twisting my perception even though I could no longer see him. With an effort, I shook off the remnants of his influence. *Go away and take your games with you.*

He had insisted the *Congé* were not my friends, but neither was he. I'd known Temple for years. I wouldn't let him tarnish our relationship by planting doubts and paranoia for no apparent reason other than to isolate me.

"I was told I could find you here," she called gaily. "So this is where you've been hiding out all summer!"

I rose and peeled off my work gloves as I monitored her approach. Her attire was almost identical to mine—T-shirt, cargoes and work boots. But unlike me, she'd taken the time to apply lipstick and mascara and I could detect a hint of her perfume on the breeze.

Tossing my gloves to the ground, I gave her a tentative smile. "What a surprise. I had no idea you were coming here so soon. I thought you were busy until next week."

"Oh, I am. We've been swamped for months. You know how it is." She bent to give Angus a quick pet when he trotted over to investigate her arrival. "I had business in the area and thought I'd drive down for a quick visit. Actually, I wanted a look at those cages before anything happens to them." She paused, giving me a worried scrutiny. "Are you okay? You look a little out of it."

"I'm just tired. I've been working in the heat all day. But what did you mean, before anything happens to the cages?"

"According to James Rushing, the plan is to try and excavate the graves through the gates rather than remove the mortsafes altogether. It seems they're cemented in place and there's a worry about how much damage will be done if they try to pry them loose. But I don't have to tell you how tedious and time-consuming that will be. The police aren't usually so patient. I wouldn't be at all surprised if Detective Kendrick decides to have them dismantled."

"Wait a minute." I shook my head in confusion. "When did you talk to James Rushing?"

"Just now."

"You've already been down to the circle? I didn't see you drive up."

"I followed Detective Kendrick out here from town and apparently he took the long way around. He was adamant about not disturbing your work by coming through the cemetery." Temple lifted a brow as she observed me curiously. "So adamant, in fact, I had to wonder if there was a reason why he wanted to avoid you."

"None that I can think of."

She shrugged. "In any case, if he decides to remove the cages, I won't be able to stop him. The graves aren't old enough to fall under my jurisdiction. But I still believe those mortsafes have historical value and I'd at least like the chance to study them before they're destroyed."

"Yes, so would I. You know about the center grave?"

She nodded. "And about the missing skull. You and I both know that skulls have a tendency to disarticulate and roll, but I gather they don't think that's the case here."

"There is evidence of a prior exhumation and reburial," I said.

"So I was told. I'd like to hear your thoughts on that, as well, but I don't want to keep you from your work. I'm hoping I can persuade you to knock off early so that we can grab a drink and catch up before I head out."

"Yes, I'd love to, but I'll need to stop by the house first." I glanced down at my grubby work clothes. "No respectable establishment will allow me in the front door until I shower and change."

"I'm inclined to agree," Temple said with her usual frankness. "Take your time and give me a call when you're ready. I'll be down at the circle with

James and Detective Kendrick. Fascinating place," she said with a strange smile.

My curiosity about the activity in the circle tempted me to halt work and follow her. But if Kendrick really was avoiding me for whatever reason, maybe it was best that I also keep my distance.

Dropping to my knees, I pulled on my gloves and set to work once more, determined not to dwell on Kendrick and the excavations or my conversation with Darius Goodwine. But it was hard to discount Darius's warning about the cold-blooded nature of the *Congé* when Dr. Shaw had told me something similar. He'd even gone so far as to warn me to keep our discussion private. How strange to think that for most of my life I'd feared the ravenous appetites of ghosts when my greatest threat might now lurk among the living.

I worked for another hour or so and then loaded up the car and called to Angus. Once home, I left him in the backyard to explore while I went from room to room making sure everything was as I'd left it that morning. The added precaution had become a daily routine. Checking and rechecking doors and windows, glancing inside closets and underneath beds. With everything that had happened, I couldn't be too careful. I had no one I could trust down here, no one I could turn to for help. Angus and I were on our own and maybe we always had been.

Satisfied that the premises were secure, I filled his food and water bowls and then hurried into the bathroom for a cool shower. A little while later, dressed in a pair of jeans and a sleeveless blouse, I headed into town to meet Temple.

I'd chosen a small establishment that I thought would be mostly empty at such an early hour because we had a lot to discuss. I no longer suspected her of having anything to do with the *Congé*—an utterly preposterous notion—but despite her modest background, she was well connected. She'd attended Emerson University with the offspring of the rich and powerful and she still traveled in privileged circles. If anyone would know about a secret organization affiliated with the Order of the Coffin and the Claw, it would be her. However, I had to take care that no one overheard us. Darius Goodwine's motives might still be in question, but I trusted Dr. Shaw with my life.

As I strode along the sidewalk on my way to the restaurant, my gaze strayed to the locksmith's shop and to that gilded key painted on the window. I thought back to the lurking shadow behind the key and to the flash of those ruby earrings. I'd caught a glimpse of the victim just days before her death, but I couldn't have known then what lay in wait for her, perhaps in the shadows of that very shop.

I had a few minutes before meeting Temple and so I crossed the street and tried the door. When I found it unlocked, I stepped inside before I could change my mind.

I didn't know what to expect. Some dark, sinister place, I supposed, but the shop was well lit and tidy. Display cabinets formed a U around the narrow room and the walls were lined with dozens of old padlocks, reminding me once again of all those hanging keys in Rose's sanctuary.

As my gaze moved over the shop, I experienced the same sensation I'd felt in the courtyard. I'd been led to this place for a reason. Whatever Martin Stark's relationship to the victim, whatever his family's history with Atticus Pope, I had a feeling he was somehow a piece of my larger puzzle.

He stood behind the back counter, head lowered to his work, but as I moved into the shop, he pushed up his headband magnifier to observe me. He wasn't much older than Annalee Nash, mid- to late thirties, I guessed, but sunlight glinted on silvery strands in his hair.

He showed no reaction to my presence and that surprised me. A part of me had expected him to share in that odd feeling of providence, but he didn't seem to recognize me. Not at first. Then as I approached the counter, his eyes flared with the same hostility I'd noticed in the clearing. Our paths had never crossed, but for whatever reason my presence provoked a negative reaction in him.

"Can I help you?" he asked coolly.

"I was told you had an impressive collection of antique locks, but I never dreamed there'd be so many. I hardly know where to look."

"If you're interested in something specific, I can point you in the right direction," he said.

"Nothing specific. As a matter of fact, I'm hoping you can tell me something about an antique key that I own." I stepped up to the counter and removed Rose's key from my blouse, extending the ribbon so that he could study the intricate scrollwork. "I inherited it from my great-grandmother. She was a collector of lost keys. I don't know where she happened upon this one. I don't know anything about it at all except that it looks very old. I was told there was once a sister key, but I have no idea what happened to it."

"Might be helpful if I could have a closer look," he said as he pulled the lighted magnifier down over his eyes.

I was reluctant to remove the key from around my neck. I'd grown too accustomed to relying on its protection, but I sometimes wondered if the key was nothing more than a symbol through which I could harness the power that I already possessed. If I lost the key, would I still be able to keep the ghosts at bay with the unbound energy of death? I didn't want to take that chance. However, I was the one who had approached Martin Stark so I could hardly balk at his request. I slipped the ribbon over my head and placed the key in his hand.

At the moment of contact, his fingers parted and the key clattered against the glass top of the display case.

"Sorry," he muttered. He clenched his fingers into a tight fist as if the key had somehow burned him. Not such a far-fetched notion. I'd also experienced a warming sensation from the metal, usually in the presence of ghosts.

He bent over the counter. "The scrollwork is extraordinary," he muttered.

"Could you make a guess as to the age?"

"Eighteenth century at least. It's been well taken care of. Treasured, I would say. Even the bit is in good shape, but something has been scuffed out on the shank." He pushed back the magnifier as he glanced up at me. "Do you see what I mean?" He ran a fingertip across the metal near the bow.

"Aren't those just scratches from ordinary wear and tear? It is an old key, after all."

"They may look random to the naked eye, but with sufficient magnification, you can tell the marks were deliberately etched into the metal. My guess is to cover up a number." He took out a powerful-looking scope from beneath the counter and once again bent over the key as he adjusted the light. "I can make out a deeper engraving beneath the scratches. Maybe a three or an eight."

I leaned in for a closer look. I'd worn that key every day for over a year, ever since it had been placed on my bedside table. How was it that Martin Stark had discovered something in the metal that I'd failed to notice in all that time?

"Why would someone scratch out a number?" I asked.

"Probably to insure the key wouldn't be associated with a certain house or building if it fell into the wrong hands. The Carolinas have always been home to dozens of secret meeting places, especially during times of war."

I was instantly intrigued. Was that why I'd been led to this shop? Was that Martin Stark's role in my bigger puzzle? To alert me to the snuffed-out number?

"Is there anything else you can tell me?" I asked anxiously.

"You're aware of the signature of the locksmith?"

I shook my head.

"It's integrated into the scrollwork of the bow. See the way the metal curls around on either side to form double *S*'s? Samuel Story was a renowned Charleston metal smith. Many of the homes in the historic district still have original Story locks." He glanced up. "Is that where your great-grandmother lived?"

Was that suspicion I heard in his voice? "She came from humble beginnings so I'm certain she never lived in the historic district. She may have spent time in Charleston as a girl, but she moved to the Blue Ridge Mountains after she married. She lived in Aiken County at the time of her death, but that was a long time ago."

The bells over the door jangled as someone came into the shop. For a moment, Martin Stark remained fixated on Rose's key. He seemed reluctant to part with it. Then picking up the ribbon, he dangled the key in the air for a moment before dropping it into my palm. "If you ever decide to sell it…"

"I won't. But thank you so much for your help."

Twenty

Temple was seated in the bar when I arrived at the restaurant. She waved me over and smiled a greeting as I slid onto the stool across from her. We ordered drinks and then sat sipping wine while we caught up on our current projects.

"You've certainly been busy," she remarked after I'd told her all about my current restoration.

"It's been a challenging project," I said.

"I'm not talking about work. I haven't spoken to you in a while and now I find out you've embroiled yourself in yet another murder investigation."

I frowned at her assessment. "I wouldn't say embroiled. I stumbled across a body and called the police."

"You seem to have a knack for finding crime scenes," she murmured. "What do you make of that whole circle situation? The mortsafes and the dead woman. Not to mention the missing skull. They must all be related in some way."

"Didn't you ask Detective Kendrick?"

"He wasn't at all forthcoming. A very taciturn man, your Detective Kendrick."

"*My* Detective Kendrick?"

She shrugged. "He's very attractive but a little too intense for my taste. You definitely seem to have a type, though." She lifted her drink, eyeing me over the rim. "What's going on between you two, anyway?"

"Nothing's going on. Why do you imply that there is?"

"He had a noticeable reaction when I mentioned your name and he went out of his way to avoid running into you in the cemetery. In much the same way, I might add, that you're avoiding eye contact with me at this very moment."

"I'm not." I gave her a deliberate stare. "And there's nothing going on with Detective Kendrick and me."

She gave me one of her knowing smiles. "If you say so. But if there were, you'd have no reason to feel guilty about it."

"Why would I feel guilty?"

"Because you've always been loyal to a fault. But you don't owe John Devlin anything. Whatever you had with him is over. He's in the past. Although I can certainly understand why you'd feel a little gun-shy after what happened." She paused thoughtfully. "What did happen, exactly? I've never been clear on that."

Nor was I. All I'd been told was that his grandfather had gotten mixed up with some very bad people and Devlin thought it dangerous for us to be together. Of course, I knew there was more to his reasoning than that. Somehow his departure was linked to his past and to his legacy as a Devlin. I had to wonder if it might be connected to my legacy, as well. He and I had shared an experience during our time at Kroll Cemetery, a supernatural encounter that should have brought us closer together, but instead had deepened the chasm between us. I hadn't understood our estrangement then and I still didn't understand it now.

"It was a matter of timing," I said uneasily. "His grandfather became ill and Devlin had commitments and responsibilities."

"What utter nonsense," Temple said bluntly. "I hope you didn't buy that flimsy excuse. And I must say, if his grandfather really was so ill, he appears to have made a full recovery. He looked perfectly fine when I saw him last week."

I scowled across the table at her. "When did you see him? And how do you even know Jonathan Devlin?"

"Oh, I don't know him. But I happened to be at a restaurant in Charleston the other night when he and Devlin came in together. The resemblance and age difference were sufficient for me to assume he was the grandfather."

I toyed with my wineglass. "Did you talk to Devlin?"

"Just to say hello. He was with a strange party of mostly elderly gentlemen. Very staid and conservative. Old-money types. With the exception of the amazon in red, they looked as if they were headed to a wake."

I told myself to let the matter drop, but I couldn't

seem to stop myself from asking, "The amazon in red?"

Temple rolled her eyes dreamily. "Elegantly wind-blown and legs for days."

"And you say she was with Devlin's party?"

"Yes. In fact…" Temple trailed off as her gaze turned anxious. "I got the impression she was with Devlin. The two of them appeared close."

My heart jolted painfully. "How close?"

"No PDAs but lots of whispering and meaning-ful gazes." She reached across the table and put her hand over mine. "I'm not telling you this to hurt you. I hope you realize that. I just thought you should know in case you're letting something pass you by out of misplaced loyalty to Devlin."

"Thank you," I managed, even though I couldn't catch my breath for a second. I felt as if I'd fallen from a very high place and landed on my chest, knocking the wind from my lungs. I was devastated by Temple's revelation, but not really surprised. A part of me had been waiting for this moment ever since Devlin had ended things in Kroll Cemetery. I knew there was the possibility, even the probability, that he would move on, especially now that he had returned to the Devlin fold.

"He introduced us, but I don't remember her name," Temple went on. "Claire something-or-other, I think."

Of course her name would be Claire or Char-lotte or Caroline. I had a very clear picture of her. Blonde, beautiful, sophisticated. Smart, too, I imag-ined, and from just the right kind of family. A golden woman. The kind I'd always imagined with Devlin, this Claire something-or-other.

Claire.

How I hated that beautiful name.

I gulped air and then some wine.

"Are you okay?" Temple asked worriedly.

"I'm fine." I forced a normal tone to my voice. No easy feat considering the lump in my throat and the ringing in my ears.

"Do you want to talk about it?"

"No," I said flatly. "I don't want to talk about Devlin or Kendrick or any other man, for that matter. I want to ask you about the Order of the Coffin and the Claw." I'd planned to bring up the subject more casually, but I needed an immediate diversion. Something to erase the images floating around inside my head of a beautiful blonde on Devlin's arm and in his bed. Claire. Claire something-or-other.

I shuddered and gripped the stem of my wineglass.

"Why do you want to talk about the Claws?" Temple asked in annoyance. "I've never understood your fascination for that group, especially now that you're no longer with John Devlin. This doesn't have anything to do with the reason you two broke up, does it?"

"No, not really. At least, I don't think so. But it may have something to do with the body I found in the caged grave."

Temple's eyes widened. "My God, really? How?"

"I don't know yet. I'm still trying to figure it all out."

"But you're not embroiled in the investigation. Oh, no, not at all."

"Okay, maybe I am a little," I relented. "It's only natural to be curious. And to be honest, I've always had a feeling that you know more about the Order of the Coffin and the Claw than you've ever admitted."

She sighed and took a sip of her wine. "You and your conspiracy theories. I told you before, even if I'd had the right pedigree for those people, I was never a joiner."

"I know that's what you said, but you did go to school with them. You attended their parties. You must have heard things."

"Like what?"

I glanced around the restaurant, feeling the same kind of paranoia that Dr. Shaw had displayed in his office. "This is going to sound strange, but bear with me, okay?"

"Sound strange? Coming from you?"

"Have you ever heard of another secret group that recruits from the Order?"

She gave me a doubtful look. "What do you mean, 'recruits'?"

"The elite chosen from the elite. I can't say much more than that. I just wondered if you'd ever heard of such a thing."

I expected her to brush me off or laugh again in my face, but instead she fell silent as she stared into her wineglass.

I leaned in. "What is it? What are you thinking?"

She glanced up. "Call me crazy, but I actually think I know what you're talking about for once."

"You do? What have you heard?" I pressed.

Now she was the one who leaned across the table, lowering her voice conspiratorially. "There was this guy I dated briefly at Emerson. Aaron, I think his name was. Cute boy. Very sweet. He wasn't like the other Claws I knew. Not at all arrogant or full of himself. He was quiet and unassuming. A deep thinker. He seemed to abhor everything that the Order of the Coffin and the Claw stood for. All the parties and ceremonies. The secrecy. He told me once he'd only agreed to the initiation because he was legacy and it was expected of him. Anyway, we went out a few times and then he just stopped coming around. We were hardly serious so I wasn't bothered by his behavior, but I did find it odd. It wasn't like him just to disappear without a word."

"You never saw him again?"

"Not for months. Then I ran into him one day in Charleston. It was the strangest thing, Amelia. He'd changed so much I almost didn't recognize him. Not just his physical appearance, but also the way he carried himself, the way he spoke…everything about him was different. I found his transformation very unsettling."

"Did he give you any explanation for his disappearance?"

"He said he'd had to go away suddenly after his father died. He'd learned some things about his family, about what was expected of him, and it wasn't safe for him to be in a relationship."

I stared at her in shock, recalling a similar conversation I'd had with Devlin. "Did he tell you why it wasn't safe?"

"All he said was that the Order of the Coffin and the Claw was just the beginning. A test, so to speak. The initiations and the rituals and the dabbling in the occult...child's play was how he put it."

A chill crept up my backbone. "What did he mean by that?"

"He said that if he told me what he'd seen and done since the last time we were together, I wouldn't believe him. And if I did believe him, I'd never sleep again."

I drew a sharp breath. "Listen to me, Temple. This is important. Did he mention a group called the *Congé*?"

"The *Congé*?" She shook her head. "I don't think so, but the conversation took place a long time ago. I hadn't thought about him in years. But I seem to recall his family was in banking. Or maybe insurance. I'm not sure. I do know they were wealthy. South of Broad kind of rich. Like most of the Claws, he could trace his roots back to the founding of Charleston." She shrugged and folded her arms on the table. "That's it. That's all I remember. Now tell me what this is all about."

"I don't really know myself. As I said, I'm still trying to figure it all out."

"Figure what out? One moment you tell me you're not involved in the investigation and the next thing I know, you're grilling me about the Order of the Coffin and the Claw and some other mysterious group because you think they're somehow related to a woman's murder." She searched my face. "Tell me the truth. What have you gotten yourself into?"

"Nothing. This doesn't have anything to do with me." A lie, of course. If what Darius Goodwine had told me was true, the *Congé* and their mission had everything to do with me. "I'm fine. You don't need to worry about me. But you can't tell anyone what we just talked about. The Order of the Coffin and the Claw, the *Congé*, any of it."

She looked taken aback. "Now you're starting to scare me."

I was frightened, too, though I hadn't realized how deeply until that very moment.

I'd been drawn to that circle of caged graves by the watcher in the woods for a purpose I still didn't understand. I'd been told by Darius Goodwine that only I could end this, only I could unmask Atticus Pope. Only I could save Rhapsody from the man with two souls.

But who would save me from the centuries-old forces that seemed to be bearing down on me with each passing day?

Twenty-One

Twilight hadn't yet fallen when we left the restaurant. Scarlet clouds scuttled across the sky and the horizon still glowed from the sunset. A warm breeze blew in from the sea, ruffling my ponytail as I said goodbye to Temple. I headed back to the car, glancing over my shoulder now and then because it was too easy to imagine the sound of stealthy footfalls coming up behind me or eyes peering at me through plate-glass windows.

As I strode along the quiet street, my thoughts turned to Devlin and I drew a deep breath. I wouldn't let myself break down, certainly not in public. I'd had a year to adjust to life without him and if I needed a moment to wallow in self-pity, then I would do so at home with Angus. He wouldn't pass judgment on my tears. Right now I needed to keep my wits about me because danger seemed to lurk on every corner.

I no longer questioned the existence of the *Congé*, nor did I doubt that I would become the target of their fanaticism if they learned of my gift. I'd heard too much from Dr. Shaw and Darius Goodwine and now from Temple to downplay the menace. They were real and they were dangerous.

As deadly in their own way as Atticus Pope, Darius had told me, but I found that hard to believe. Since childhood, I'd witnessed many disturbing things and I'd encountered evil in all manner of outlets. But a witch doctor that used the blood and organs of the young and innocent to strengthen his magic was a level of obscenity I could barely comprehend.

Was he out there at this very moment prowling the streets and back roads looking for his next victim?

For all I knew, his spirit could be hiding in the woman walking behind me or in the man crossing the street ahead of me. He could even be concealed deep within the cleric standing in a church doorway or the young mother shepherding her toddler from the park.

I shivered as I stared into the faces of strangers, searching for something that would give him away.

As I approached Martin Stark's shop, I slowed my steps, inadvertently glancing beyond the gilded key into the window. If Pope had lured the woman in the caged grave to Ascension out of revenge for his murdered disciples or for his own perverted appetites, what had she been doing at this shop just days before her death? How had she known Martin Stark?

The interior lights were off and a closed sign hung in the door. I moved to the alley and peered down the side of the building. The courtyard beyond lay in deep shadows. Curiosity stirred, but I warned myself not to tempt fate. There was nothing to be discovered behind the closed gate. No clues to be gleaned from all those old locks. I wanted to believe that Martin Stark's role had been fulfilled by revealing the scratched-out number on Rose's key, but I couldn't forget his inexplicable hostility toward me. Nor could I discount the photograph of Pope's disciples that Essie had shown to me on her front porch. One of the men had born a remarkable resemblance to Stark.

Pope had been captured in that shot, too, along with two children playing at the edge of the orchard. I'd recognized the girl as Annalee Nash and I'd now come to believe that the boy was Officer Malloy. He'd said that his uncle had been a friend of the Willoughbys and he'd seemed very uneasy at the house. I couldn't help wondering what he might have witnessed during his time there and if he'd blocked those memories out of fear.

They were all tied to Pope in some way or another. Annalee, Stark and Malloy. Was it possible that Pope had returned to Ascension to resurrect the Brotherhood using the relatives and offspring of his murdered disciples? Would that explain the flash of fear in Stark's eyes when Annalee had caught his arm in the courtyard? And Officer Malloy's look of surprise when I'd mentioned Annalee's name that first day in the clearing?

It seemed to always come back to Annalee and her buried memories. To the ten-year-old girl who had been found covered in her father's blood.

Something moved in the shadows at the back of the alley. An animal, I told myself. A tomcat on the

prowl or a stray dog scavenging for food. I was perfectly safe. People were out and about on the streets.
No need to worry.

Then why had the hair lifted at the back of my
neck? Why had gooseflesh popped along my bare
arms? Why didn't I hurry away and seek the solace
of my locked vehicle?

I made no conscious decision to investigate, but
the next thing I knew, I stood inside the courtyard
gate. The place was very still and quiet. Tomb-like. I
could hear the silken rustle of palmettos, could even
discern the scratch of tiny claws against the stone
pavers. The fountain gurgled like an open heart, but
no human sound came to me.

He was there, though. I could feel his presence
down my backbone and along my every nerve ending. I sensed the icy tentacles of his magic reaching toward me, curling around me, drawing me into
his web.

The wind picked up and the pinwheels started to
clatter. The scent of ozone drifted through the ole-
anders, along with a deeper, darker smell that might
have been sulfur.

I turned in a dreamlike fog, searching the shadows. Hooded and masked, he hovered in the deepest
part of the shade. As he lifted his head, my blood
ran cold because what I had taken for a mask was,
in fact, his transformed countenance.

His bared teeth flashed as he moved toward me.
I wanted to run away, but a dangerous paralysis
gripped me. Even when he was almost upon me, I

remained frozen, unable to break free as he lifted his machete.

I felt something strange at my throat and put up a hand to grasp Rose's key. When I lowered my fingers, they were covered in blood. It seemed to be everywhere. Soaking through my clothing. Running down my arms and dripping onto the pavers. Rivers of sticky crimson that gushed from a wound I didn't even feel.

I sank to my knees gasping for breath.

"Are you okay?"

I floated out of that terrifying scene, still lost in confusion. I found myself staring up at Lucien Kendrick.

He looked very concerned. "What happened? Did you fall?"

"No—I…"

He hunkered down, putting himself at my level. For a moment, I thought I might lose myself again in his stare. The fading light glowed in his eyes, and for the first time, I noticed the motes at the bottom of his pupils. In my dreamy state, I marveled that we had that in common, but I didn't think those markings were the only thing that we shared. He had the kind of insight that went beyond experience and the five senses. I had a feeling he also lived within the looming specter of the dead world.

"Did you hit your head?" he asked. "You seem a little dazed."

"I'm fine, I think."

"You think?" He took my elbow and helped me to my feet. My behavior was so peculiar he must have thought that I was drunk or high or having a nervous breakdown. At that moment, I wouldn't have put money on my mental well-being.

"You don't look well," he said worriedly. "Should I take you to the ER?"

"I felt a little light-headed, but it's passed now."

He gave me a doubtful look. "How often does that happen?"

"Not often. Why?"

"You had an episode in the cemetery the other day."

"That was just the heat. There's no need for concern," I assured him with far more conviction that I actually felt. "I've probably just been working too hard."

He wasn't convinced. "If you won't see a doctor, at least let me drive you home."

"Thanks, but my car is parked just down the street."

He searched my face, peering deeply into my eyes. "I'm not sure you're in any condition to drive."

"I'm not intoxicated. I only had one glass of wine."

"Your sobriety isn't in question." He guided me from the street into the privacy of the alley. I shot an anxious glance toward the courtyard. Behind the closed gate, I could hear the faint click of the pinwheels.

I wanted to believe I'd been the victim of nothing more sinister than a ghastly daydream or a strange hallucination, but I knew better. Someone had been inside my head, manipulating my thoughts and perceptions and altering my reality. Someone who knew about my gifts and abilities.

Someone who would come for me when I least expected it.

I gazed up at Kendrick and shivered.

"Feeling better?" His eyes had darkened in the shadows of the alley and I caught a whiff of the ubiquitous mint that seemed to cling to his breath and skin.

"Yes. I should get going." His hand was still on my elbow, I realized. I withdrew slightly and he leaned a shoulder against the building. He wasn't exactly blocking my escape, but neither was he making it easy for me.

"You don't want to tell me what really happened?"

"I already told you, I felt a little dizzy."

"So dizzy that you had to drop to your knees to keep from falling?"

His questions burrowed under my skin, picking at my patience. Why was he standing there grilling me when all I wanted to do was go home to Angus? "I've done nothing wrong," I said, which did not at all sound defensive.

"No one is accusing you of anything. But I don't just investigate crimes, you know. I try to look out for the welfare of everyone is this town."

"Yes, of course, and I'm sorry if I sounded defensive. But the last time we spoke, you did accuse me of withholding information."

His gaze flicked over me. "I still think you're holding something back, but I can be concerned about your safety at the same time."

Guilt niggled. I should have told him days ago about the glimpse I'd had of the victim, but I hadn't trusted him or my recall. I was even less certain now of either. What if Pope really was inside my head, manipulating my thoughts and planting false memories to mislead and misdirect?

And did it really matter if Kendrick knew about those flashing rubies? According to Darius, I was the only who could stop Pope, anyway.

I glanced up at Kendrick, pondering how much I should tell him. How much I should trust him. "What is it you think I'm keeping from you?"

He shrugged. "For starters, you seem to know an awful lot about Atticus Pope and his disciples, as you called them. I'd like to know where you're getting your information."

"I'd never even heard of him until you mentioned his name to me. And then I went online and researched him and the Willoughbys as you suggested I do."

"Yes, but that's where I have a problem. I've also researched Pope. I know how little information there is about him on the internet. And I've never come across a single reference to his 'disciples.'"

"Maybe you just don't know where or how to look. I didn't mean that like it sounded," I rushed to add. "Research is an important tool of my work and I've become proficient at digging up obscure details. It didn't take me long to find out more than I ever wanted to know about Atticus Pope. By all accounts, he was an evil man."

Kendrick frowned. "Evil or not, dead or not, he's

been gone from these parts for at least twenty years. I meant what I said the other day. I don't want rumors spread about him and the victim. Murder in a small town is enough of a rarity and people are already on edge."

"Are you still trying to convince yourself those past events have no correlation to the present? I think, deep down, you know it's all connected. Otherwise, why tell me about Pope in the first place? Why bring him up now?"

"Maybe I wanted to see your reaction."

"And?"

"You're as cool as a cucumber," he said without the slightest hint of admiration.

I leaned back against the building, all too aware of his nearness. I told myself this intensifying curiosity I had for Detective Kendrick was a reaction to what I'd learned about Devlin. I was human. I needed to know that someone like Lucien Kendrick could find me attractive. I also knew that whatever might be building between us needed to be stifled. I was still wounded and raw and I didn't trust Kendrick any more than he seemed to trust me.

I drew a breath and tore my focus from his lips. "You still think I'm hiding something."

"I'm more certain of it than ever."

I shuddered. "Surely you don't think I had anything to do with that woman's death."

"No, I don't. But you're a part of this somehow. I just haven't put it all together yet."

"Is it really so hard to believe that I'm only a bystander? I stumbled across a body and reported it. Why can't that be the end of my involvement?"

He studied me for a moment as if considering his answer. His hesitation did nothing to instill confidence. "What's your relationship with the Charleston Institute for Parapsychology Studies?"

I was taken aback by the question. Just how deeply had he delved into my life? And why? Surely his suspicions didn't warrant that kind of invasion. "How do you even know about the institute?"

"You were there the other day, weren't you?"

"Are you having me followed?" I managed to ask coolly.

"Having you followed? No. I saw you there myself. You were pulling out of the drive just as I arrived. The receptionist told me you had a meeting with the director. She said the two of you are old friends."

"How very helpful of her." I folded my arms. "I don't see how my visit to the institute is any of your concern. And what were you doing there if not following me?"

"I was hoping to speak with Rupert Shaw."

My own suspicions erupted. "How do you know Dr. Shaw?"

"I'm not personally acquainted with him, but before I came to Ascension, I worked on a couple of cases that used him as a consultant."

"What kind of cases?"

"The kind with no easy answers," he said.

I unfolded my arms and relaxed my posture a bit. "Was he able to help you?"

"I didn't get a chance to talk to him, unfortunately. I was told he no longer consults with law enforcement."

I was unaware that he ever had. "May I ask why you wanted to see him?"

A frown played across Kendrick's brow as he turned to scour the street. I wondered if he was making sure we wouldn't be overheard or if he needed time to figure out how much he wanted to tell me. "The other day at the cemetery…" His gaze came back to me in a way that made my heart flutter. "Maybe I'm wrong, but I thought we had a moment. Do you know what I'm talking about?"

I swallowed. "Yes, I think so."

"I went to see Dr. Shaw because there is something extraordinary going on with this case. I can't explain it. It goes beyond a normal investigation." He paused again as if to gauge my reaction. Finding no judgment, he went on. "Every time I go down to that circle, I feel something in those woods. Something or someone. I've searched the area at least a dozen times and I've never spotted anything out of the ordinary. But I know something's there. A presence. I can feel it watching me. Whatever it is, I think it may be trying to tell me something."

I didn't say anything to that. I couldn't. To have confirmation that he also felt the watcher was almost more than I could process at the moment.

This was dangerous territory we'd entered.

A part of me wanted to confide my own experiences, but Darius's warning was still too fresh. If the

Congé found out about my gifts and abilities, they'd
hunt me down, he'd said.

They mark themselves with symbols and creeds.

My gaze went to the tattoo on the back of Kendrick's hand and then to the strange scar that looked
like a brand at his neck. Was he *Congé*? Was this
some kind of test?

My pulse raced as our gazes held for another long
moment.

"You don't have anything to say about what I just
told you?" he finally asked.

"What is it you want me to say?"

"You can be honest. I know how crazy it sounds."

I glanced away, but his intensity pulled me back.
"I guess I'm wondering why you felt the need to
tell me."

"Because you may be the only person I can tell."
A shadow moved in his eyes. A quiet, almost desperate emotion that made me shiver.

"I have an open mind, but I'm not..." My hand
fluttered to Rose's key. "I think you may have the
wrong idea about me."

He smiled sadly. "Or could it be, you have the
wrong idea about me?"

At home, I made my usual rounds through the
house with Angus at my heels. I didn't want to let
him out of my sight. His presence was a comfort and
I leaned down to pet his head as we made our way
down the narrow hallway.

He balked at the front bedroom to pace back and
forth in front of the doorway as he eyed me warily. I

entered alone, rattled by his behavior and by everything else that had happened to me that day. Things had gotten a little too cozy between Detective Kendrick and me and I wasn't at all comfortable with this new layer of intimacy.

I moved about the bedroom, assuring myself there was no cause for alarm. If the Willoughbys haunted that airy space, I saw no evidence of a manifestation. Nor did I hear anything out of the ordinary, but certain areas did seem cooler than the rest of the house.

Quickly, I left the room and closed the door.

Angus and I retreated to the kitchen where I fixed a light supper for myself and supplemented his earlier dinner with a few treats. I even opened a bottle of wine, which was unusual for me. I rarely drank alone, but for so many reasons, I needed a little more fortification than the single glass of chardonnay I'd had earlier with Temple.

Carrying the bottle to the table along with my laptop, I occupied myself with busywork until Angus needed to go out. Then I stood and stretched, rubbing the back of my neck as I followed him out to the porch. He bounded down the steps and dashed off into the night.

"Don't go far," I cautioned as I stood behind the latched screen door. During the months we'd lived in the house, his nocturnal wanderings hadn't concerned me. He could go almost all the way to the marsh and still remain safely confined within the fence. But I did worry now. The same barrier that kept him in wouldn't keep out the beings, living or dead, that might come looking for me.

When he didn't return as quickly as I thought he should, I stepped outside to call to him. "Angus, come!"

He trotted out of the shadows and came straight over to me, nudging my leg with his snout. The gesture was the closest thing to affection he'd shown me in ages and I fell to my knees, caressing his scarred head and scratching behind his ear nubs.

"You don't know how much I needed that tonight," I murmured, wrapping my arms around him. He acquiesced for a moment and then pulled away with a little whine of protest.

We turned as one to go up the steps, but just as I reached for the door, I heard a sound behind me. The chant drifted out of the darkness, a distant singsong that seemed to ebb and flow on the breeze.

Beside me, Angus growled a warning. Not my imagination, then, or someone prowling around inside my head. He'd heard it, too. The chant seemed to come from the orchard. Swelling and swelling as the wind rose.

The single word now became clear to me, perhaps because Darius had forced me to open myself up to the vibrations of the dead and Rose's key could no longer protect me. Whatever the reason, I listened in dread to the ominous mantra undulating through the orange grove.

Rise, those phantom voices chanted.

Rise. Rise. Rise.

Twenty-Two

I sat at the kitchen table drinking alone. I didn't want to think about the meaning of that chant, but images kept floating through my head as I topped off my glass. Were Pope's dead disciples calling out to me? Imploring me to help them rise from their graves?

It was one thing to be lured to a cemetery where the trapped spirits were of the wronged and the innocent or to the ruins of an old church where ghost children cried out for justice. I was very much afraid that what called to me from beneath those mortsafes was a different kind of entity.

I wanted no part in the resurrection or release of Pope's disciples, but I wasn't certain I had the power to pick and choose. Like my great-grandmother, I had a light inside me that beckoned the unquiet. Since my time at Kroll Cemetery, I'd reluctantly come to accept that for the sake of my mental and physical well-being, it might sometimes be necessary to help trapped souls cross over.

But Papa had warned me about those spirits that wished to remain in the living world because of their hunger for human warmth and energy or their malicious penchant for creating chaos. And in some cases, I believed because of their fear of what awaited them on the other side. The desire to remain earthbound might be so great, he'd said, that the entities would try to snuff out the very light that drew them.

So, no, I didn't want to awaken those dead disciples any more than I wanted to face off against the zealots who waged war on the unnatural. Rose's key and Essie's charm could only do so much to protect me from the ghosts and they offered no safeguard at all against the human *Congé*. From here on out, I would have to rely on my sharpened senses and every last one of my abilities to keep from falling into the traps that I suspected had been set all around me.

Sufficiently numbed by yet another glass of wine, I headed off to bed, but sleep didn't come easy. When I finally managed to doze off, my dreams were filled with terrible images. Bestial faces grinning from the shadows. Hands reaching up to me from the caged graves. My own body parts strewn about the church ruins.

When the alarm went off at dawn, I felt nothing but relief. I crawled out of bed, packed up the car and headed with Angus for Seven Gates.

The cemetery was eerily silent. I saw no parked cars at the side of the road or boys on bicycles hanging about the entrance. No kids with fishing poles heading for the swamp, no policemen hurrying to and from the circle. It was as if the whole area had been abandoned and no one had thought to tell me.

The displaced sensation lasted all day and I had a strong sense that someone was messing with me, meddling with my reality.

My courage had been tested in the deepest part of the night, but now I refused to be driven from my work. Instead, I threw myself into the backbreaking tasks until my arms quivered and my legs felt like jelly. By the end of the day, I wanted nothing so much as a cool shower and an early bedtime, but instead I came home to find a strange car parked in front of the house and two people waiting for me on the porch.

As I pulled into the driveway, the man came down the steps and strode across the yard to greet me. He was nearly upon me before I recognized Officer Malloy in his plainclothes attire of plaid shirt, jeans and boots.

I wondered if there had been more trouble. Another body discovered in the circle, perhaps. A dozen scenarios flashed through my head, but all I could seem to focus on was my suspicion about the young police officer and his possible connection to Atticus Pope.

I slid out of the vehicle to confront him. "What's going on, Officer? Has something happened?"

He put up a hand to reassure me. "Everything's fine. Don't worry."

My gaze darted to the woman on the front porch. "Is that Annalee Nash?"

"Yes. I'll explain everything, but you may want to calm your dog first."

By this time, Angus was creating quite a ruckus. I got back in the car and fastened a leash to his collar. Then we both climbed out and I led him through the back gate where I spent a few moments stroking his fur. Satisfied that neither of us was in imminent danger, he settled down and I removed the leash so he could roam the fenced property.

When I walked back around the house, I found Malloy pacing in the driveway.

"What's going on? Why are you both here?" I didn't want to sound overly wary or to let my imagination run away with me, but I thought it odd that Annalee hadn't come over to greet me. She hadn't moved at all so far as I could tell. She just sat there staring out across the yard. "Is she okay?"

Malloy stopped pacing and glanced over his shoulder. "She'll be fine. I happened to be driving by earlier when I spotted her on the porch. I didn't think anything of it at the time. I assumed she was here visiting. Then I saw your vehicle at the cemetery so I knew you weren't home."

"You were at the cemetery? I didn't see you," I said, trying to soften the accusatory edge in my tone.

"Kendrick asked me to have a look around, make sure everything was okay. He's beefed up the patrols since you reported a disturbance, but I'm sure you already knew that."

"I still don't understand how I could have missed you at the cemetery."

"I don't know what to tell you," he said with a

shrug. "I went all the way down to the circle and back. You seemed fine so I didn't see any need to disturb you. Annalee was still sitting on the porch when I came back this way. I stopped to check on her because I thought she might be having one of her spells."

"What kind of spell?" I asked in alarm.

He took my elbow and moved me out of earshot. "I don't think she can hear us, but you never know. From what I understand, she sometimes slips into these fugue states. She can move about if she wants to and sometimes she'll even speak to you, but she's basically unaware of what's going on around her. It's a little like sleepwalking, I guess. From a distance, she seems fine, but when you get close, you can tell by the glazed look in her eyes that she's not really there."

Despite my suspicions, I couldn't help feeling for Annalee. I knew what it was like to awaken from a spell or a dream with no idea what had transpired during those lost moments. "How often does it happen?"

"Often enough that most people around here know to look out for her. If anyone sees her wandering around, they'll take her home and sit with her until she comes out of it."

"Should we call someone? A doctor? Does she have any family close by?"

"Her family's all gone and the doctor would likely tell us to keep an eye on her and make sure she doesn't do anything to hurt herself. There's always the danger that she could walk out in front of a car or fall down a flight of stairs. Or worse," he added ominously.

"That sounds terrifying. Has anything like that ever happened?"

"Not that I know of. Maybe she has a special instinct or sixth sense that keeps her safe. Anyway, there's really no point in both of us staying out here with her. You must be tired and probably hungry. Why don't you go on inside? I'll make sure she gets home safely."

I was tempted by the offer, but I didn't feel at all comfortable going about my business with Annalee Nash lost in a trance on my front porch. "If you don't mind, I'd like to see for myself that she's okay."

Malloy looked surprised but not particularly offended by my request. "Suit yourself, but I should probably prepare you first. It can be a shock the first time you see her like that. A little creepy, if you want to know the truth."

"Thanks. I'll be fine."

We walked across the yard together, and as we approached the porch, I measured my movements so as not to startle or frighten her. She looked as if she'd dressed hastily in an oversize T-shirt and shorts. Her hair had curled in the heat, and in the fading light I could see dark circles beneath her eyes. She sat hunched over on the steps, arms wrapped around her middle as her gaze remained fixed on something only she could see.

Then, as if a switch had been flipped, she tilted her head to stare down at me. "Oh, hello. I hope I haven't come at a bad time."

The sudden shift caught me off guard. I didn't know how to react, nor was I certain I could trust her abrupt transformation. "Not at all," I tried to say easily. "I just got home from work."

Her gaze flicked over me. "I should have called before coming over. I'm sorry."

"No, you're fine. Did you need to see me?"

"Yes. I'd like to discuss the restoration with you if you have a few moments." She looked very young and innocent sitting there in her shorts and T-shirt with curls falling across her forehead. Under ordinary circumstances, I would have had great empathy for everything she'd been through, but now I couldn't help wondering what was really going on inside her head. If I peered too deeply into her eyes, would I find a wounded bird or the soul of a monster?

"What is it?" I asked as my fingers sought Rose's key.

"I know it's getting late so I promise I won't take up much of your time." She glanced at Malloy, who lingered beside me at the bottom of the steps. "You can go now, Tommy. I'm sure you've better things to do than babysit me."

"I'll take off in a bit, but I want to make sure you're okay first."

"I'll be fine once you stop hovering. You know how I hate that."

"Old habits die hard," he muttered.

"Apparently so."

I had a feeling something was going on between them that I didn't understand. An inside dynamic I wasn't privy to.

"I'll go wait for you in the car," he said. "I really don't think you should walk home alone. This road gets pitch-black after sunset."

"You don't have to tell me how dark it gets out here," she said, still with that unsettling undertone. "Wait in the car if you must. I won't be long."

As he disappeared across the yard, I became very aware of her proximity. Aware of her history with this house. I wasn't afraid of her, but I couldn't deny my uneasiness as I sat down on a step below her.

"I shouldn't have been so hard on him," she said as she drew up her knees and wrapped her arms around her legs. She began to rock back and forth. The movement was oddly hypnotic and I glanced away. "He means well. Everyone in town means well. But the way they look at me sometimes..." She trailed off with a sigh. "Being the local freak can get a little tiresome."

"I'm sure that's not how they see you."

"Oh, I'm pretty sure that's exactly how they see me."

"Then why come back here?"

"Because this is my home, and despite all the looks and whispers, the people here are unfailingly kind. They've always been very protective of me and I'm grateful for that. I'm not the easiest person to care about," she said frankly.

"What do you mean?"

"I'm different. I know that. I always have been even before things changed." She glanced over her shoulder at the house. "You know what I mean."

"I've heard a little about what happened here."

She rested her chin on her knees. "I knew you would as soon as that body was found. It was bound to stir up talk."

I leaned back against the railing, watching her carefully. "Can I ask you something? Did you know about those caged graves?"

"No," she said in surprise. "Why would you think so?"

"It just seems odd that no one around here knew anything about them."

"They're in a remote location. No one even goes out to the cemetery anymore, let alone down into those woods."

"Why is that?"

"Superstition, mostly."

"Superstition about Seven Gates or about what happened here?"

"A little of both, I think."

We were silent for a moment. Dusk was falling rapidly now. I could hear bullfrogs in the marsh and the closer serenade of the cicadas. Out on the road, the interior light in the car flashed and then the door clicked softly. I saw Malloy's face in the flare. He was looking up at the house and I wondered if he'd been standing outside his car listening to us.

I turned back to Annalee. When she didn't pick up the conversation, I said, "You wanted to talk to me about the restoration?"

"The historical committee is getting a little concerned about the schedule."

I nodded. "I've had some interruptions in the past

few days. I'm running behind but I can easily make up the time by putting in a few weekends."

"That's not the concern. We all agree that you've made remarkable progress. I think the other members just want reassurance that you aren't going to pack up and leave us in the lurch."

"Why would I do that?"

She gazed down at me. "With everything that's happened…who could blame you?"

"A lot has happened," I agreed. "But I like to finish what I start. I've no intention of leaving. I am curious about something, though. Why didn't you tell me about what happened in this house before I moved in? You must have known someone would let it slip."

"You seemed so adamant about wanting to get away from Charleston for the summer and there just aren't that many rental properties available in Ascension. I was afraid if I couldn't find you a place, you'd accept another offer and you have no idea how hard it was to raise enough money to even approach you. I've been trying to get the whole town involved in cleaning up that cemetery for years. Not just for personal reasons, but for the sake of everyone who was laid to rest there. If we lose our reverence for the dead, where does that leave us?"

It was an argument I'd made many times and Annalee sounded sincere. But I still couldn't get past the suspicion that she might somehow be playing me. That she might have an ulterior motive for wanting to keep me in Ascension.

"I should go." She stood and then sank back down as if her knees had collapsed.

"What's wrong?"

She put a hand to her forehead. "I feel…there's a strange buzzing in my ears."

"Are you okay?"

She didn't answer, nor did she seem to hear me. Her gaze moved to the road, but I didn't think she was searching for Malloy. A muscle at the corner of her eye began to twitch and her fingers tapped a frantic staccato against her knees. She seemed to be having another episode and I didn't know if it was wise to try and rouse her.

I lifted a hand to motion to Malloy, but then my arm fell back to my side. My ears were also buzzing, and behind my eyes images started to flash as though I were clicking through shots on a camera.

I'd once told Dr. Shaw that I had no control over when and how I entered other people's memories. The instances had mostly occurred with Devlin, presumably because of our deep emotional connection. I had no such bond with Annalee or anyone else in this town, but a strange nexus was at work here. Reality seemed fluid. I did know one thing with certainty, though. Those strobing images were not from *my* past. Annalee seemed to be searching back through her memory banks, sorting through a gallery of mental photographs until she finally came upon the time and place that she sought.

Suddenly, I was inside the church ruins, peering into the darkest corners. Torches burned outside in the graveyard, casting long shadows across the crumbling walls and into the woods beyond. I felt anxious and frightened, but I was in no danger. Whatever had happened inside that dank place had nothing to do with me. I was a reluctant voyeur to something that had occurred twenty years ago.

As my eyes adjusted to the gloom, I could pick out human forms and human faces. At the very back of the ruins, two young girls had been chained to the brick. With their free hands, they clutched each other tightly, sobbing in terror while a ten-year-old Annalee sat on the stone floor watching them. Her knees were drawn up, her arms wrapped around her legs as she rocked back and forth.

It was a strange and unnerving sensation because I was fully aware of the adult Annalee sitting on the porch steps above me. I observed that Annalee for a moment, taking in the twitching muscles and tapping fingers before allowing myself to sink back into her past.

The child Annalee made no effort to help the captives. She remained unfazed by their cries. I thought she must have fallen into a trance both in the present and in the past, but something outside the ruins caught her attention and she turned to peer through the arches. I followed her gaze to where robed and hooded figures chanted in a circle by firelight.

From deep within the cemetery, I could see other forms moving among the headstones. I could hear nearby whispers and faraway laughter and the guttural moans of people having sex on top of the graves. My stomach churned at the scene and I turned back to Annalee, wanting to shield her young eyes from the perversion. Wanting even more to spare those poor chained girls from the agony and horror that awaited them. But I could do nothing to help them because the past couldn't be changed.

Laughter rumbled from the shadows and I realized that Pope was there, too, watching from the dark as he transformed. I caught a glimpse of his savage features as he moved toward Annalee.

A barefoot woman I knew instinctively as Mary Willoughby appeared at his side. She wore a cotton dress that fell open at the neck and hemline, revealing her bare breasts and thighs. A tangle of curls cascaded across her shoulders and swayed down her back. She looked wanton and feral, her eyes gleaming unnaturally as she went to Annalee, smoothing her hair and crooning to her as she drew her down to the floor. Annalee tried to rise, but her mother held her fast and the girl began to whimper. "No, Mama, no."

Pope knelt beside Annalee and lowered his mouth to hers. But he didn't kiss her. He didn't touch her at all. Her body stiffened and her muscles began to jerk as he blew a dark mist deep into her lungs.

The images flashed again, sorting and sorting until we were back on the front porch. It was daylight and the child Annalee now wore a nightgown covered in blood. Even her bare feet were stained crimson, her hair matted with gore.

Her fingers tapped fiercely on top of her knees as she rocked back and forth, a strange keening sound emanating from the back of her throat. I made no move toward her because we were still in her past and I remained nothing more than an observer. But when she turned her head, peering down the road to track a distant siren, I could have sworn that our gazes locked. Her eyes were a very clear blue and a smile played at the corners of her mouth.

"Momento mori," she whispered.

Remember to die.

Twenty-Three

Had I really been able to access Annalee's memories or had she somehow orchestrated the whole thing, allowing me to see only what she wanted me to see?

I thought about those disturbing visuals for a long time after Officer Malloy had driven her home. The scene in the graveyard was so much like the illustration in Dr. Shaw's book about black magic and witchcraft that I wondered if Annalee had somehow accessed *my* memories.

I didn't like all these head games. I didn't like being manipulated and toyed with until I no longer trusted my own thoughts and experiences.

Why had Annalee really come back to this town? And why had she gone to so much trouble to seek out my website all those months ago? If she had spent years trying to get Seven Gates Cemetery cleaned up, then why had nothing been done until my arrival? I didn't always advocate amateur restorations, but at the very least, trash could have been hauled off and the worst of the vines and brush chopped down.

Had superstition really kept the townspeople away

or were they afraid of their silent complicity in what had taken place in the cemetery and inside those ruins?

They must have had an inkling of the ceremonies and rituals being conducted there. They must have been aware of the disappearances and yet no one had tried to stop Atticus Pope and his disciples until Darius Goodwine had brought in the *Congé*. By then it was too late. Pope's soul had already migrated into another.

Ascension was no longer the haven I'd once thought it and I couldn't wait for this job to be over. I'd accepted the restoration because I'd wanted desperately to escape Charleston and so many painful memories. Now I couldn't wait to get back to the city, even if it meant running into Devlin and a beautiful blonde named Claire.

Climbing into bed later that night, I clung to Rose's key as I slipped Essie's charm beneath my pillow. Their protection might be slight, but at the very least they offered a placebo comfort. That was enough at the moment. My muscles were so fatigued and I was so mentally exhausted that I dozed off almost immediately, only to be awakened sometime later by a cold nuzzle against my cheek.

A gasp rose to my throat and I was already reaching for the pepper spray on the nightstand when I recognized Angus's shape in the dark. He stood at the side of the bed using his snout to fully nudge me awake. Still in a panic, I flung off the covers and swung my legs over the side of the bed as my gaze darted about the shadowy bedroom.

"What's wrong? What's the matter?" I was certain something dire must be afoot. A ghost…a prowler…

Angus whimpered and trotted over to the bedroom door, then came back.

Relief swept over me as I wiped sleep from my eyes. "You need to go out again?"

A more urgent whine brought me to my feet at once. "When you have to go, you have to go," I muttered as I shuffled across the room to the door, groping for the light switch so I wouldn't stub a toe in the dark.

I turned on the hallway light to guide us through the silent house. It was a hot night and I didn't bother with shoes or a robe. The white cotton of my nightgown floated ghostlike about my legs as I padded out the kitchen door and onto the porch. I took a moment to scan the darkness before unlatching the screen.

A breeze had risen during the night. I could smell rain in the air, but the moon was still up, casting a misty glow over the orange grove. Through the scattered cloud coverage a few stars twinkled out.

I pushed open the door for Angus. "Make it quick, okay?"

He bounded down the steps without a sound, rooting in the damp grass around the porch before modesty led him to the deeper shadows at the back of the yard. I latched the screen door while I waited for him to finish. When he didn't come back after a few moments, I called out to him.

"Angus!"

He didn't respond, but I could see his darker silhouette against the shadows. When I called to him again, he shot a glance in my direction before spinning back to the orchard. He stood motionless, his attention riveted by something I couldn't yet hear or see.

"Angus, come!" I unfastened the door and hurried down the steps, pausing just at the edge of the light. *"Angus!"*

He didn't so much as glance at me this time. He remained transfixed by something far more compelling than my command. He didn't appear alarmed so I dismissed the idea of an intruder or even a ghost. He had undoubtedly caught the scent of some night creature. A raccoon or opossum, more than likely.

I huddled at the bottom of the steps and trained my senses on the night, trying to pick up any suspicious sound or scent. The breeze tangled my hair and I tucked the unruly strands behind my ears as I closed my eyes in concentration. I heard nothing more than the ripple of wind in the trees and the distant bang of a loose shutter. I made an effort to tune out those ordinary noises so that, like Angus, I could focus on the orchard. On what lay hidden in the shadows. Squeezing my eyes closed, I let my senses guide me into the trees.

My concentration was so rapt that I had what almost seemed an out of body experience as I imagined myself floating across the yard. Angus pressed up against me, perhaps to ground me. I put a hand on his back, smoothing his ruffled fur as I drifted deeper into the night. Nocturnal sounds assailed me. A rustle in the underbrush. The drone of a mosquito. The squeak of a bat.

The banging grew louder and now I could tell the sound came from beyond the orchard, from the shed where George Willoughby had killed himself. But the building didn't have shutters and the door was padlocked. So what could be banging in the wind?

Not banging, I realized.

Hammering.

Someone was inside the building hammering in the middle of the night.

My first thought was of Kendrick, which made no sense at all except that he had expressed a keen curiosity about the shed. He'd wondered aloud what might still be found there. But if he really had a desire to search the premises, all he needed to do was ask Annalee to let him inside. I doubted she'd refuse a police detective's request.

So, no, Detective Kendrick wasn't a likely culprit. Who, then? Annalee herself?

My mind flashed back to her hunkering form at the edge of the orchard. And then to her trance on the front porch and that whispered missive: *memento mori.*

Had that message been intended for me?

Focus!

I tucked away all thoughts of Annalee Nash and Lucien Kendrick, guiding my senses out of the trees and along the dirt path that would lead me to the shed. The hammering seemed loud to me now, but in reality, the sound was little more than a muffled thumping as though whoever had gained entrance took great care not to give himself away.

Over the muted thud came another noise. The

softest of cries. Like the mewling of a hungry kitten or the keening of a frightened child.

I'd heard a similar sound in the front bedroom a few nights ago. That indefinable hollowness once again lifted the hair at the back of my neck and sent a shock wave down my spine.

First he took their blood and then their hands, their eyes, their tongues.

My knees almost gave way as Darius Goodwine's disturbing words pounded in my head.

Don't think about that now! Don't think about what lies in wait in the darkness. Just focus on the sound!

Closing my eyes, I visualized the white facade of the shed in the moonlight. In my mind, the door hung open so that I could peer inside. The hammering was louder than ever now, a steady *thump, thump, thump* as though boards were being pounded into place.

Drifting up to the door, I hovered on the threshold as I searched the darkness, detecting nothing more threatening than the vague shapes of furniture and garden equipment that I'd noted on my real-life visits.

Across the crowded storage space, I could see a flickering light and, against the far wall, the looming silhouette of someone bent to his work.

Thump, thump, thump.

I ignored the muted din of the hammer as I zeroed in on the mewling. Where were those cries coming from? Not from the silhouette across the room, I felt certain. From who, then? From what?

I kept my eyes closed and poured all my concentration into those hushed howls as I pictured myself stepping inside that cluttered room and floating like a ghost toward the flickering light. The thumping stopped and I heard a voice, strange and yet somehow eerily familiar. "Save your breath. No one knows you're here. No one is even looking for you. You've already been forgotten so you may as well accept your fate."

I retreated then as the shadow rose and I heard a soft exhalation of breath. A moment later, a door closed and a chain jangled as the padlock clicked shut.

A low growl from Angus drew my focus away from the outbuilding, back through the orchard and across the yard to where we both stood at the bottom of the steps. I stroked his back, trying to convince myself I had imagined the hammering, the looming shadow and those soft, piteous cries. But Angus's behavior told me otherwise. He stood rigid, his earless head lowered, and when I took a step toward the orchard, he pushed up against me as if warning me to remain still.

I stood frozen for the longest time listening to the night. The clouds had thinned and the moon was so bright now I could see a few feet into the orange grove. I no longer heard the banging, but my normal senses picked up the sound of thudding footsteps on hard ground. Someone was coming toward us, moving fast through the trees.

A part of me wanted to wait and see who emerged from the darkness, but the wiser part of my brain told me to hide. I raced up the porch steps, turning only once to glance over my shoulder. I could see a shadow moving through the trees as he rapidly approached the house.

Slipping inside the screen door, I beckoned to Angus and then sank to the floor, concealing myself behind the half wall before the intruder could spot me. I reached up to latch the screen as I stroked along the dog's back to keep him calm. His eyes gleamed as he turned his head, listening to the footfalls that were now thudding across the backyard.

"Stay," I whispered into his ear nub. "Good dog."

A shadow fell across the back porch as the latch rattled. The hair on Angus's back bristled and I could feel the tension in his muscles as he crouched in the dark, prepared to fight for our lives if need be.

It would have taken very little effort for the intruder to snap the latch or to kick in the screen, but he hovered at the top of the steps as if vexed by the simple lock.

My gaze shifted to his shadow as I conjured an inhuman face in the moonlight. I imagined the scent of ozone from his magic and the sulfuric smell of his presence. Atticus Pope was out there in whatever guise he now used. I could sense him with every fiber of my being. All I had to do was rise up and peer at him through the screen to know him in his present form.

I hunched even lower as I tried to quiet my breath. I heard him go down the steps and I thought for a moment he'd given up. Odd that a screen door latch would thwart him so easily, but perhaps it was something in this house, a spell or Essie's charm, that re-pelled him.

I could no longer hear him, but Angus's head turned as he tracked an indistinguishable scent or sound. His teeth bared and he leaped forward to push me out of danger a split second before the blade of a machete slashed through the screen only inches from where my head had been.

Scrambling across the porch and into the kitchen, I called breathlessly to Angus. He reluctantly came and I slammed the wooden door and turned the lock. Then I ran for my phone and the pepper spray on the bedside table. As I waited for the police to arrive, I made sure the premises were secure even though I felt certain no lock could keep Pope out.

Somewhere down the road, a car door slammed and an engine gunned. Such an ordinary means of transportation for a man of witchcraft and black magic, but then I reminded myself that even Atticus Pope had frailties. So long as he resided in a human body, he could be stopped.

Unless the heart of a Goodwine made him invincible.

Twenty-Four

"**Y**ou're sure you didn't get a look at him?" Kendrick asked as he examined the sliced screen. "Not even a glimpse?"

"I only saw a shadow."

He flicked the light in my direction, stopping short of catching me in the face. "Why did you hide on the porch? If you thought you were in danger, why not hurry inside and lock all the doors?"

"Because I didn't have time to get inside without him seeing me. And I didn't want him to know that I'd seen him." I tugged at the tail of my T-shirt, feeling unkempt and half-dressed even though I basically had on the same clothing that I wore to work every day.

Kendrick scratched the back of his neck. "I've been around the house twice now and I've searched all over the yard. Other than the damaged screen, I haven't found any evidence of an attempted break-in. I'll have the latch dusted for prints, but I have to say, if someone really wanted in, that flimsy lock wouldn't keep him out. He could have easily cut through the screen on the door."

"I agree."

"So what do you think he really wanted?"

I had my suspicions, but I bit my lip and shrugged. "I don't know."

Kendrick studied me for a moment. "You said you heard him at the shed first."

"I heard someone in the shed."

He arced the light over the orchard. "Let's go down there and take a look."

I started to call to Angus, but then I decided it would be best to leave him guarding the premises. If anyone came skulking about, he would alert us.

The moon was still up, casting that same fragile glow over the landscape as we made for the trees. I was secretly relieved that Kendrick had been the one to answer my call rather than Malloy. As wary as I still was of the detective, I'd come to distrust the officer even less. His earlier interaction with Annalee had unnerved me and I couldn't shake the notion that the two of them, along with Martin Stark, might somehow be involved in all this.

Despite the hot night, I shivered as we emerged on the other side of the orchard and I caught sight of the outbuilding. Angus's nightly wanderings had taken him all over the property, but I'd only been down this way by daylight. Even with the moon shining so brightly and a police detective walking beside me, I felt the tug of yet another premonition. *If a place could be haunted, it would be that shed.*

I hung back as Kendrick began a slow walk around the structure, angling his flashlight beam all along the ground, up the walls and back toward the fence.

"Nothing here, either," he concluded as he came back around the corner. "The door is still padlocked and the windows are all closed."

"What about footprints?"

Kendrick trained the beam on the ground in front of the door and then knelt to have a closer look. "Maybe when it's daylight, we'll find something." He didn't sound hopeful.

"I was so certain someone had broken into this place. I even heard a voice. At least, I thought I did. I'm sorry if I called you out here at this time of night for nothing."

He glanced up at me. "I wouldn't call that slashed screen nothing."

I suppressed a shudder. "No, but as you said, if he'd really wanted in, the latch on the screen door wouldn't have discouraged him. Maybe someone really is trying to scare me." Or test me. I had no doubt that Pope's perception was at least as keen as mine. If he had been sensing supernatural vibes, he may have been trying to find the source or even to confirm his suspicions by luring me out into the open. Or perhaps he was trying to ascertain how much of a threat I posed.

There was an even more chilling explanation based on something Dr. Shaw had told me about the victims of medicine murder. Their terror and agony made the *muti* more powerful. Was it possible Pope was toying with me, picking at my doubts and fears so that my weakened resolve would strengthen his magic?

Unmindful of my churning thoughts, Kendrick clinked his flashlight against the padlock. "You don't have a key?"

"Only to the house."

"Do you know of anyone besides Annalee who would have access to this place?"

"No. I've never seen anyone down here."

"Did you call her about a possible intruder? Or to see if she knew who might have been out here?"

"I didn't want to alarm her with a phone call in the middle of the night. But she was here earlier."

"At the shed? When was this?"

"Not at the shed, at the house. She and Officer Malloy were sitting on the front porch when I got home from work. He said she was having one of her spells—that's how he described it—but she snapped out of it pretty quickly once I arrived."

Kendrick straightened from the lock. "What was Malloy doing here with her?"

"Apparently, he saw her on his way to and from the cemetery and stopped to make sure she was okay."

"Did he say what he was doing at the cemetery?"

The question surprised me. "Yes. He said you sent him to have a look around."

"He said *I* sent him?"

"Didn't you? He also said you'd beefed up patrols since the disturbance I reported in the cemetery."

"He said an awful lot, sounds like." I could see

Kendrick's face in the moonlight, but his expression remained inscrutable.

I watched him for a moment. "Are you saying none of what he told me is true?"

"It seems as if some wires got crossed. It happens. I did put the word out to keep an eye on the cemetery and the house. Maybe Malloy was just being unusually proactive."

Was that a hint of sarcasm I detected in his voice? I was quickly coming to the conclusion that very little love was lost between Kendrick and the younger officer.

"I'll get in touch with Annalee first thing in the morning and see if she has any idea who may have been out here," he said. "Could have been the same kids that scared you at the cemetery."

I frowned. "Assuming that it was a kid I saw. That hasn't been proven, has it?"

"Not conclusively, but it's still the best theory we have. People react differently when they hear about a murder, especially one that hits a little too close to home. Some are curious, some hide behind locked doors and others use it as an excuse to act out."

"I hope that's not what you think I'm doing," I said uneasily.

"I meant whoever is trying to scare you. But it would only be natural if you were reactive. We haven't caught the killer yet and you live alone, you work alone. I'd be worried if you weren't on edge."

"I have my moments," I admitted. "Can you tell me anything about the investigation? How it's going? You must have leads."

"None that I can talk about."

"Can you at least tell me if the victim has been identified? She's been on my mind lately."

He hesitated as if pondering his need for discretion. "We don't have a positive ID yet."

I pictured the victim as she'd looked in the morgue, tiny and forsaken and yet still with an indomitable air. If she really was *Congé*, I supposed that explained a lot. She was probably from a well-to-do family, likely well educated and, for all I knew, well trained, though apparently no match for Atticus Pope. "Don't you find it odd that no one has come forward to claim the body? Someone must be out there looking for her."

"People die alone all the time," he said.

"Not people like her. I doubt she was a runaway or homeless."

"What makes you say that?"

"Her jewelry, for one thing. All those ruby studs. Her silver ring looked custom or even heirloom. It could be traceable."

I saw a brow lift in the moonlight. "Go on."

"She wore a band shirt. I've never heard of the group, but if they're local, you could canvas the clubs where they last played, maybe find someone who remembers her. It's a thought," I finished with a shrug.

"Interesting observations," he said. "It seems my earlier assessment was right on the money. Nothing much gets by you, does it?"

"Details are also important in my line of work, Detective."

He gave a slight nod. "Then you'll be relieved to

know that everything you mentioned has already been checked out, plus a few leads you may not have considered. Believe it or not, the investigation is in capable hands."

"I didn't mean to imply otherwise."

"We'll find out who she is and we'll catch her killer. Sooner or later, he'll give himself away. They almost always do. In the meantime, you haven't remembered anything that could help us out, have you?"

I glanced away. "No, I'm afraid not."

He followed my gaze with the light, running it all along the perimeter of the orchard and up into the trees. "Tell me again about that noise you heard. You said you thought at first it was a loose shutter banging in the wind. Was it loud enough to wake you up?"

"It didn't wake me up. My dog had to go out. I heard the noise while I waited for him on the back porch."

Kendrick focused the light over my shoulder. "Isn't that your dog over there?"

I whirled, surprised to find Angus hovering in the shadows at the tree line. He didn't growl or bare his teeth, but I could tell he was wary of Kendrick, which was undoubtedly why he'd followed us.

Kendrick crouched and put out a hand.

"He doesn't always warm up to strangers," I warned.

"*Au pied*, Angus."

The dog lifted his head at the sound of Kendrick's voice. He eyed him suspiciously for another long moment before trotting over to inspect Kendrick's out-stretched hand, going so far as to nuzzle his palm.

"I guess you're one of the exceptions," I murmured.

"I've always been good with dogs. They're a lot easier to relate to than most people."

"I don't disagree. Do you have one of your own?"

"Not now," he said with regret. "Not for a long time, but always as a child. My grandmother used to say that you could tell a lot about a person's character by how well they got on with animals. I've always found that to be a pretty reliable gauge."

"Would you have said as much if Angus hadn't accepted you so readily?"

"Probably not." I saw a grin flash as he cupped Angus's scarred snout. "What happened to him?"

"He was used as a bait dog before I found him. Or rather, he found me in the Blue Ridge Mountains."

"*Bon chien*, Angus." He bent forward, speaking softly into the dog's ear nub. *"Tu es un doux guerrier. Non? Un gardien féroce. Nous sommes semblables toi et moi. Nous portons les cicatrices de nos défaites aussi fièrement que nous célébrons nos victoires."*

I'd had a couple of years of high school French, enough to get by on when I'd gone to Paris after graduation, but Kendrick spoke so rapidly I could pick out only a word here and there. Warrior. Protector. Angus gave a sharp bark and wagged his tail fiercely as if he had understood every word. But, of course, it wasn't the language that he responded to. It was the inflections and nuances in Kendrick's voice. It was the man himself, I imagined.

"What did you say to him?"

"That's between Angus and me," Kendrick said, scratching behind the ear nubs and then smoothing the fur along the dog's backbone. "He's a good animal. Gentle and proud. Ferocious when he has to be and loyal to a fault."

"Yes, that's Angus."

Kendrick stood, his gaze finding me in the dark. "His attachment to you is strong. You've been together for a long time?"

"No, not really. Not quite two years."

"Sometimes it only takes a moment."

"Yes." A moment like the one we'd shared in the cemetery?

I didn't want to think about that right now. Kendrick was standing a little too close and I was still feeling a little too vulnerable. But I couldn't keep my gaze from straying back to him and I found myself searching his face, tracing along his strong jawline and then lingering on his lips. He looked dark and mysterious in the moonlight, very Byron-esque, and I remembered Temple's comment about my having a type.

He didn't seem aware of my scrutiny. He'd turned toward the orange grove, tilting his head as he listened to the wind in the leaves. "There's a strong breeze tonight. Maybe you heard a loose shutter at a neighbor's house. Sound carries at night. Could have been farther away than you thought."

"Yes, that's possible, I suppose."

"The voice you heard. Male or female?"

I thought back, frowning. "It was very low, but I had the impression it was a man's voice."

"Could you make out anything he said?"

"'Save your breath. No one knows you're here. No one is even looking for you. You've already been forgotten so you may as well accept your fate.'"

He stared at me for the longest moment. "You picked that up all the way back at the house?"

"I have good hearing." Admitting to my uncanny senses made me nervous so I quickly added, "And as you said, sound carries at night."

"I did say that, but your recall is very specific."

I folded my arms. "What he said made an impression. And it made me wonder if someone could be locked up inside this building. Or, if not in here, somewhere nearby."

Kendrick's gaze seemed relentless in the moonlight. "That's unlikely."

"Maybe. I'm just telling you what I heard and what I thought."

"It couldn't have been a neighbor's TV or radio?"

"Anything's possible."

He returned his attention to the lock. I noticed that he took care not to touch the metal even though he'd found no evidence of tampering.

"Do you know anything about padlocks?" he asked.

"Not really. Not beyond the obvious. Why?"

"Come take a look at this one."

I walked over to the door, bending to get a better look but taking care not to brush up against him.

He adjusted the light for me. "Does anything about that lock seem strange to you?"

"Strange in what way? It looks like a normal padlock to me."

"Keep looking."

I leaned in closer, searching for aberrations in the steel or in the design. Then the importance of the engraved emblem struck me and I glanced up at Kendrick in surprise. "It's an owl's head. The same symbol that was on the mortsafe padlock. I heard Martin Stark talking about it when he came to the clearing that day." I took another look. "This can't be a coincidence, can it?"

"Depends on the popularity of the lock and local availability. I'm not about to jump to any conclusions, but I'll admit it's piqued my curiosity. I'd be interested in finding out when this lock was purchased and by whom."

"Maybe you should talk to Stark about that," I said, remembering my own enlightening conversation with the locksmith. "You said the emblem has piqued your curiosity, but I think it's done more than that. It confirms something you already suspected, doesn't it? You always try to downplay or even deny it, but there's a connection between what happened twenty years ago and what's happening now. No matter what you say, I still think that's why you felt compelled to warn me about the Willoughby house."

His gaze deepened. "I told you about the house because I thought you had a right to know."

"Why? The Willoughbys died a long time ago.

Why was it necessary for me to know their history if it has nothing to do with the present-day murder?"

"You know why."

"I have no idea."

We were still standing close, a mere breath apart. The light was angled at the lock, but the way it bounced off the building cast shadows across Kendrick's face, making my pulse race.

He lifted a hand as if to touch my hair, then seemed to think better of it. But his gaze was still on me, peering into my eyes and whispering over my lips until my knees grew weak.

"I understand your reluctance." His voice was low and unbearably intimate in the dark. "The world is full of disbelievers, but I'm not one of them. You don't have to hide from me."

"I don't..." Whatever I'd meant to say vanished as I became mesmerized by his golden stare. His eyes were at once dark and softly glowing and I felt inexorably drawn to him in a way I never would have thought possible after Devlin.

The scruff on his lower face was more pronounced in the reflected light and I had the strongest urge to run the back of my hand along the prickly texture, to trace a finger down that mysterious raised scar tissue at the back of his neck. My heart beat very hard against my chest and I felt breathless and anxious because I knew something was about to happen. A step was about to be taken that could change everything or perhaps nothing at all.

I didn't see Kendrick move toward me, but suddenly I felt a hand on my arm, warm and slightly roughened from calluses. It was a light touch, neither threatening nor seductive. The gesture was meant to reassure, but the contact made me tremble just the same.

His expression flickered, and for a moment, his guard dropped and an air of loneliness descended. I saw pain and longing in his eyes and the shadow of an old fear that made me want to offer him comfort. I thought again about that moment in the cemetery when a look had passed between us, a fleeting solidarity that had forged a bond whether I wanted to acknowledge it or not.

Without warning, my mind cleared and I found myself drifting into his past, settling into one of his memories. Before me was a young Lucien Kendrick with unkempt hair and an already jaded demeanor. He stoodstanding outside an old train station in Paris, a duffel bag in one hand and a backpack thrown over his shoulder. I recognized the writing on the building from my short stay in the city of lights. *Gare de l'Est*.

It was just getting on dusk and he was dressed for the cold. His frosted breath floated out among the ghosts that hovered in the recessed doorways and alleys.

"Ils sont déjà là. Partout." A woman stood just beyond the fringes of the streetlamp. She wore a heavy wool coat and a silk headscarf that covered her hair and part of her face, but I somehow knew she was Kendrick's grandmother.

"Do you see them?" she asked in English as she pulled her coat tightly about her frail body.

"Only glimpses," he said. "But even in this weather, I can feel their cold."

She stepped out of the shadows and put a hand to his cheek. "You understand why they are drawn to us? What we must do because of our gift?"

"Oui."

"Ours is a noble calling. Remember that in the dark times, *mon petit prince*. Remember me."

"Always, *Mamiluce*."

"Bon voyage." She hugged him fiercely, kissing both of his cheeks before fading back into the shadows of his memory.

He stepped into the glow of the streetlamp, his gaze meeting mine across the wet street, across the long years and through the misty twilight, before a wall finally came up. That was all he would allow me to see, but it was enough.

He wasn't *Congé*. He was a ghost-seer. He had walked my dark path. He had known my fears and loneliness. And now he was offering me, what? Solace? Understanding?

And what would he expect in return? I wondered with a shiver.

Twenty-Five

Far more important questions needed to be asked. How had Kendrick known about me in the first place? What had I done to give myself away to him?

From the moment we met, I'd sensed that he knew things about me. I had assumed that he'd researched me on his way to the caged graves that first day, but now I was forced to consider the possibility that his interest went beyond my role as a material witness in a murder investigation. Perhaps even beyond the ghosts. Could he have been the watcher in the woods? Was he the one who had summoned me to that airless circle?

His eyes shimmered in that strange, yellow light. I didn't trust myself to speak, but so many more questions bubbled inside me. Had he always been aware of the ghosts or, like me, had he acquired the sensitivity in early childhood? Had he been sent to live with his grandmother because she shared his sight? Did he know about hallowed ground? Had he been given rules to follow?

And what had his grandmother meant by the nobleness of their calling?

"Do you understand now why I felt compelled to warn you?" He slid his hand up my arm, a feathery touch that made my breath catch. "I was afraid of what you might find in that house. Of what might find you."

I still couldn't bring myself to open up about my gift. So much was at stake and secrecy had been too deeply ingrained. "I don't understand anything. This house, this town…you."

He trailed both hands over my shoulders, cupping my neck as he gently caressed my jawline with his thumbs. His touch mesmerized me and yet I felt anything but languid.

"I don't know if we should," I said, my voice raw with nerves.

"Is there someone else?"

My hesitation was slight. "Not anymore."

"But there was. Someone important."

I nodded.

He stared into my eyes, searching for a way in. I tried to glance away, but he wouldn't let me. His fingers slid into my tangled hair as he lowered his lips to mine. But he didn't kiss me. He remained so close and my chest was suddenly so tight that I wondered if he'd stolen my breath.

I kept my hands at my sides, but they itched to touch him. I wanted more than anything to thread my fingers through his hair and tug him to me until that minuscule distance between our lips had closed. I wanted to run my hands over his biceps and shoulders and press myself against him as my tongue tasted his skin. I pictured myself opening his shirt and unfastening his belt as I sank slowly to the ground.

In that moment, I craved him as surely as a ghost hungers for life and that desperate longing should have worried me. I was a careful person. I'd paid dearly for throwing caution to the wind and now I knew better. Lowering my guard was never a wise option, especially when I couldn't be certain that my feelings were even real.

Tread carefully, a voice whispered through the haze. *And trust no one.*

Kendrick's head came up. "What was that?"

I was still so lost in my fantasy that his question barely registered. "What?"

"You didn't hear that noise?"

"No... I..."

"Shush. There it is again." He cocked his head toward the door, his expression grim as his hands fell away from me. "You were right. Something is locked inside the shed."

That jarred me back to earth. "Oh, my God."

"It's not a person," he quickly assured me. "I think it's a cat. A stray, most likely. Sounds like it may be wounded."

"Wounded?" I shook off the last of that betraying fog as I pressed my ear to the door. I heard it then, a soft, faraway mewling that tugged at my heart. "Oh, it's a kitten! We can't just leave it in there. We have to help it."

"If we're not too late."

His words conjured distressing images and I said urgently, "We still have to try."

He nodded. "I'll see if I can get one of the windows open." He moved away from the door, brushing my shoulder and making me all too aware of my momentary lapse and my still-thudding heart. I felt dismayed and not a little embarrassed as I followed him around to the side of the building.

"Can you see anything?" I asked anxiously as he shined the flashlight beam into the window.

"Looks like a bunch of old furniture and equipment." He placed the flashlight on the ledge and tried the window. Layers of paint and grime had sealed the frame tight, but after a few tries, he managed to get it open. Hitching himself over the sill, he reached for the flashlight, and then ran the beam over the walls and floors as he searched the interior.

"I smell decay," he said. "Probably a dead rat."

"What about the kitten?"

"No sign of life yet. Unless you count spiders."

I braced myself against a twinge of arachnophobia. "Is there a light?"

He disappeared for a moment and then came back to the window. "No power."

"That's too bad."

He reached a hand down to me. "Are you coming in?"

"Yes," I said without hesitation.

He clasped my wrists and easily lifted me off the ground. Once I had my upper body over the sill, I pulled myself through, and then glanced around as he passed the light over the piles of furniture. I caught a glimpse of his face in a mirror. The sight startled and intrigued me because somehow his reflection looked different. Or had my perception of him changed?

"All this stuff must be leftovers from the Willoughbys' antique business," he said.

I turned in a slow circle, lifting my gaze to the roof. "The place is literally packed to the rafters."

"Some of it may even be valuable. Strange that Annalee would leave it out here to mildew and rot."

"Maybe she found the memories too painful to deal with it. Then again, she claims to have no recall of what happened in here."

Kendrick turned. "Claims?"

"That's what you said, isn't it?" But Annalee did have memories. Perhaps buried so deeply that the images only surfaced during her blackouts, but they were there just the same. "Officer Malloy told me a story of when he and Annalee were children. She once lured him in here and locked him inside an old wardrobe. He wasn't found for hours."

"Sounds like a typical kid prank."

"I suppose so. But it's easy to imagine his terror, isn't it? To be trapped inside a confined space, not knowing whether you'll ever get out."

We both fell silent, listening for the telltale cries. I sensed nothing unnatural in the building. No ghosts or the evil that had allegedly taken possession of Mary Willoughby's body, driving her husband to murder her while she slept. And yet there was something disquieting about that place, apart from the spiders and the smell.

Kendrick was still moving the light slowly over

the stacks of furniture and up under some of the larger pieces.

"Do you see anything?" I asked.

"Not yet," he muttered as he knelt to run the beam across the floorboards.

I watched him curiously. "Why do I get the feeling you're looking for something besides a wounded kitten?"

"Someone was in here earlier. We need to figure out what they were up to."

"So you believe me now," I said on a breath.

"I've seen no evidence, but I doubt it's wise to bet against your intuition and observations."

I told myself now was the perfect time to open up a little about my gift, return the insight he had allowed me earlier. But our moment of bonding had passed and my self-preservation had returned. I needed to watch myself with Kendrick. Whether intentional or not, he'd shown me a memory that mirrored the loneliness of my childhood and I had to be careful that I didn't succumb to a false sense of kinship.

I watched him in silence as he moved about the crowded space, squeezing between heavy pieces of furniture to peer into web-draped corners.

"What about the other rooms?" I asked. "Can you go all the way to the back of the building?"

"Not easily. There's too much stuff in the way and it looks as if the doorway has been barricaded."

"Maybe that explains the hammering."

Stepping onto a box, Kendrick hoisted himself to the top of an old wardrobe—perhaps the very one that Malloy had been confined in—and then used the wooden beams to propel himself over the furniture.

He had only progressed a short distance when I heard the mewling. "There! Did you hear it? I think it's coming from beneath the floorboards."

"Hold on." He backtracked along the beams and swung down from a rafter to land at my feet. We both stood listening for a moment.

"I think you're right," he said. "It's under the floor."

"Should we go outside and look?"

"I don't think we can get to it from outside. If the animal is sick or wounded, its mother may have abandoned him. He probably crawled up under the floor as far as he could to hide from predators."

I thought of the way Angus had looked, beaten and starved, when he crept out of the woods in Asher Falls. I hated to think what would have happened to him if he hadn't found me, just as I hated to think about a frightened and possibly wounded kitten cowering beneath our feet.

I was fully prepared to rip up the floorboards with my bare hands if need be, but Kendrick reasonably suggested we try and pinpoint the cries first. He cleared some of the lighter pieces of furniture out of the way and then knelt to glance under an old library table. From what I could see in the dim light, the piece looked massive. We were both strong, but I doubted our ability to move the heavy table without help.

"Can you still hear it?" I asked worriedly.

"You're the one with the superhuman hearing," he said. "You tell me."

I crouched beside him, listening so intently that I fancied I could hear the scurry of spider legs up the walls. But the mewling had stopped and I wondered if we'd scared the poor creature back into a hidey-hole. I remained frozen, my senses attuned to the darkness. After a moment, a plaintive cry rose up through the floorboards.

"There," I whispered, pointing to the spot where the sound had apparently emanated.

Kendrick maneuvered under the table and flattened himself on the floor as he ran his hands over the planks.

"I feel a slight draft coming up through the cracks," he said, sweeping aside cobwebs that hung from beneath the table. "Which is odd because the shed sits on a concrete foundation. This place is solidly built. You can tell by walking across the floor. Not much give and take or even creaking for an old building."

"Then how did the kitten get up under the floor?"

"Who knows? Right now I'm trying to figure out where that draft is coming from. Roll the light to me, please."

I upended the flashlight and gave it a shove. The arcing beam cast leaping shadows on the walls, making the place seem truly haunted. I had no trouble imagining a distraught George Willoughby closed up in that desolate room, brooding about what he had done to his wife as he worked up the courage to take his own life. The images were so vivid that I wondered if I had somehow slipped into his memory. But George Willoughby had been dead for a long time and so far I'd yet to encounter even his ghost.

Kendrick rapped on one of the planks and then moved his hand over a few inches. "Do you hear the difference?" He repeated the knocking.

"Sounds hollow," I said.

"There's a hole beneath the floor. I don't know how an animal managed to get inside, but I think that's where we'll find our stray." He glanced back at me. "I saw some tools on a table near the window. See if you can find a crowbar or hammer, anything we can use to pry up these boards."

I collected the tools and then hurried back over to shimmy up under the table.

"The draft is coming from this spot," Kendrick said. "Can you feel it?"

"Yes, but…" I stopped to listen.

"What's the matter?"

"The cries are getting weaker."

"He's probably just frightened by all the noise. But we should hurry before he decides to crawl off somewhere out of reach. Move back a little so I don't hit you with my elbow."

I pushed away, holding the light steady for him. He fitted the claw of the hammer beneath a nail, taking care not to splinter the wood as he prized it loose. Within a matter of moments, he'd removed several boards, revealing the source of the draft.

A circle had been cut in the concrete subfloor and fitted with a metal grate that was roughly the size of a manhole cover.

"What is that?" I asked as I moved back up beside him.

"Could be an old well or cistern." He shined the light down through the grate. "The cover was probably put in place before the shed was built to keep someone from falling in."

"I wonder why they didn't fill it with concrete when they poured the foundation."

"Too costly, maybe. It looks pretty deep."

A terrible dread came over me. There was something strange about that hole. Something sinister. I felt a powerful urge to look over my shoulder as I remembered Dr. Shaw's warnings about sacrifices and torture and young girls being held against their will.

From the bottom of the pit came a piercing yowl. If the kitten had been frightened into silence before, now he seemed determined to alert us of his whereabouts.

I moved in closer, trying to get a glimpse through the grate as Kendrick aimed the flashlight straight down through the layers of cobwebs and shadows.

"Can you see the bottom?" I asked.

"No. It's pretty murky down there. Too many spiderwebs."

I could feel those tiny feet crawling all over me now, but I ignored the sensation as I focused on helping Kendrick remove the metal grid. The hinges had rusted in place and we couldn't get leverage in such cramped quarters.

After a few minutes of pulling and tugging, I pushed back in frustration. "The thing won't budge. We'll never get it off without moving the table and I don't think we can do that by ourselves." I hated to think of the hours that would be eaten away if we had to wait for help. Who knew how badly the kitten was injured or how long it had been constrained in that terrible place. If we didn't get it out of there now, we might be too late.

"We'll have to break the hinges," Kendrick said. "Or figure out how the cat got down there in the first place. I can still feel that draft. Maybe there's another way in." He moved the flashlight to a different angle as he searched the confines of the pit. "I'm guessing it's at least twenty or thirty feet deep. Maybe more."

"Can you see water?" I had visions of a wet and trembling kitten desperately clinging to the walls to keep from drowning.

"It's not a well."

Something in his voice made gooseflesh pop on my arms. "What is it, then?"

"A cylinder."

"Like a silo?"

He hesitated. "I don't think it's a silo, either."

"What do you think it was used for, then?"

He met my gaze over the grid. "From what I can tell, the walls are solid. I doubt we'll find another opening."

"You're saying our only way in is to remove the grate?"

"I'm saying there's no way a cat could have gotten into that hole of its own volition. Someone put it down there."

Twenty-Six

I stared at Kendrick wide-eyed as his revelation sank in. Even the yowling had stopped, as if the kitten could sense my horror. I could picture that looming shadow hammering the floorboards back into place, admonishing his feline prisoner that no one would come looking after all this time.

My heart started to pound in agitation. "But the hinges are rusted in place. The cobwebs haven't been disturbed. You said yourself there's no sign that anyone has been in here in years."

"I realize that."

"Then how..."

His gaze was still on me. "I don't know."

I bit my lip, trying to quell a terrible trembling. Who we were up against...*what* we were up against...

How did one combat spells and witchcraft and a reality that transcended concrete walls and a metal grate? How did one catch a killer that left no footprints and buried his prey alive?

I was as frightened as I'd ever been by the prospect of confronting Atticus Pope in whatever body he now occupied. But as I stared down into that swirling darkness, visions of his mutilated victims flashed through mind, stirring another emotion. The same thirst for vengeance I experienced in the church ruins with Darius Goodwine.

"Why would he put a kitten down there? Why would he harm such a defenseless creature?"

I never expected an answer and Kendrick didn't offer one. Instead, he set to work on the hinges, using both hammer and crowbar to break the rusty fasteners. With that done, we were able to lift the grate a few inches and slide it aside so that we now had access to the pit.

I called down to the animal, trying to soothe its fears along with my own.

"I saw a coil of rope earlier," Kendrick said. "I'll fasten it off to one of the table legs and lower myself down."

"No."

He glanced up. "No?"

"It has to be me." The last thing I wanted was to go down in that hole. I could hardly catch my breath just thinking about the confines of those circular walls and the layers of cobwebs that obscured the bottom. But it had to be done and it had to be me.

"Why you?" Kendrick asked with a scowl.

I couldn't explain my rationale. I hardly understood it myself. But I somehow knew I was still being tested. My fears and phobias were being prodded by Pope in order to strengthen his magic. The only way to thwart him was to overcome my weaknesses.

Or maybe I just needed to prove something to myself. Maybe confronting whatever lurked in that hole was a way to strengthen my own magic.

"I'm still waiting to hear why it has to be you," Kendrick said.

"I'm lighter and you're stronger. Judging by your performance on those beams earlier, you have a lot of upper body strength. You'd have a much easier time pulling me back up."

"But I don't have claustrophobia."

"Who says I do?"

His gaze swept over me. "You don't have to say it. I can tell by your body language and by the look on your face. You're trembling at just the thought of being lowered into that hole."

"Maybe I am, but I can control it." I took another deep breath and gritted my teeth. "I can do it."

A part of me hoped he would find a way to talk me out of such folly. I wouldn't have taken much convincing. But instead he nodded. "Okay, if you're that determined, we'll do it your way. But if anything happens or you panic, just scream or yank on the rope and I'll pull you back up."

He scooted out from under the table and disappeared. I pushed myself up to the verge of the cylinder, calling down to the trapped kitten as I tried to peer through all those restless shadows. Did something stir at the bottom? Was the draft we'd felt earlier a manifestation?

What if those piteous cries were another trick to lure me into that pit? What if Kendrick couldn't or wouldn't pull me back up? My stomach churned with the realization that I was literally placing my life in the hands of a man I barely knew.

All too soon, he returned with the rope. He fashioned a sling and then slipped the loop up my legs and over my hips. He wrapped the other end of the rope around a table leg so that he could control the speed of my descent.

Once he had everything in place, he rechecked all the knots. "Ready?"

I swallowed and nodded. We crawled back under the table and I hovered at the edge, staring down into all that blackness.

"Just remember, the rope is secured around the table leg and that table isn't going anywhere. Even if were to drop you, which I won't, you wouldn't fall far."

"That's some comfort."

"When you get settled, I'll hand you the flashlight." He checked the knots one last time to reassure me. "Just ease yourself over the side and then let go whenever you're ready."

I went into the opening backward, my heart racing and my breath shallow. When I let go of the edge, the rope jerked and I fell a few feet before Kendrick was able to take out the slack.

"You okay?" he called down.

His voice bounced off the walls as I swung back and forth. I was seated on the sling, grasping the rope with both hands as I tried to calm my thudding pulse. "I'm fine."

He appeared over the edge. "I'm going to hand the flashlight down to you."

I nodded even though I had no idea if he could see me. I clutched the rope so tightly I could feel the abrasive fibers burn into my palms. This was not a good idea. Test or no, I was sorely tempted to have Kendrick pull me back up, but then I heard the echo of those tiny cries below me. I needed to do this. Not just to thwart Atticus Pope or even to face my fears, but to rescue a tiny being whose life had become precious to me.

I reached for the flashlight. Clinging to the rope with one hand, I shined the beam all around the cylinder and then down into the pit. I could still see very little and the sway of the sling disoriented me. I drew in several breaths and tried to focus on the mission. As long as I could hear those cries below me, I could do this. *I could do this.*

"Hold tight," Kendrick called from above. "I'm going to lower you down, okay?"

"I'm ready."

I splayed the beam over the walls as I began to descend. Cobwebs clung to my clothing and hair and I didn't want to think about the size and proximity of all those spiders. I didn't want to think about the purpose of that hole or why a helpless kitten had been left in there to die.

It seemed as though I had been descending forever and I began to think we might run out of rope before I reached the bottom. But as I tunneled through those cobweb clouds, the cries from below grew louder. I angled the beam down through the gossamer threads and saw glowing eyes staring up at me.

"Almost there," I called up. My feet touched the

floor and I swung the light quickly around the space to make sure that nothing else lurked in the darkness. The cylinder widened at the bottom and I breathed a little easier now that the walls didn't seem so close. But I still had to watch my step because the floor was littered with debris, giving the terrified kitten plenty of places to hide until he decided whether he could trust me.

"You okay?" Kendrick called down.

I angled the light up, trying to catch a glimpse of his face. "Yes. I'm at the bottom now. Just taking a look around."

"Is the cat down there?"

"Yes, but he's hiding from me."

"I'll toss down a box," Kendrick said. "If you can trap him inside, we'll have an easier time getting him out of there."

I backed out of the way, keeping the rope around me as I flattened myself against the wall. The concrete felt cold and moist against my back. I could smell dirt and mold and the unmistakable musk of old death. I thought about all the snakes that might be hiding in the cracks and crevices of the concrete and all those spiders weaving their webs above me.

A small box landed on the floor at my feet. I stepped out of the harness and bent to retrieve it. Then I shined the beam all around the cylinder, searching for the kitten until the light once again caught those glowing eyes.

I knelt and called to him softly. "Here, kitty. Don't be afraid. I won't hurt you. I'm going to get you out of here." But as I slowly advanced, he darted behind another pile of debris. This wasn't going to be easy. His self-preservation was strong.

I started to hum an inane tune that was meant to soothe us both. As I knelt there waiting for him to get used to my presence, I once again lifted the light to the walls to take stock of that strange, circular room. Amid all the cracks and discoloration in the concrete, I saw something that made my heart still.

"Someone's been down here," I said. "There's writing on the wall."

"What does it say?" Kendrick called down.

"It's hard to make out. The ink is faded and flaking. It must have been here for a long time." I moved in closer, mindful of the skittish kitten. "I can still feel a draft, but I don't see any other way in. It's odd." I glanced over my shoulder, shivering from the chill of my own uneasiness.

"Maybe you better come up out of there," Kendrick said.

"Good idea." But that writing worried me. I had a feeling I was missing something important. A clue or a message. I moved closer still and now I could detect scratches in the concrete that looked like claw marks.

The chill deepened as I studied those scratches. A premonition tugged. That draft...where was it coming from...?

I said urgently, "Here, kitty, kitty, kitty."

The light shimmered in those glowing eyes as he crawled out of his hiding place to stare at me warily.

"It's okay, it's okay," I whispered.

I crept forward, my hand outstretched. This time

he didn't dart away, but folded into a tiny bundle as if he could disappear from sheer force of will. When I was only a few inches away, I paused and continued to murmur to him. I couldn't tell if he was hurt, but he was certainly frightened and possibly starved. Setting the flashlight aside, I eased nearer until I could cup my hands around him. He resisted, but I held him fast, feeling the quiver of his frail little body as I lifted him. Then I placed him against my chest so that he could feel my warmth and the beat of my heart. He was still frightened, but he clung to my shirt like a lifeline.

The flashlight beam was still directed at his hiding place and as I knelt there, holding him close, my gazed moved over the mound. I thought at first it was just a bunch of old rags, but then I saw bits of bone hidden within the folds of the fabric. Human bones picked clean by rodents and insects and a grinning skull with hanks of grayish hair sprouting from the cranium.

I must have made some involuntary move or sound that frightened the kitten even more. Tiny claws dug into my flesh as he climbed from my chest to burrow underneath my chin. I cradled him there with one hand as I picked up the flashlight, refocusing the beam on the writing. Now I understood why the words were faded and flaking. They had been scrawled there in blood by the same person who had gouged those claw marks into the cement. By the same someone who had been thrown down into the pit and left to die.

So intent was I on deciphering those cryptic words

that I hadn't registered the sudden drop in temperature. As the cold seeped through me, I turned to glance over my shoulder. Mary Willoughby was there in the pit with me. Not the ghost of the seductive sycophant I'd glimpsed in Annalee's memory, but the wraith of a woman driven mad by a slow, agonizing death.

She wore the same dress from Annalee's memory, but the fabric was now filthy and torn and much of her hair had been pulled from the roots in her madness. I could smell her. Phantom scents were not unusual for ghosts and my keen senses had become adept at picking up the eerie perfume that was unique to each manifestation. Mary Willoughby's was very unpleasant. A dank foulness that I had come to associate with evil.

Her lips moved, but I couldn't hear her. Drawn by my warmth and energy, she reached out a hand to me. Her spirit had been trapped in that pit for a very long time and I could sense her hunger. I could feel her iciness as she tried to touch me, tried to crawl through my skin.

The light inside me was an irresistible lure, but I felt no rushing wind, none of that strange suction that I had experienced in Kroll Cemetery. The souls that had been trapped behind the walls of that graveyard had been desperate for release, but Mary Willoughby's spirit resisted the pull. She craved my warmth and coveted my humanness. She might even regard my vessel as a means of escaping her prison. But she did not want to move on.

She remained earthbound, I suspected, because

of her fear of the unknown. Her association with the likes of Atticus Pope and her complicity in the brutal murder of children and the abuse of her own daughter had surely destined her soul for a place even worse than this pit.

The thought of such a dark presence entering my body even to pass through terrified me. I backed away, pressing against the wall as if I could somehow sink through the concrete. The kitten clung to me and I clung to the kitten. We were both quivering now. I placed the flashlight on the floor and reached for Rose's key.

The manifestation faded until she was nearly transparent, but I could still see her features. Her lips continued to move frantically as if repeating the same missive over and over and I thought of that chant in the woods. Those twelve caged graves in the clearing. Was she trying to summon Pope's disciples?

My gaze flicked back to those scrawled words on the circular wall of her prison and suddenly I knew what she had written. I knew what she was trying to tell me. It was neither a message nor a warning, but a terrifying reminder.

Memento mori.

Remember to die.

Twenty-Seven

Dawn hadn't broken, but the light was already thinning as a fine mist settled over the country-side. I stood shivering at the edge of the orchard as I watched uniformed officers come and go from the shed. Angus huddled at my side and I was grateful for his company. I knelt and buried my fingers in his coat. He looked at me with those liquid eyes as if to reassure me that everything would be fine now. Nothing could get to me so long as he remained near. Not even Mary Willoughby's ghost.

I hadn't told Kendrick about her manifestation. I'd had no chance to even if I'd wanted to share such a harrowing experience. Everything had happened so quickly once he found out about the remains. He'd hauled me up and then busied himself placing calls to the necessary authorities. Within half an hour, a number of uniformed cops had descended on the property, followed by the county coroner and then James Rushing, who had insisted on examining the remains in situ.

One of the officers had offered to take my rescued kitten to a local veterinary clinic owned by a relative and I'd reluctantly turned over my charge.

Another officer had been dispatched to Annalee Nash's house to alert her of the discovery. She had arrived on the scene a few minutes earlier dressed in shorts and a baggy T-shirt that reminded me again of the enigmatic ten-year-old I'd witnessed in her memory.

She'd nodded briefly when she first walked up, but I had the impression she wanted to be alone so I hadn't tried to approach her. But I studied her from a distance as images flashed in my head. Not her buried recollections this time, but my own creations based on what I knew of her past and what I'd seen in that pit. I had a very clear picture of her leaning over the edge of the cylinder and whispering down to her trapped mother: *Memento mori, Mama.*

She had only been a child at the time. It was a little far-fetched to believe that she had violently attacked her mother while she slept, somehow dragged her body all the way through the orchard to the shed and then pushed her down into that pit. A far more likely explanation was the one that had become local canon. George Willoughby was responsible for his wife's demise.

I turned back to the shed as those images continued to strobe in my head. What had been the original purpose of that cylinder? How had George Willoughby known about it? And who now knew of its existence?

I was still kneeling beside Angus when I looked up to find Annalee Nash standing over me. I'd been so lost in thought and so focused on the comings and goings at the shed that I hadn't seen her approach. Her sudden appearance startled me. I rose quickly and Angus pressed up against me as he watched her with wary eyes.

"I didn't see you come up," I said.

"I didn't mean to startle you. You seemed a million miles away."

"I'm just a little distracted."

"With good reason. First you stumble across a body in the clearing and now my mother's remains."

"We don't know for sure that the remains are your mother's," I pointed out. *I* knew, of course. I'd seen her ghost. But I could hardly offer that as confirmation. "Dr. Rushing is a forensic anthropologist. He should be able to make that determination fairly quickly, especially if your mother had any broken bones or other identifying markers. Otherwise, he can use dental records and DNA testing if necessary."

"It's her. I know it's her." Annalee glanced back at the shed. "All these years and she was right there. So close. It's hard to wrap my head around that."

"You couldn't have known," I murmured. Unless she had seen her mother go into that pit.

Her smile seemed appropriately wan. "I suppose not. But I feel like I should have known. Like I should have somehow sensed her nearness." She paused. "I know in my head that feeling isn't rational. After all, I wasn't even here. They took me away the morning they discovered my father's body."

"You're probably still in shock," I said, for lack of a better platitude.

"Maybe. Or maybe I just don't know how I'm supposed to feel about all this. She's been gone for such a long time. Most of my life. I can barely even remember what she looked like."

I thought of the barefoot woman in the ruins, the way her eyes had gleamed as she held her daughter to the ground. Maybe it was best if those memories of her mother never surfaced.

Annalee slipped her hands into the pockets of her shorts as she rocked back and forth on her heels. "Sometimes I do have vague images of her. Mostly flashes of her doing some mundane chore—in the kitchen washing dishes or out in the backyard hanging laundry. Sometimes I'll catch a whiff of a certain perfume, and if I close my eyes, I can see her at her dressing table, brushing her hair as she smiles at me in the mirror. I do remember that she was very beautiful."

I thought of those grayish clumps of hair still clinging to the skull. Those empty eye sockets and that hideous grin…

"Maybe that's the way you should remember her," I said.

Annalee gave me a sharp glance. "Yes. Maybe it is for the best."

She still rocked back and forth, her eyes so distant that I thought she might have drifted off into one of her states. But then I caught her watching me out of the corner of her eye. Her scrutiny unnerved me.

"I'm glad you're here," she said unexpectedly.

"It's good to have someone to talk to while this is going on."

"I'm happy to help in any way I can."

"Would you mind if I ask you a question?"

"No, of course not."

Her gaze was very direct now. "I was told you're the one who found her remains."

"Yes, along with Detective Kendrick."

"The details are still a bit fuzzy, but the officer who came to my house said something about an intruder."

"I thought someone had broken into the storage shed so I called the police. Then Detective Kendrick and I heard what sounded like an animal in distress and we crawled through a window to investigate. That's when we found the hole beneath the floorboards." I hesitated, uncertain how much I should reveal since the case would undoubtedly be reopened. "If you have any more questions, it's probably best to talk to Detective Kendrick."

She gave a slight nod as her gaze moved back to the shed. "I wonder how much longer they'll be."

"A while, I imagine. Would you like some tea while you wait? I could go up to the house and fix you a cup. Or you could wait there if you'd prefer. I'm sure Detective Kendrick wouldn't mind stopping by when he's finished."

"That's kind of you, but I don't want to leave. I feel like I should be here."

"I understand."

"After all these years." She shook her head in wonder. "What were the chances that you would stumble across a hole beneath the floorboards while trying to rescue a stray cat?"

"Did you have any idea that hole was there?" I asked carefully.

"No. How could I? I'm sure it was boarded up before we ever moved here."

"But someone knew about it."

She shot me another glance. "My father, you mean."

I didn't ask any more questions even though there were so many things I still wanted to know. Had she noticed anything unusual in her mother's demeanor in the days leading up to the tragedy? Had Annalee shared her father's conviction that something evil had taken over her mother's body?

If she remembered nothing of that night, why hadn't she moved into the house upon her return to Ascension? What was she afraid of here?

But, of course, I asked none of those things because, as badly as I wanted the answers, interrogating Annalee Nash wasn't my place.

Kendrick came out of the shed just then and I saw him glance over at us. I started to lift a hand in acknowledgment, but then I saw a look pass between him and Annalee.

I was still shaken by the night's events and my suspicions lurked a little too close to the surface. Even if they had exchanged glances, it didn't have to mean anything. But the rationale did little to ease my mind because suddenly I was remembering the confrontation between Annalee and Martin Stark. The secretive nuances in her conversation with Officer Malloy. I'd had a feeling for days now that she and Stark and Malloy were all somehow involved in this. Was Kendrick a part of that cabal, as well?

I toyed with the idea of clearing my mind to see if I could slip into her head, but I had the disturbing notion that she might have the power to block me. The last thing I wanted was to pit myself against Annalee Nash and I certainly had no intention of revealing my abilities to her.

She moved away after that and I hung around for only a few minutes longer. Then, calling to Angus, I walked back to the house. The light was still gray and the mist that clung to the trees had thickened. There was a hushed quality to the orchard that had me glancing over my shoulder even though the voices from the shed should have been a comfort.

Hooking the screen door behind us, I plopped down on the hammock and Angus curled up nearby, snout on crossed paws as he watched the yard through the screen door. The air had cooled and I pulled a light throw over me, hunkering down under the soft cotton as if I could hide from the day's revelations.

My thoughts churned as I lay there in the dark, listening to the sounds from the other side of the orchard. Even from this distance and without much focus at all, I could distinguish Kendrick's voice from all the others. His accent seemed more pronounced and I wondered if the grimness of our discovery had caused him to revert back to his natural inclinations. Or had I exaggerated the lilting edges of his vowels and the slightly elongated *e*'s now that I'd had that glimpse into his past?

The hammock swung gently beneath me. I grew drowsy and it became a struggle to keep my eyes open. I'd had a long day, but I wasn't yet ready to succumb to sleep. There was a chance Kendrick would stop by before he left and I had a thousand questions I wanted to ask him.

Who else could have known about that hole besides George Willoughby? Who had imprisoned a helpless cat and for what purpose except to lure me down there?

I couldn't help but think of Kendrick's description of Annalee Nash when the police had found her on the porch. I couldn't help but conjure the image of the girl I'd glimpsed in her memory. Catatonic and covered in blood. So traumatized she hadn't spoken a word for months and only then after her mind had been able to thoroughly suppress the memories of that night.

What had she seen? I wondered. What did she know?

Despite all those disturbing questions, I fell into a deep sleep. Strangely, it wasn't Annalee or Malloy or Kendrick I saw in my dreams. It wasn't even the ghost of Mary Willoughby. I stood on a darkened street in Charleston peering through a wrought-iron gate that opened into a long, narrow alley. I could hear the ocean behind me and laughter from across the street, but my gaze was riveted on a tall figure lurking in the shadows behind the gate. I couldn't see his face, but I knew him. It was Devlin. I felt an urgent need to go to him but I couldn't find a way inside.

"Use the key," he whispered.

His familiar drawl sent a shiver through me as I removed Rose's key from around my neck and fitted it into the lock. The gate swung open, but when I tried to enter, he lifted a finger to his lips and glanced uneasily over his shoulder.

"What is it?" I asked.

"Danger," he said, and then faded away.

I woke up with a start, thinking the dream had awakened me. But then I heard voices nearby. Devlin's presence had seemed so real that, for a moment, I thought he had come to find me. I was still so gripped by the sensation that I almost called out to him. Then as the haze cleared, I realized that someone was talking out on the road.

A moment later, I heard the sound of vehicles heading off into the night. I assumed all the authorities had cleared out, but then I heard Kendrick. He sounded very near, as if he were standing right outside the porch, yet his voice was muted so that I couldn't make out his words. A woman answered him and I thought his companion must be Annalee.

I hadn't even realized that I'd gotten up from the hammock, but the next thing I knew I was unlatching the screen door and slipping silently down the porch steps, padding through the damp grass and around the corner of the house to the front drive where I had a view of the road. Only one vehicle remained—Kendrick's black SUV.

Mist swirled in the postdawn light, but I could

make out two silhouettes at the side of the vehicle. Annalee was gazing up at Kendrick and he was gazing down at her, one hand propped on the open door. They were standing very close as he spoke softly to her in French.

Twenty-Eight

Despite so little sleep, I rose at my normal time, expecting to find a line of police cars parked in front of my house, but the road was deserted and the countryside quiet. I carried a cup of tea out to the back porch as I waited for Angus to finish his morning routine. He nosed all around the yard, sniffing and pawing, but he didn't go beyond the orchard. He didn't seem to want to let me out of his sight and I was grateful for that. Today I needed him close.

As he came back up on the porch, my gaze fell again on the slashed screen. Strange how that event now seemed almost dreamlike in light of all the other discoveries. I thought about Mary Willoughby's ghost trapped in that hole, restless and ravenous but unwilling to move on because of her sins. I thought of those twelve disciples buried beneath cages, calling out for relief but reluctant to transcend their earthly bonds because of what awaited them on the other side.

What part was I to play in all this? I wondered.

As much as I had learned about myself and about my gift, I still sometimes puzzled over my destiny. I could endure, if not embrace, my role in helping trapped spirits move on. In time, I might even learn to accept my great-grandmother's legacy of tracking those supernatural beings she and Papa had called malcontents—entities with no other earthbound purpose than to create chaos among the living.

But unmasking Atticus Pope, an evil witch doctor with the power to enter my mind and manipulate my thoughts, required a whole different level of abilities. I wanted to believe I was strong enough to withstand his diabolical machinations. I was a Gray, a Wysong and a Pattershaw. My gift was a coalescence of all those powerful bloodlines, of all those ethereal senses. But I was also an Asher. The weaknesses that came from my birth father's family had also been encoded in my DNA. What if I succumbed to Pope in the same way that Mary Willoughby had? What if I did things under his influence that couldn't be undone? That unwittingly put not only my life but also my soul in jeopardy? Would I, too, remain trapped in an earthly prison because of my fear for what awaited me on the other side?

I often pondered my purpose and place in this world and the next, but I didn't like to dwell on my mortality. I didn't want to think of myself as a ghost. I strived to lead a good and productive life, but sometimes I worried about where my gift would lead me. I'd already come so far—from ghost-seer to death walker to detective of lost souls. What would ultimately be required of me—here and on other the other side?

Shrugging off that weighty question, I went back inside to tidy up the kitchen and then ready myself for work. The sun was just popping over the horizon when Angus and I arrived at Seven Gates Cemetery. I stood inside the fence watching the red-gold light fan across the sky as it burnished the pine boughs.

Angus made every step with me as I carried my tools through the gate, pausing when I stopped to click the lock behind us. It seemed we'd turned a corner and were slowly but surely settling back into our old relationship.

Safely inside the fence, he explored the perimeter and nosed around all the gates as if to satisfy us both that all was well. Then he found his usual place beneath the cottonwood grove to watch the squirrels as I set to work. A light breeze rattled through the palmettos and swept away the last of the ground fog. With the sun warm on my back and Angus on guard nearby, it was easy to lose myself in the routine task of cleaning headstones. It was easy to believe that nothing more sinister than all those layers of lichen and moss awaited me.

I cleared my mind, refusing to think about the exchange between Kendrick and Annalee the night before or the strange dream I'd had of Devlin. The morning passed peacefully. Angus and I had lunch in the shade and then I pulled on my gloves and got right back to work.

By late afternoon, my back and shoulders protested and I stood to stretch, going through a series of exercises to work out the kinks. My gaze fell on the north gate and I experienced a familiar tug. The summons wasn't as strong as before, but I felt compelled to return to those cages just the same. After everything that had happened, I wanted a fresh look at that circle.

Angus trotted at my heels as I strode along the rugged trail. The rich, loamy scent of the woods soon engulfed us. Patches of primrose and buttercups grew along the path and the air swirled with the cottony seeds from the cattails.

The dreaminess of the day persisted until I stopped to detangle a burr from Angus's fur. Then I sensed something moving toward us through the trees. I turned an ear to the woods, trying to home in on the snap of a twig or the scrape of a low-hanging branch. Closer and closer the presence came until goose bumps tingled along my arms. But Angus remained unruffled. His calm eased my fears and I chided myself for allowing my imagination to run away with me.

We continued down the trail without incident, and as we rounded the last curve, I was struck again by the unexpectedness of the mortsafes. I put up a hand to shade my eyes, thinking once more of those trapped spirits beneath the cages and wondering if Pope's disciples had been calling out to me, beseeching me to free them from their prisons. Or, like Mary Willoughby's specter, did they fear what awaited them on the other side?

I shuddered and paused to glance over my shoulder, peering deep into the woods. I couldn't shake the feeling that we were not alone, and this time Angus sensed it, too. His head came up and the fur along his backbone bristled. He stood for a moment, head slightly cocked, before dashing off toward the woods.

"Angus, stay!"

He halted but he didn't come back to me. His head was still tilted as if something he'd heard or sensed in the trees confused him. It came to me then that something was calling to him. Something was luring him into those woods as surely as I had been compelled to that circle.

"Angus, come!"

He glanced back at me, torn by my command and the summons from the woods. Then he whirled and darted off into the trees.

"Angus!"

I ran after him, following the crackle of dead leaves as he rushed toward some unknown destination. Sunlight shimmered down through the branches and the air thickened with seed tufts. The ethereal quality of the woods seemed discordant with the dark premonition that suddenly gripped me. Angus wasn't the only one who had been lured into the forest.

I could feel a presence all around me now. When I turned in a circle, those invisible eyes followed me. The sensation was so strong that I thought a figure with an animalistic face must surely hover nearby. How foolish I'd been to come into these woods alone. No one knew where I was. If I disappeared, no one would miss me for a very long time. My parents knew that I was away for the summer. Neither they nor Devlin had any reason to be alarmed by my absence.

Devlin. I could almost hear his deep drawl in my head: *Danger.*

My breath came harsh and fast as I scanned the trees, the brush and the piles of windswept leaves where a flesh-and-blood presence might hide. Where something from the underworld might lurk.

I saw nothing suspicious, heard nothing untoward. Still, I stood there clutching Rose's key until the sensation faded. Then I hurried after Angus, emerging a few minutes later at the swamp. Cypress knees jutted gnomelike from the shallows and long curtains of Spanish moss draped the soft bank. The landscape was dark and primordial, unlike the wetlands of reeds and rushes that I was used to.

Angus huddled at the water's edge staring back into the woods. I thought for a moment he waited for me, but his gaze was fixed on something behind and above me.

My fingers tightened around Rose's key as I turned. From deep within the forest, sounds came to me. The rustle of brush. The whisper of leaves. Soft sounds. Innocent sounds.

Then my gaze lifted.

I felt the cold penetration of the watcher's gaze from the shadows, but I couldn't tear my focus from the sight above me.

Someone had carved a primitive-looking skull into a tree trunk and fashioned dead branches on either side of it to create a winged effigy. A death's-head. A symbol of mortality and the transcendence of the soul.

My first thought was not of Atticus Pope, but

of Darius Goodwine's revelation about the *Congé*. They marked themselves with symbols and creeds, he'd said. What better representation for a faction intent on stamping out the supernatural than a death's-head? What better creed than a reminder of our own mortality?

Warily, I searched the trees. Were the *Congé* out there at this very moment tracking Atticus Pope? Had they returned to Ascension to seek revenge for their fallen comrade? Or had they refocused their attention onto me? Were they watching me now, waiting in the shadows for proof that I was their enemy, one of the unnatural?

Memento mori, the leaves seemed to whisper.

Kendrick hunkered in front of the symbol, observing the effigy from a different angle. "Someone went to a great deal of trouble to create this," he finally said. "Do you have any idea what it means?"

"It appears to be a death's-head, a symbol that represents mortality and the flight of the soul. You'll see it on headstones in very old graveyards. The kind of *memento mori* art we talked about the other day."

"It's impressive," he said. "The wingspan must be at least twenty feet across."

I folded my arms as I stared up at the symbol. "I can't imagine how someone managed to haul all that brush up there, let alone fashion it into wings. And then to carve that symbol at such a height. I wouldn't have noticed it at all if Angus hadn't been with me." When he heard his name, he trotted over to stand beside me and I reached down to absently scratch his scarred head.

Kendrick seemed unaware of either of us at that moment. He stared up at the effigy, deep in thought. "Maybe it's not meant to be noticed from this vantage," he murmured.

"What do you mean?"

He got up and walked to the water's edge, staring out across the tangle of water lilies and duckweed before turning to lift his gaze back to the symbol. "Maybe it's meant to be viewed from out there." He nodded toward the shadowy water. "Remember I told you the other day that the killer would have had to bring the victim through or near the cemetery unless he came by way of the swamp."

"Yes, I remember. So you think the symbol is part of his ritual?"

"His ritual?" He gave me a frowning glance. "You're still trying to put him in the box of a fictionalized serial killer. You're trying to ascribe to him the kinds of motives and compulsions you've seen on television. The symbol may well be ritualistic, but I think it also serves the practical purpose of being a marker."

"What kind of marker?"

"The body of water you see here is not so much a lake as a series of sloughs and channels. It goes on for miles and it's easy to get lost in all that vegetation, especially at night when the landscape looks the same. You'd need a way to distinguish the place to put in if your destination is the circle or even the cemetery."

"Yes, but even as big as that symbol is, you'd still need a powerful spotlight to find it in the dark. And in that case, why go to so much trouble? If it's not ritualistic, why not just tie a ribbon around a tree or paint an *X* on the trunk?"

"I never said it wasn't ritualistic or symbolic. Nor do I think it was put up there for the soul purpose of guiding the killer through the swamp. It looks to me like this thing has been up there for years."

"As a marker?"

He was silent for a moment. "You seem to know an awful lot about Atticus Pope so I'm assuming you've heard the rumors of ceremonies and sacrifices that were supposedly conducted in the church ruins."

I flashed back to Annalee's memory and nodded. I'd not only heard about the rituals, but also I'd witnessed one through the buried recollection of a ten-year-old girl. "Yes, but anytime I've brought up the possibility of a Pope connection, you've been quick to discount it."

"Because I haven't wanted to muddy the investigation."

"And now?"

He hesitated. "Let's just say, I'm willing to admit there are aspects of this case I can't reconcile."

"Like this symbol?"

He shrugged.

"I have another theory about it," I said.

"I'd love to hear it."

We were both standing on the bank now, shoulder to shoulder, and I found myself reacting to his nearness. But there was another reason for the prickles across my scalp and the bristle of my every nerve ending. I could still feel the watcher in the woods. The sensation had diminished upon Kendrick's arrival, but the presence was still there. Still watching me. Still waiting.

I shivered again as I forced my attention back to the symbol. "I don't think it was erected to guide Pope's followers to the ruins. I think someone put it up there as a warning to those who would continue to do his bidding after his disciples were buried beneath the cages."

"Correct me if I'm wrong, but we've yet to determine the identities of those interred beneath the cages," Kendrick said.

"Maybe we don't have proof, but as we've previously discussed, it's not a far-fetched assumption. Mary Willoughby disappeared twenty years ago and we found her remains at the bottom of a pit. Twelve of Pope's closest disciples vanished at around the same time and there are a dozen mortsafes in that circle. I'll say it again, that can't be a coincidence."

"And you think whoever murdered them put this symbol up as a warning to Pope's remaining followers."

"It's one theory."

His expression remained inscrutable. "Do you also have a theory about the murderer?"

That gave me pause as I remembered Dr. Shaw's warning to speak of the *Congé* to no one. They were a powerful faction, he'd said, their reach wide and merciless. And once upon a time, I'd entertained the notion that Kendrick might be one of them. Now I knew that he was a ghost-seer like me, anathema to the zealots and all that they stood for. Surely someone with his gift and background would never have been allowed to infiltrate such an aristocratic covenant.

But I was also remembering something Darius Goodwine had told me. *Someone close to you has been assimilated into the ranks of the Congé. Someone you think you know well. Someone you think you can trust. But don't be fooled.*

"I'm waiting," Kendrick prodded. "Who do you think buried Pope's disciples in that circle?"

"A person or persons who wanted to make sure Pope's soul couldn't transmigrate."

"Transmigrate?"

"The transference of the soul upon death into the body of another."

"I know what it means," he said. "I'm just having a little difficulty following your logic."

"Then stop trying to look at it logically. Surely you of all people can't be shocked by the notion of soul transference."

"Shocked, no. But I've never seen any evidence that such a thing can occur."

"You don't believe in possession?"

"I don't *not* believe—I've just never witnessed it for myself. I take it you have?"

I didn't answer him. My arms were still folded and I clutched them to my body because the conversation made me feel too exposed. I had revealed nothing about myself to Kendrick and yet I had revealed everything to him. "Pope claimed he was the descendant of a powerful witch doctor, right? Maybe he wasn't a descendant at all. Maybe the witch doctor's soul migrated from body to body over the course of centuries making him virtually immortal."

Kendrick was looking at me strangely now and I could hardly blame him. An open mind was one thing, but even a true believer had his limits. "You think Pope's soul was trapped in one of the buried disciples?"

"Actually, no. I think that was the intention, but something went wrong. Pope's soul had already migrated by the time the disciples were buried."

"And where is his soul now?"

"That I don't know, but if he has come back, I think he's the one who buried that poor woman alive. Either she was on to him or he wanted revenge for his murdered disciples. Maybe she was somehow connected to the person or persons responsible for what happened to them twenty years ago."

He grew pensive. "Assuming all of what you say is true, why wait until now to exact his revenge?"

I glanced up at the symbol. "I think he was constrained somehow. If his soul was transferred into the body of a child, for instance, he would have had to wait until his new vessel was old enough and strong enough to carry out his wishes."

"You're talking about Annalee Nash."

My heart thudded as I recalled their closeness out on the road in the wee hours. Was that anger that flashed in his eyes now? Defensiveness I heard in his voice?

I tried to keep my tone neutral. "I wasn't talking about her specifically, but it might explain the catatonic state she was found in and her current blackouts. Do you know her very well?"

"It's a small town. Everyone knows everyone to a certain extent."

Which didn't at all answer my question.

He rubbed a hand along the scruff on his chin. "You've come up with an interesting premise, I'll give you that. But we need to be careful about throwing around too many wild accusations."

"I don't think they're so wild and I'm not throwing them around to anyone but you. You can make of them what you will. But you just said there are certain aspects of this case that you find hard to reconcile. Haven't you already thought of some of these things yourself? Isn't that why you drove to Charleston to speak with Dr. Shaw? Because he's an expert in alternative explanations?"

A frown darted across Kendrick's features. "It may have been a mistake to tell you about my visit to the institute."

"Why?"

"I think I've shared too much with you."

Now it was I who gave him a puzzled look. "You can say that after everything I've just said to you?"

"That was different. You shared a theory about a murder investigation, but you've told me nothing about yourself."

To the contrary, I'd just told him everything about myself.

He turned to face me, his eyes softly glowing in the waning sunlight. "The last thing I want is to make you uncomfortable around me."

"I'm not uncomfortable."

"Are you sure about that?" He paused. "I've sensed wariness in you ever since I got here."

"Maybe you're imagining things."

"I don't think so. I felt your reluctance last night before we discovered the cylinder. I felt it that day in the alley when I told you about the presence in the woods. I don't blame you for protecting yourself. I understand the need for secrecy. I know only too well the dangers of letting the wrong people in."

I tried to glance away but he had a way of trapping me—of enthralling me. Maybe it was the hypnotic quality of his eyes or the intensity of his stare. Or his own kind of magic. Whatever the cause, I found myself immobile as my breath grew shallow and my heart pounded an uneasy staccato inside my chest.

"You're right. I am discomfited by all this," I admitted. "It's not a conversation one has every day."

"If ever."

"If ever," I agreed.

He made no move to touch me, but I could feel his fingers in my hair, the whisper of his knuckles along my jawline. Without physical contact, the connection was somehow more powerful and I couldn't help but tremble.

"You don't have to tell me anything you don't want to," he said. "Your personal life is your own."

"I know that."

"But I also meant what I said last night." He moved infinitesimally closer but he still didn't touch me. "You don't have to hide from me."

I could see the reflection of the setting sun in his eyes as he continued to regard me. I could see those tiny motes beneath his irises that were so much like my own and the shimmer of something in those golden depths that I thought might be desire.

How quickly our focus had shifted. How easily I'd forgotten about the implication of that symbol and the lurking danger that it represented. The *Congé* and Atticus Pope seemed far, far away as I found myself fantasizing again about Kendrick's lips on mine.

"Are you okay?" He seemed bemused by something he'd glimpsed in my eyes.

I swallowed. "Yes, I'm fine. Just lost in thought."

"About...?"

"A lot of things. That symbol. Atticus Pope." I drew a breath. "You."

His gaze flickered and he seemed on the verge of saying something else before he turned back to the effigy. The moment shifted and I felt oddly bereft even though I knew it was for the best. Our shared gift was a powerful bond and a part of me did want to let him in. I felt something for Kendrick. Certainly not love, but my desire for him went well beyond the physical.

For as long as I could remember, I'd wanted nothing more than to be normal, but maybe what I'd craved all along was acceptance. Kendrick offered me a sense of belonging and I couldn't deny the potency of such a promise. I'd been a loner since childhood. An outsider who had never fit in. I'd had to guard my gift and everything I saw and felt, even with Devlin. Especially with Devlin. In some ways, his refusal to acknowledge even the possibility of the supernatural repudiated my very existence and I hadn't realized until now how much of myself I'd had to withhold from him and how much I'd come to resent it.

As I stared into Kendrick's golden eyes, something dormant stirred to life. In that moment, I could almost believe the estrangement with Devlin was for the best and I really was ready to move on. But I also remembered the glance Kendrick had shared with Annalee Nash outside the shed and later, on the road, the way he'd spoken to her so softly in French.

I wanted to let him in, but not yet. Not until I knew that I could trust him.

"Would you like to take a boat ride?" he asked.

I'd been so lost in my reverie that it took me a beat to process his unexpected question. "A boat ride?"

He nodded toward the symbol. "Don't you want to see that thing from out on the water?"

I glanced up at the primitive death's-head, shivering as sunlight gilded the wings. For a moment I could have sworn I saw the tips flutter. It was an illusion, of course. A trick of light and shadow.

Or was I even now under the influence of a powerful witch doctor's magic?

Twenty-Nine

I fed and watered Angus and then hurried to shower and dress before Kendrick arrived to pick me up. When he pulled up a little while later, I was waiting for him on the front porch. I ran down the steps, feeling anxious about the excursion and not really knowing why. He opened the passenger door from inside and I climbed in.

"Are you sure you don't want to bring Angus?" he asked. "The two of you seem inseparable."

"He'll be fine until I get back. He's been on a ferry before, but I'm not sure how he'd react to a boat ride."

Kendrick backed out of the drive and put the vehicle in gear. "What's the news on your latest rescue?"

"The kitten? I called the clinic a little while ago. He has a number of issues, not the least of which is malnutrition, but he doesn't have any injuries. He'll need to be quarantined for a few days while they run the usual tests."

"Will you take him in when he's released?" Kendrick asked.

"I travel too much, but I may have another solution. My mother lost a beloved tabby a few years ago. She's had some health problems that prevented her from getting another pet, but I think she may be ready now. If not, then I'll talk to my aunt. She's fastidious about her house, but she also happens to be a cat lover."

Kendrick shot me a glance. "You have an affinity for strays, don't you? You're willing to go to all that trouble just to find that cat a home."

I shrugged. "It's no trouble to me and I don't like to see any animal mistreated or homeless. I can't imagine why someone would put a defenseless kitten down in that awful hole. Or *how*, for that matter, since we saw no sign of an intruder in the shed."

"I'm still trying to figure that out myself," he said. "I noticed a number of cracks in the wall, especially toward the bottom. None of them are very large, but it's possible the kitten managed to squeeze through somehow."

We were passing by a cluster of homes now and I waved to a woman tending her yard before I turned back to Kendrick. "Do you think there could be other cylinders on the property?"

"It's possible." He glanced at me again. "Is there a reason you're asking that question?"

"I've seen no evidence, if that's what you mean. But I can't help wondering about the original purpose of such a thing. If not a silo or well, then what was it built for?"

"Maybe we already know the purpose," Kendrick said.

"To hide Mary Willoughby's body?"

"Not just her. If someone were to be taken against their will, they could be hidden in a place like that indefinitely."

According to Darius Goodwine, Pope had kidnapped innocent children to use in his rituals. He'd also taken runaways and homeless victims that no one had looked for or missed. I imagined a whole series of those cylinders with human claw marks gouged in the walls and bones heaped on the floors.

"I've been thinking about your theory regarding Atticus Pope," Kendrick said. "If he has come back, it would explain certain things."

"Such as?"

"His family used to own the Willoughby house. They moved away for a time, and when Pope returned to the area, he tried to buy the place back, but George Willoughby refused to sell. Maybe the reason he took up with Mary Willoughby was so he'd have unlimited access to the property and to that cylinder. Maybe he knew it was there because he was the one who built it. And in that case, he would still know about it."

"But that doesn't tell us who murdered Mary Willoughby."

"Her association with Pope gave her husband a strong motive. Why else would he commit suicide if he wasn't guilty of killing his wife?"

"Maybe it wasn't suicide."

Kendrick lifted a hand from the steering wheel to rub the back of his neck. "You have a theory about that, too, I'm guessing."

"Maybe whoever put Mary in that hole and shot

her husband was the same person or persons who buried Pope's disciples beneath the cages. And for the same reason."

"To trap Pope's soul?"

"That would explain George Willoughby's insistence that something had taken possession of his wife's body, wouldn't it?"

"But how does that jibe with your theory about Annalee?"

"A soul can migrate more than once."

Kendrick turned to study my features. "What did you see down in that hole last night?"

His question caught me off guard. "What do you mean?"

"I saw your face when I pulled you up. I heard something in your voice when you called out to me."

"You think finding those remains wasn't enough to put that look on my face?"

"Was it her ghost?" he pressed. "Mary Willoughby's spirit?"

"You're right," I said. "I'm not comfortable talking about this."

"I understand." He turned back to the road. "Maybe it would help if I tell you about some of my experiences."

"What kind of experiences?"

"I've had supernatural encounters since early adolescence, but I never actually saw a manifestation until I went to live with my grandmother. Paris is a haunted city. But even there, my sightings were rare. I would sometimes glimpse shimmers and darting shadows from the corner of my eye, but mostly I could just sense them."

I said nothing to that, but I watched him carefully, taking in the set of his jaw and the pulse at his throat. He didn't seem at all hesitant or wary to confide in me. I wondered if he had always been that open or if he trusted me so easily because he had been inside my head. He'd trespassed in my memories and now he knew that we were the same.

"My earliest recollection of an encounter happened when I was thirteen or fourteen," he said. "We had been living in New Orleans for a couple of years by then, but we'd come back to Beaufort County one summer so that my father could operate his cousin's shrimp boat. One night I woke up with the sensation of something hovering over me. I sensed other entities gathered around my bed, watching and whispering, but this one seemed to want something from me. I could feel icy fingers scratching at my chest as if the thing intended to claw out my heart."

"What did you do?"

"I huddled under the covers for the rest of the night, and then the next day, I told my father. He didn't believe me, of course. Or at least he pretended not to."

"Did it ever happen again?"

"Almost every night before we returned to New Orleans. I never knew what the entity wanted. What any of them wanted. It was almost as if they were testing me somehow."

The base of my spine prickled. "Testing you for what?"

"I don't know. After that conversation with my father, I never mentioned the encounters again. I never told anyone about them until I went to live with my grandmother. I learned from her that the sight runs in our family and that my father was frightened of it. And then he grew frightened of me so he sent me away."

"What about your mother? You mentioned that she still lives in this area. You don't have any contact with her?"

"She left us when I was a baby. I don't really have a desire to see her."

"Then why did you come back to Beaufort County?"

"For a lot of reasons. I've always loved the area." He paused and I saw his fingers tighten around the steering wheel. "Maybe there is something to be said for roots."

I didn't think he was quite as blasé about his mother's abandonment as he tried to let on. I had a feeling his history was as dark and muddled as my own, but far from repelling me, his complicated nature drew me in deeper.

"You told me the other day that you feel a presence in the woods every time you go to the circle. Did you feel it today at the symbol?" I asked him.

A frown fleeted across his brow. "For a moment."

"What do you think it is?"

"I don't know, but whatever it is, it came when you came."

I turned in shock. "What?"

Something flashed in his eyes, an emotion I didn't want to name. "Don't you feel it, too?"

My suspicions bristled as my heart flailed in trepidation. I said slowly, "How do you know it came when I came? I was under the impression you'd never been to the circle before the day I found the body."

"That's true. But I don't just feel it in the woods," he said. "Not anymore. I sensed it briefly that day we spoke in the alley. I felt it even stronger last night in the shed. That's when I realized that I'm only aware of it when you're around."

A chill shot through me as I moistened suddenly dry lips. "How do you know it's not here because of you?"

His gaze was dark and steady. "It's not. I can't explain how I know, but I do. Call it a hunch or a premonition. Whatever that presence is, I think it's here to protect you."

"From what? From who?"

"That's what we need to find out."

I said almost fearfully, "Is it here now? Can you feel it in the car with us?"

"No." A smile twitched at the corners of his mouth. "There's no one here but us. Maybe that means it's decided you aren't in any danger from me."

Wasn't I?

I sat back, gazing out the window at the passing scenery as I wondered again at the wisdom of our excursion. Being alone in the swamp with a virtual stranger wasn't a good idea. "How much farther?"

"We're almost there."

He pulled onto a narrow road with a blue mail-box at the end.

I sat up as a clapboard cottage came into view. Built on stilts, the house was shaded by a grove of water oaks dripping with Spanish moss. "Is this where you live?"

"Yes. What do think?"

"It's a beautiful place, but very isolated."

"I like the quiet." Kendrick parked the vehicle and turned with an enigmatic smile. "Gives me plenty of space to think."

We went down the sloping yard to a small dock and boathouse where a fiberglass fishing boat with an outboard motor was moored alongside a wooden rowboat. Kendrick climbed into the fishing boat first and then helped me down. The boat rocked beneath our feet and he grabbed both my arms to steady me.

He didn't immediately let me go, but instead stared down into my upturned face. His gaze dark-ened as his lips parted slightly, and for a moment, I thought he might kiss me. Despite my reservations, I probably wouldn't have stopped him. I was curi-ous to know what it would be like. But he didn't kiss me. Instead, he moved away to untie the rope and push off.

We cruised the narrow channels as the sun sank and the water lilies began to close. I sat facing for-ward, the breeze cool on my face. Every so often, we passed the blackened skeleton of a cypress tree that had been struck by lightning, and I couldn't help but note the juxtaposition of life and death in the swamp.

Turtles huddled on fallen logs as water snakes glided among the bladderwort. A glossy ibis stepped delicately through the shallows, searching for dinner. Insects skimmed over the water and buzzed in my ears. An owl took flight from the treetops. Beneath the surface serenity of the primal landscape, life teemed.

We glided onward, deeper and deeper into the swamp. Spanish moss hung so thick in places I could hardly glimpse the bank. The scenery was eerily beautiful, but a more menacing landscape I could hardly imagine.

We rounded a bend and suddenly I caught sight of the symbol. Wings lit by the crimson glow of a fiery sunset, the death's-head loomed over the treetops—to guide or to warn? I wondered. As I stared up at the macabre creation, I had the strangest sensation that the thing was alive somehow and that it might swoop down on us at any moment.

"Do you see it?" Kendrick asked over the rumble of the outboard.

"Yes. The wings look on fire."

He steered the boat to the center of the channel and then cut the motor. We drifted toward the bank as the light faded and the wings turned dark against the sky. It was very quiet on the water. I could hear the lap of waves against the hull and, somewhere downstream, a loon called to his mate.

Kendrick moved up behind me and spoke softly in my ear. "It's out there now," he said. "Can you feel it?"

I shivered as his breath fanned against my neck. "Is it a ghost?"

"It's not a ghost." He spoke so definitively I turned to observe him. He knelt behind me, eyes closed, head slightly cocked as he concentrated his senses. "It's not a flesh-and-blood presence, but it's human. The energy and intelligence is alive. It's a traveler, I think."

Gooseflesh exploded along my bare arms. "A traveler?"

"Someone with the ability to separate the spiritual self from the corporeal self."

"You mean an astral traveler?"

A smile tugged at his lips. "You say that with such skepticism and yet only a little while ago you spoke so convincingly about transmigration."

I wasn't skeptical. I believed in body and spirit separation. Wasn't that how gray dust worked? I'd once experienced the effects of the mysterious botanical myself when I'd crossed over to the other side.

Kendrick searched the bank, his demeanor suddenly uneasy. "I can't say for certain what it is, but it's a powerful presence. I've never encountered anything like it."

Nor had I. I wanted to believe he was right and the presence meant no harm, but I didn't think the watcher's intent was benign. If anything, I felt an undercurrent of malice in the breeze. The presence had manipulated me from the first, compelling me to those cages and then to the winged effigy. Whatever lurked in those woods had an agenda.

"We should head back," Kendrick said. He seemed as spooked now as I was by the watcher.

"It'll be dark soon. Not a good idea to be caught out here once we lose all the light."

He fired up the motor and turned the boat, steering us back toward the center of the channel. I glanced over my shoulder. The wings were nearly invisible against the deepening sky, but I could see bits of light between the branches. Maybe it was the eeriness of our surroundings that fueled my already overwrought imagination, but for a moment, I could have sworn the effigy took flight. I watched in horror as it swooped down from its perch, skull face gleaming in the twilight as it dove for our boat. I actually put my hands over my head and ducked. But when I looked again the wings were still fastened to the treetop.

I turned to glance at Kendrick but he faced away from me. I sat huddled on the seat, clutching Rose's key as we made for home.

I didn't tell Kendrick what I'd seen. What would be the point since the animation of that symbol could have been nothing more than a strange hallucination or a nasty mind trick? But he must have sensed my disquiet because he insisted on taking a look around the yard and orchard when we got home.

While he searched the grounds, I went through the house. Angus met me at the front door and followed my every step. I started at the back and worked my way up to the front bedroom where he once again refused to enter. He waited at the threshold while I made my usual inspection. Then he trailed me outside and plopped down on the mat in front of the door.

"I suppose this means I won't be invited in for a nightcap," Kendrick teased as he climbed the steps and went over to give my guard dog a quick scratch.

"It's a little early for a nightcap," I said. "But Angus and I can offer you a cup of tea or a glass of wine."

He rose and came back over to where I stood at the edge of the porch. "I should head back to the station. I've got a mountain of paperwork waiting on my desk."

"I sympathize. I've got plenty of work to do myself."

"I won't keep you, then."

We stood at the top of the steps, gazing at each other as black clouds deepened the twilight. Lightning flickered in the distance and the air felt heavy with static.

"Looks like we got off the water just in time," I said.

He glanced at the sky. "It'll blow over. I doubt we get even a drop of rain from that cloud."

"You sound pretty certain."

"I know the weather patterns around here." He paused, his gaze returning to me. "Amelia…"

"Yes?" My breath caught in spite of myself. It was only the second time he'd ever said my name and the slight elongation of the *e* made me wonder again about his background. About his French grandmother who saw ghosts and the time he'd spent with her in Paris. He seemed very exotic to me at that moment. A man with an affinity for the super-natural.

He was still staring down into my eyes, search-ing my features anxiously. "You'll be all right here, won't you?"

"I have been so far."

He frowned. "I don't like leaving you alone. Not after everything that has happened."

"I'm not alone. I have Angus."

"Your gentle warrior," he said with a smile. "You also have my number. Call me anytime. I mean that. I can be here in a matter of minutes."

"I'll call if I need you."

"I should go," he said again.

But he made no move toward the steps or to me. I leaned back against the porch post, hands behind me as I gazed into those mesmerizing eyes. He wasn't touching me at all and yet I could feel him just as I had earlier. His hands sliding up my arms. His mouth pressing against mine.

My lips parted and I saw something flare in his eyes, but he still didn't reach for me. I could still feel him, though. I wasn't hallucinating or imagining his touch. It was real. He never moved a muscle and yet somehow his fingers wove through my hair, tilting my head as he deepened the kiss with his tongue.

"How are…"

"Shush," he said.

My head fell back against the post and I closed my eyes, seeing him at the back of my mind as he lifted my shirt over my head and tossed it aside. He un-dressed me completely and yet I stood on the porch with all my clothes on. I could feel his hands on my bare skin now, skimming over my breasts and trailing along my inner thighs. Teasing and teasing until I heard myself gasp.

My eyes flew open.

How could this be? How could I experience something so intensely intimate and pleasurable when we had never even touched?

How had I allowed him to infiltrate my head and entice me so easily? Why did I not push him out now and slam the door against his carnal manipulations?

But I didn't push him out. Instead, I visualized myself unbuttoning his shirt and shoving it aside as I trailed my mouth along his shoulder.

"How are you doing this?" I whispered.

His eyes were dark and glowing and so intensely focused I worried the glare might burn right through me.

"It's not me," he murmured. "It's you."

"I'm not doing anything."

"But you are. You're making it happen because it's what you want. And only you can stop it. You have the power to send me away with the blink of an eye."

I told myself to do exactly that. *Go inside, lock the door and end this dangerous fantasy right this minute.*

But I remained motionless, and the next thing I knew, we were both inside the house, entwined inside the front bedroom. That room gave me pause, but he silenced my protest with an even deeper kiss. We moved to the bed, embracing and peeling off clothing until we were both naked. His hands were all over me now, making me burn with hunger. Unchained from my earthly reservations, I moved down his body, touching and stroking and tasting. I couldn't seem to get enough of him.

We kissed and kissed and when I invited him in, he turned me, drawing me back against him as he rose behind me. He was moving inside me now, on and on and on until I felt consumed and half-crazed with need. Until a violent shudder brought me back out to the front porch where I stood fully clothed and shivering.

He did touch me then, a mere brush of his knuckles down my cheek. "Sweet dreams," he murmured.

"Good night" was all I could manage.

Thirty

The next afternoon, I drove to Charleston to have an early dinner with Dr. Shaw. Angus rode with me and I left him at the house on Rutledge, curled up in my office with food and water bowls brimming.

I had allotted myself enough time to take a pre-dinner stroll through the historic district. I missed my morning walks and wanted to savor a bit of the city before I met up with Dr. Shaw.

I started out on Tradd and headed toward the water. The houses along this street were very old and in varying states of disrepair and renovation. One could always tell the season by the delectable scents drifting over the garden walls—jasmine in the spring, magnolia in early summer and the elusive tea olive in fall and winter. The four-o'clocks were blooming now and I enjoyed their subtle perfume as I sauntered along the cracked sidewalks, peering into the wrought-iron gates that opened into mysterious alleyways and lush courtyards.

When I reached East Bay, I paused. I could cross the street and stroll along the Battery or I could turn right and continue down the peninsula to White

Point Garden. This time of day, the fragrances spilling from the park would be captivating. But that walk would take me past Devlin's ancestral mansion, a white, three-storied confection of gleaming pillars and shady piazzas. I'd never been inside the home, nor had I met Devlin's grandfather. They'd been estranged until last year when Jonathan Devlin had taken ill and Devlin had been lured back into his grandfather's orbit, back into the world he'd left behind when he married Mariama Goodwine.

But dwelling on his relationship with Mariama never led to a good place. I would be better off not thinking about Devlin at all if I could help it. I was still shaken by the episode with Kendrick the evening before and I felt vulnerable to forces I didn't understand. I wanted to put those fears behind me, shove aside all my worries and premonitions so that I could enjoy my brief stay in Charleston.

I turned left on East Bay, wandering past the colorful houses on Rainbow Row and eventually making my way past the shops and eateries to Queen Street. Dr. Shaw was already at the restaurant by the time I arrived. I found him in the bar sipping a double dram of Scotch. It was still early and we had no trouble being seated near a window where we could watch the hustle and bustle on the street.

"How have you been?" he asked as he observed me from across the table.

"I'm well, but a lot has happened since the last time we spoke."

"So I gathered from your email. You must tell me everything, my dear. Don't leave out a single detail."

"We could be here for hours," I said drily.

His eyes gleamed from the prospect. "I'm yours for the evening," he said as he motioned for the waiter. He ordered a fresh Scotch for himself and a glass of wine for me, and once the drinks were served, he sat back to listen with relish as I recounted my latest experiences in Ascension.

I told him about my conversation with Essie Goodwine, about my sighting of the man in the mask at the cemetery, about the toxic smoke, the slashed screen and the strange cylinder beneath the floor of the shed. I took my time with each revelation and he was quick to have our glasses replenished when the libations ran low. By the time I finished, I was feeling flushed and light-headed from all the wine.

"We should order something to eat," I said as I glanced out the window to find that twilight had fallen. The restaurant was starting to fill up and I was glad we'd had the place to ourselves while I spoke of ghosts and witch doctors and transmigration of souls.

We studied our menus until Dr. Shaw finally settled on the scallops and bacon and I chose a root vegetable salad with a side of ricotta gnocchi. While we waited for our food, I told him a little more about the watcher in the woods and Kendrick's assertion that the presence was human.

"Have you ever heard of such a traveler?" I asked.

I could have sworn I saw something dark flash in his eyes before he glanced down at his Scotch. "Astral projection has been practiced for aeons," he said. "Although there are some who would argue the experiences are nothing more than lucid dreams."

"Have you ever experienced it for yourself?" I asked.

"No. For all my otherworldly interests, I seem to be stubbornly earthbound," he said with no small amount of irony. Absently he toyed with the pinkie ring he wore on his right hand, the snake and claw symbol identical to the one on Devlin's medallion. "But I would suggest that you yourself are a traveler. Perhaps not in the sense that one normally thinks of astral projection, but when a ghost passes through you, do you not leave your body to help it cross over, even if only for the blink of an eye?"

"I don't like to think so," I said. "I don't like to think about ghosts passing through me at all. What if one decides not to leave?"

"Like the ghost in the pit that you spoke of?"

I shuddered. "Yes, exactly like that one. I've encountered some very evil spirits, Dr. Shaw, but the ghost of Mary Willoughby was a special kind of malevolency, perhaps because of what she let happen to her own daughter."

"You're right to fear the dark ones," he said. "Not only because they might try to possess you, but also because they could conceivably drag you with them through the veil."

I had felt that very tug to the other side, so his concern wasn't without merit.

"In mythology, there's a designated place for the darkest of souls," he said. "A place beyond hell if one is a believer. The Greeks called it Tartarus, a pit of torture and despair as far below Hades as earth is to heaven. I knew a young man once, a traveler who claimed to have looked into such an abyss. He was so shaken by the sight that he tried for years to convince himself what he experienced was nothing more than a nightmare. I don't think he ever traveled again—at least not consciously. He had a fear of being trapped in such a place."

"Is that possible?"

"According to some, if the astral cord snaps or is cut, the traveler could become lost for all eternity. The physical body would eventually wither and die unless something else took possession of it."

"Something else?"

"A ghost, a lost soul...or worse."

I shuddered as I stared down into my glass.

The discussion had taken a disturbing turn, even for us. I was glad when our dinners were served and the conversation trickled to a halt as we luxuriated in the Lowcountry delicacies. We ate in silence until both of us pushed back our plates with satisfied sighs.

"That was wonderful," I said. "I haven't had a meal like that in ages."

"You look a little peeked to my eye," Dr. Shaw said with a frown. "Have you been working too hard on top of everything else that's occupying your time?"

"No harder than usual. I like to keep busy. What about you? I've dominated the conversation all evening and I got the distinct impression from your email that you also have news."

"Yes, as a matter of fact, I have turned up something of interest." He glanced around uneasily at the well-heeled clientele. "This may not be the best place to discuss it, though."

I took a look around, too, noting the proximity of the other patrons. "Let's take a walk," I said.

We sorted the check and then headed out into the evening, retracing my steps on East Bay. We crossed the street and walked along the Battery until we found a private spot where we could look out on the harbor as we chatted. We weren't far from the place where Devlin had first appeared to me out of the mist, and I wondered why, after all this time, he was still so much on my mind. Why couldn't I forget him and move on?

"You're very quiet all of a sudden. Are you all right?" Dr. Shaw asked solicitously.

"Yes, I'm fine. I'm just happy to be back in Charleston for the evening. I didn't realize how much I missed it."

"The holy city. There's no place like it." He watched the lights in the harbor. "When will you be finished with your current restoration?"

"I'll be there for a few more weeks at least." I turned, peeling a strand of hair from my face that had blown loose from my ponytail. "What have you found out, Dr. Shaw?"

He glanced around at our surroundings to make certain we couldn't be overheard. "Since we last spoke, I've put together a list of people I believe may be affiliated with the *Congé*, culled from those families rumored to have had an association with the Order of the Coffin and the Claw going back all the way to the city's founding fathers. Names you'll find on the oldest gravestones in our oldest churchyards. As you can imagine, the project has been quite an undertaking, but I haven't been alone in my endeavor. I've had a great deal of input from my contacts, people who know far more about these clandestine organizations than you or I could ever hope to learn. They risk a lot by even speaking with me so it's important that we keep this information to ourselves."

"I understand, but how do your contacts even know about the *Congé* if they have so much power and they guard their identities so assiduously?"

"Secrets always have a way of coming out," he said. "I don't have to tell you how dangerous it would be for all concerned if the existence of such a list were ever made public. Having said that, there is a name that keeps turning up, one I think you'll find most enlightening."

I leaned in, searching his face in the glow of the security lights. "Is it Kendrick?" I asked on a breath.

He said in surprise, "The police detective you've been working with? No, not Kendrick, my dear. Devlin."

The name shocked me into silence, though I wasn't sure why it should catch me so off guard. Hadn't that notion been swirling around in my subconscious ever since I'd first heard of the group from Darius Goodwine? My suspicion had flitted to the surface again after my conversation with Temple, but

I hadn't allowed it to foment into anything stronger than vague doubt.

I said shakily, "Are you sure?"

"As sure as one can be. It fits with the reason he gave you for distancing himself, does it not? He said it would be dangerous for you to be with him because his grandfather had gotten mixed up with some very dangerous people. John must have found out about the *Congé* during the old man's illness last year. He would have quickly concluded that his continued association with you could call attention to your gift and abilities, thus putting your life in imminent danger."

"But he wouldn't have known about my gift then. We never addressed it directly or even indirectly until at the very end when he'd already made his decision."

"Oh, I'm quite certain he knew." Dr. Shaw leaned an arm on the railing as he studied me. "I once told you that John has the kind of sensitivity I've rarely come across, so at the very least he must have strongly suspected. Didn't you say the two of you had experienced a supernatural encounter together?"

My mind raced back to our time in Kroll Cemetery to the sighting of the malcontent in my bedroom and the ghost of my great-grandmother in the window of a burning house. Devlin had denied it all, but Dr. Shaw was right. He *knew*.

Even so, I still found his name on that list hard to accept. "Wouldn't his sensitivity to the supernatural pit him *against* the *Congé*?"

"It's my contention that many of the members are

sensitive to some degree or another. Originally, they used their powers to track and combat the evil they feared had infiltrated Charleston. Those were dark times and they considered themselves the spiritual guardians of the city. Aristocratic sentinels with a noble purpose, but over time their arrogance and fanaticism corrupted the mission."

My mind reeled from Dr. Shaw's stunning revelation and perhaps from the lingering buzz of the wine. I stared down at the spot where the Ashley and Cooper rivers merged in the harbor. The churning waters seemed to mirror my internal agitation. "You said membership is legacy. A recruit is only brought in when an old member dies. Devlin's grandfather is still very much alive."

"Yes, I did say that, but possibly exceptions are made when a member becomes infirm and unable to carry out his duties. Perhaps John is being groomed for the inevitable. A man of his talents would be an invaluable asset to such a faction."

"His talents?"

Dr. Shaw turned back to the water. "I'm speaking about his experiences in law enforcement, of course."

But I didn't think that was what he meant, far from it. For all our confessions and revelations, I had a feeling Dr. Shaw still kept things from me, especially where Devlin was concerned.

I gripped the railing as my thoughts continued to whirl. "I'm sorry, Dr. Shaw, but after everything you've told me about the *Congé*, I have a hard time believing this. They're as ruthless and deadly in their mission as the Brotherhood is in their black pursuits. That's what you said. How can you expect me to think that John would be involved with such a group? I can't accept it. I *won't* accept it until I hear it from him."

Dr. Shaw turned in consternation. "You must consider the consequences before you do anything so rash as to confront him. A provocation of any kind is a very bad idea for many reasons."

"What reasons? What are you still keeping from me?"

He couldn't meet my eyes. "There hasn't been an announcement yet, but I hear through the grapevine that the formalities are forthcoming any day now. My dear…" He placed his hand on my arm. "John is engaged."

Thirty-One

I walked Dr. Shaw back to Waterfront Park where he'd left his car and then I headed up Tradd Street. As I hurried along the darkened sidewalk, my head spun, but not from the wine. I felt stone-cold somber now. Outwardly, I remained steady. Maybe there had been so many revelations over the course of the evening and I'd had so many experiences and encounters during my time in Ascension I was now immune to shock. Or, I suspected, my composure was merely a defense mechanism. When I finally allowed my emotions to surface, I wasn't sure which disclosure would distress me more—Devlin's engagement or his possible affiliation with the *Congé*.

A breeze rippled through the trees, carrying the scent of butterfly ginger over a walled garden. I could glimpse the dark shapes of trimmed evergreens behind wrought-iron gates and the ethereal gleam of marble faces in dappled moonlight. The evening was balmy and fragrant, the city as alive and lovely as it had ever been, but I couldn't wait to leave it now. I couldn't disassociate Charleston from Devlin and tonight I needed to be free of both.

I was so lost in thought that the sudden glare of headlights startled me. I reacted reflexively, stepping back into the shadows as a car pulled to the curb across the street. The vehicle was sleek and black and sexy, and for a moment, as I admired the low profile, I was pulled right back into Devlin's world. Even the silhouette of the driver reminded me of Devlin. It wasn't him, of course. It couldn't be him. The possibility was too slim and the irony too cruel.

As I stood in the shadows observing from a distance, the driver climbed out of the vehicle and turned to glance down the street as another car appeared behind him. Caught in the headlights, he squinted into the brilliance and my heart started to beat in hard, painful strokes as my gaze glided over familiar features. He was dressed in dark slacks and a dark shirt exquisitely tailored to his tall form. He wore his hair longer than when I'd last seen him, and in the glare of the headlights, I could detect the hint of a beard on his lower face, but I knew him just the same. I would always know that face because I still dreamed about it nearly every night.

He watched the car until it was out of sight and then he turned and strode down the sidewalk to one of the largest houses on the block. He took out a key, unlocked the gate and then glanced over his shoulder as if to make certain he hadn't been followed. For a moment, I thought he might see me huddled there in the shadows. That he must surely hear the sound of my pounding heart. But he did not. He turned back to the gate and disappeared inside, leaving me alone, puzzled and trembling.

I left the shadows and crossed the street to peer through the intricate wrought iron as a feeling of déjà vu tingled over me. I had been there before in a dream. To that very gate. Or had my spiritual self left my body and traveled back to Charleston to find Devlin? Had I encountered him on another plane where he had warned me of danger?

I glanced down the narrow alley, past a lush courtyard to a dimly lit carriage house nearly smothered by bowers of crape myrtle and lemon trees. I tried the gate, but it had locked behind Devlin.

"Use the key," I could almost hear him whisper.

But I wasn't that brave. I wasn't sure I wanted to know what business he had behind that locked gate. Still, I stood there vacillating until the dazzle of headlights chased me into the shadows of a recessed doorway.

A car even sleeker than Devlin's pulled in behind his. A woman got out, and though I had never seen her before, I somehow knew her. Knew that her name was Claire.

She was dressed all in black, her slacks and top as elegantly molded to her body as Devlin's attire had been to his. Her hair was long and straight and glimmered silvery gold in the moonlight. She was very beautiful. Quite possibly the most beautiful woman I had ever laid eyes on and it took no effort at all to picture her with Devlin.

She walked to the gate and paused to glance over her shoulder just as he had done, but she was more careful than he. She scanned both sides of the street and then turned to peer into the very doorway where

I lurked. I drew back holding my breath. When I chanced another glance, her gaze had moved on, but I had a feeling she knew I was there. The way she looked in the moonlight…the half smile that played at her lips. For a moment she reminded me of Annalee Nash. Physically, they looked nothing alike, but there was something about her demeanor. Something about that smile.

She had secrets, I thought with a shiver. Dark secrets buried deep.

She waited another beat and then unlocking the gate, she, too, disappeared inside. I remained hidden in the doorway for several long minutes because I didn't want to risk an encounter with her. Another car pulled up and deposited two older gentlemen at the gate. I didn't recognize either of them, but I imagined that I would find their names on the oldest headstones in the city's oldest churchyards.

Once they were safely ensconced behind the wrought iron, I left my hiding place, but I didn't return to the gate. The night had suddenly become far too dangerous and I would be foolish to linger so near to what I assumed was a congregation of the deadly *Congé*.

Thirty-Two

A short while later, Angus and I were back on the road. I had originally intended to spend the night in the city and head out early for Ascension. But plans changed. Things happened. Old loves got engaged and suddenly became mortal enemies. I couldn't remain in Charleston a moment longer. It wasn't safe for me there.

I drove with the windows down and the smell of pluff mud permeated the night air, that singular, sulfuric perfume of the Lowcountry. We had left the secrets and intrigue of Charleston far behind us and were now heading back into the pungent world of tidal flats and root working. Of salt marshes, folk magic and, as I had recently discovered, the darker rituals of witchcraft and black magic.

I almost expected Kendrick to be waiting for me when I pulled into the drive. I wasn't particularly in the mood for company and I was still a little wary of him, of *us*, after the incident on the front porch. But I would have gladly accepted his offer to check the grounds while I made sure the house was secure. He wasn't there, though, and I had no intention of calling him. I didn't need Kendrick or Devlin or anyone else to keep me safe. I had been on my own for a very long time. I knew how to take care of myself. Even so, I couldn't suppress a shiver of apprehension as I unlocked the front door and reached for the light switch.

Angus padded beside me as we began our nightly ritual at the back of the house and slowly worked our way up to the front bedroom where he balked at the threshold and whimpered. I went in alone to search the closet and corners and underneath the bed. Nothing appeared out of place. Everything was just as I'd left it a few hours ago, and yet I couldn't shake the feeling that something was different. Something was horribly wrong inside that room.

I thought about the hollow sound of the mewling I'd heard from the bedroom and wondered if there might be a tunnel or passageway underneath the house that ran all the way back to the shed. Maybe that would explain how the kitten had ended up at the bottom of that concrete cylinder when the outbuilding had appeared untouched.

Then I thought about the entity that had been trapped beneath my great-grandmother's house near Kroll Cemetery and I hurried from the room, closing the door firmly behind me.

I retreated to the smaller back bedroom to change out of the dress and sandals I'd worn to dinner. I was too keyed up for bed and I felt a little too vulnerable to go outside and search the grounds in my nightgown so I put on the fresh work clothes I'd laid out earlier. Transferring keys, phone and pepper spray to the pocket of my cargoes, I went into the kitchen to put on the teakettle. While the water heated, I walked Angus outside.

I stood at the bottom of the steps shining the flashlight over the yard and as far into the orchard as the beam would reach. Closing my eyes, I focused on the night sounds, trying to project my senses out into the trees where someone might lurk.

The shrill whistle of the kettle startled me back to the porch steps and I hurried inside to turn off the burner. As the sound subsided, I glanced over my shoulder. I felt on edge for no discernible reason. I'd checked the house and all around the backyard. Angus was still outside. If anything or anyone were about, he would let me know. But the outside no longer concerned me. I felt a sense of wrongness inside the house that no amount of logic could dispel.

I walked across the kitchen to peer down the hallway. Shadows lurked. I had left the light on in the entry when Angus and I first got home, but now it was off and the door to the front bedroom hung open. Either someone had come in while I was outside or they had been here all along. Or more likely, it wasn't a some*one* at all.

The floor creaked from an invisible weight and I felt a shudder go through me. I took a few steps into the hallway and another floorboard creaked beneath my feet. I froze and the house fell into a waiting silence.

I wished that I had brought Angus in with me, but I didn't dare go out to the backyard to call him. I was afraid to take my eyes off the hallway. I stood there for the longest time, straining to hear a sound or pick up a scent that would provide me with an explanation for the creeping fear that prickled my scalp.

I moved deeper into the hallway, telling myself all the while that nothing was wrong. I was just anxious from everything Dr. Shaw had revealed to me. From everything that had happened since I'd seen those hands clutching the mortsafe. I had nothing to fear. The house remained secure and Angus patrolled the yard. And anyway, when had running away ever solved my problems? When had denial and pretense ever chased away my bogeymen? Best to face those lurking shadows head-on. Best to do battle on my own terms.

I reached in my pocket for the pepper spray, thumbing off the top of the canister as I inched forward. Despite my resolve, a voice in my head screamed for me to get out of the house. *Get out now while you still can!*

But I couldn't run away. I couldn't seem to fight the compulsion that drew me steadily toward George and Mary Willoughby's bedroom. When I got to the threshold, I balked just as Angus had done, sliding my hand along the wall to feel for the light switch. Then my hand fell away as my heart jerked in shock.

Moonlight spilled in through the tall windows and I had no trouble discerning the tall figure that perched on the edge of the bed. A stray draft rippled his loose clothing and I could see the sheen of a metal talisman at his throat and another at his wrist as he sat motionless, head bowed, shoulders uncharacteristically slumped.

I wanted to turn away from Darius Goodwine. I wanted to run from that house and the secret that was about to be exposed, but I could not. I stood frozen as he finally lifted his head to observe me.

"How did you get in here?" I demanded. But, of course, he wasn't really there at all. He was inside my head. Or was I inside his? It was all too confusing and I couldn't seem to settle my nerves enough to make sense of his visit.

I summoned shaky indignation. "You shouldn't be here. How dare you come into my home uninvited? What do you want?"

He pointed to a spot on the floor at the end of the bed.

My gaze flicked to the large floral area rug and then back to him. "What is it? What do you want? Enough of these games. Just tell me!"

I noticed the smell then. Not the ozone of his magic or the must of an old house, but a thin metallic trace of fresh blood.

My gaze shot back to the unstained rug and then once more slowly returned to him. There was something different about his appearance. From our very first meeting, he had always come to me as a flesh-and-blood man. As real and as solid as if he actually stood before me. But his form seemed to waver in the moonlight. For a moment, I swore I could see right through him.

"Why are you here?" I asked in dread.

His gaze remained fixed on the floor. He again pointed to the rug at the end of the bed and I moved into the room with dawning horror. I knew what he wanted now. I knew what I had to do.

Kneeling at the end of the bed, I rolled back the carpet. Dust tickled my nostrils and fear slid along my backbone. The wood beneath was old and streaked with what I thought at first might be Mary Willoughby's blood. But the splotches were fresh. I ran a hand across the floor, staining my fingertips crimson.

A small indention, worn smooth by time and use, had been chiseled into one of the boards. I crooked my fingers through the handle and pulled. A section of the floor lifted on hinges, revealing a gaping hole similar to the one we'd found in the shed.

Easing to the edge, I peered down into the abyss, but I could see little beyond the opening. I fished the flashlight from my pocket and flicked on the switch, angling the beam down through all those shadows to a form huddled on the concrete floor.

I drew back in shock. My hand trembled so badly I could barely grip the light. I took a moment to compose myself and then I moved back to the rim, stabbing the beam down through the darkness to run it along a bloodstained torso and the pale, mutilated face that stared up at me.

No, no, no!

My mind screamed in protest, not wanting to accept what had already been absorbed into a part of my brain. *First he took their blood and then their hands, their eyes, their tongues.*

Almost of its own volition, the light traveled slowly down the body as I duly noted the loose clothing and the metal talisman that hung from a leather cord still wrapped around the arm above one of the stumps.

My mind exploded with a thousand images as reality rained down horror upon me. Understanding came in the blink of an eye. Darius Goodwine had been lured back from Africa out of fear for his daughter's safety, but he had badly underestimated the power and vengeful nature of his enemy. He had been ambushed by Atticus Pope, paralyzed by a powerful drug, tortured beyond any normal person's endurance and then he'd been thrown down into that hole so that the agony from his injuries would rejuvenate Pope's magic.

Without hands, Darius hadn't been able to claw his way out of his prison. Without a tongue, he couldn't call out for help. So he had come to me using the only means available to him. Had it also summoned the kitten? I wondered. To alert me of his presence. To warn me about those holes.

Sick and trembling, I stared at his ghost and he stared back at me. He had started to fade but his lips still moved. He made no sound but I could hear him inside my head.

Save her.

Perhaps it was understandable, though not admirable, that my first thought was not of protecting Rhapsody Goodwine, but of how to save myself.

Thirty-Three

I rose on watery legs and backed from the room, away from Darius Goodwine's ghost. Away from that hole and the secret at the bottom.

I fled down the hallway, through the kitchen and out to the back porch, but my call to Angus died away on a whisper as I spotted someone crouching at the edge of the orchard. Pressing my back into the wall, I tried to melt into the shadows. I almost expected the ghosts of Pope's disciples to form a circle in the yard as they chanted for me to release them. But the silhouette was female, human and, I knew now, deadly.

I had no idea where Angus was. He would have alerted me to Annalee's presence if he'd been able. The thought of him lying wounded somewhere or even worse...

No. I wouldn't think about that right now. I couldn't. The image would undo me. I had to stay focused. I had to get out of that house because I had no idea if Annalee was acting alone or if she had summoned more followers.

Sinking beneath the half-wall on the porch, I

crawled back into the kitchen and then raced down the hallway to the front door. I wouldn't look inside the front bedroom. I wouldn't search for Darius Goodwine's ghost. I had to get out of there now. Go for help. Call the police...

That thought gave me pause. Tom Malloy *was* the police and I'd had the distinct feeling that he and Annalee were in this together. Might Pope have recruited others on the force? Could I trust anyone in Ascension?

Don't think about that now. Don't think at all. Just run!

Plunging headlong down the porch steps, I dashed across the yard to my vehicle. As I started the engine, the headlights leaped to life, trapping Annalee Nash in the glare as she came through the back gate. For a moment she stood frozen, then she started forward just as I caught a movement near the porch out of the corner of my eye. Fear pounded in my chest. Maybe I was seeing things and maybe I wasn't, but I had a terrible feeling that I was being surrounded. Hemmed in by Pope's newest recruits.

Images of Darius Goodwine's mutilated body flooded my mind and I heard myself muttering, "Go, go, go."

I put the car in Reverse and backed out of the drive, barely missing the ditch. Then jerking the gearshift into Drive, I slammed on the gas pedal, fishtailing down the road in a shower of gravel.

I hadn't meant to end up at Lucien Kendrick's house. I had no clear destination in mind until I drove past the blue mailbox. My only intent was to get as far away from the Willoughby place as possible and call for help. Then I would go back and look for Angus.

No, I hadn't meant to end up at Kendrick's house at all. How did I know that I could trust him? He could be a follower, too, for all I knew.

But I'd been inside his head. I'd glimpsed a piece of his past. Surely if evil resided there I would have sensed it.

I had to place my faith in someone because I couldn't battle Atticus Pope alone. I couldn't elude his followers without help. I needed someone capable, someone armed and dangerous, to go with me back to the house to search for Angus.

Leaving the safety of my locked car, I bolted across Kendrick's yard and up the porch steps to bang on his front door. *Please be there, please be there, please be there.*

No answer.

Again and again I pounded until sanity prevailed and I accepted the reality that he wasn't home. I got out my phone and called him. From inside the house, I heard a faint ringtone. His phone was inside but where was he?

Those terrible images flashed in my head again. What if Pope had taken him? What if he lay in a heap at the bottom of another dark hole, mutilated and bleeding and perhaps already beyond help?

I rushed down the steps only to pause at the bottom as a familiar feeling stole over me. The watcher was nearby. I could feel those invisible eyes peering at me through the darkness. The sensation grew stronger until I whirled, expecting to find someone standing on the porch above me. No one was there, of course. I saw nothing in the shadows, heard nothing from inside the house. But I could feel the traveler's presence in the icy fingers that slid up my backbone. In the rush of adrenaline that pulsed through my bloodstream.

"Who are you?" I whispered.

No answer. Nothing stirred but my own heartbeat and the silent creep of fog from the water.

I told myself the sensation was just nerves. Who could blame me for being frantic? But the feeling wasn't nerves or imagination. The traveler was there. Not in the woods, not in the swamp. Right there beside me. For a moment I thought I might be able to reach out and touch a flesh-and-blood being.

"Who are you?" I whispered again. "What do you want from me?"

If I hadn't paused at the bottom of the steps, if I had not glanced down at precisely the moment the moon skirted a cloud, I might never have glimpsed the spark of red embedded beneath a splinter in one of the stairs.

Even as I bent to dig the ruby stud from the wood with my fingernail, the significance of my find hadn't fully registered. How else to explain my sudden calm when only moments earlier I had been fleeing for my life? When desperation had guided my car past that blue mailbox and down the wooded lane to this lonely, isolated destination. To this very spot at the bottom of Lucien Kendrick's porch steps.

I was still bent over the stair, prying loose the ruby stud, when my gaze lit on a darker shadow beneath the porch. Someone huddled there just beyond the reach of moonlight. I peered through the gloom, dreading yet another gruesome discovery. But the silhouette moved. The person was still alive. I suppressed a scream as Rhapsody Goodwine crawled to the edge of the light and put a finger to her lips.

I was so taken aback I could do nothing but mouth her name. She stared back at me through wide, frightened eyes. I wanted to ask her how she'd gotten there and why, but I didn't dare utter a sound. Had Pope or one of his disciples lured her to Kendrick's house? Had she come looking for Darius, drawn down that same desolate road as I by curiosity and a willful nature? I knew for certain we were both in danger. And I was the only one who could save us.

As she melted back into the shadows, I heard a voice in my head as plainly as if the traveler stood at my side, whispering into my ear. It wasn't Rhapsody's voice, nor Kendrick's, but a familiar drawl that feathered along my nerve endings like the softest caress.

Danger...danger, Amelia.

Devlin's presence was so strong at that moment and so overpowering I almost said *his* name aloud. His second warning lifted the hair on my arms and turned the blood in my veins to ice.

Careful. He's right behind you.

Thirty-Four

Kendrick had come up from the swamp, moving quietly across the yard, perhaps hoping to catch me by surprise. For a moment as moon glow fell across his face, his features seemed to contort into something dark and bestial, the *loup garou* from his grandmother's stories. Then he was Detective Kendrick again, handsome and confident and striding toward me with his head slightly cocked. But he wasn't really Kendrick at all. Not anymore. His mask had fallen and I knew that I was looking into the soul of Atticus Pope. I had a vision of him standing over the young Kendrick's bed, scratching at his chest—not to claw out his heart but to find a way in.

He hesitated a fraction as if trying to read me, but I closed him out. My heart thudded and my stomach churned in terror, but somehow I managed to raise a barrier so that he could not enter my head, so that he couldn't glimpse Rhapsody inside my memories.

I said in surprise, "So you *are* home! I was just about to give up."

As he continued toward me, I had to fight the impulse to flee. But I was all too aware of Rhapsody crouching underneath the porch, trembling and frightened and counting on me to somehow protect her.

"I was out on the water," he said.

"Really? I didn't hear the outboard."

"I took the rowboat out. I like the exercise. I find it therapeutic."

I had a sudden vision of him paddling through the swamp, looking for the symbol that would guide him to the church ruins once he had what he needed from Rhapsody Goodwine.

"Anyway, I realized I'd forgotten my phone and came back for it." He closed the distance between us and stood staring down into my upturned face, probing and probing, but I still wouldn't let him in. "What's wrong? You look upset."

What to tell him? I couldn't let him know that I'd found Darius Goodwine beneath the floor of the Willoughbys' bedroom or Rhapsody Goodwine lurking under his porch. He would never let either of us leave here alive. My only hope was to build on our previous conversations. Play on the budding intimacy that I now knew had been nothing more than a devious manipulation.

I folded my arms as I gazed up at him. "I guess I am a little upset, but that's no excuse for coming over here this time of night. It was impulsive and I'm sorry for intruding on your privacy." I hoped the remorse gave me sufficient cover for glancing away to compose myself.

He took my arms and it was all I could do not to shrink away from him. His touch made my skin crawl. Those same fingers gently digging into my flesh had wielded the knife that cut out Darius Goodwine's eyes and tongue and sawed off his hands. All for the sake of Pope's dark magic. All to satisfy his depraved nature.

"Why are you upset?" he asked.

"It's nothing. I don't want to bother you."

"What if I want to be bothered?"

I was in mortal danger from this man, but I couldn't let him sense my fear. I couldn't let him know about Rhapsody. Our only hope of escaping unscathed was to keep him out of my head.

He was still searching, still probing, still trying to find a way in as his fingers tightened around my arms, and all I could see in the back of my mind was Darius Goodwine's mutilated body in that hole…

"I was in Charleston earlier tonight having dinner with a friend. He told me some distressing news. Distressing to me, but nothing that concerns you. I really don't know why I came here except…"

"Stop apologizing. I'm glad you came." He sat down on the steps and pulled me down beside him. "Just tell me what happened."

I hugged my arms around me as I huddled next to him. "You asked the other night if there was someone else and I told you there had been. Someone important."

"I remember."

"I found out tonight that he's engaged. It's been over a year since we were together, but the news still hit me hard. Harder than it should have."

"I'm sorry."

"Don't be. It's for the best. Rationally, I know that. Now I have no reason to cling to the past. It's just…"

"I understand."

I drew a breath and nodded as I sorted through my options. My car keys were in my pocket, along with the pepper spray. My phone was still in my hand and my arms were folded in such a way that I might be able to place a 911 call without him noticing. But could I trust the local authorities to come to our rescue? What if he really had recruited Tom Malloy and Annalee Nash to do his bidding? To rebuild his dark alliance?

I didn't know if my defenses had momentarily slipped or if Kendrick's senses were so keen that he had intuited my intention, but he removed the phone from my trembling fingers and placed it on the step beside him, out of my reach.

"I should put that in my pocket," I said. "I'll forget it if I don't."

"You won't forget it. I'll make sure you don't." He turned back to me. "Now tell me why you're really here."

"But… I just told you."

"No, you told me why you're upset. Why did you come here? To me?"

"Because… I wanted to see you. I *needed* to see you."

Moonlight glinted in his golden eyes. "Lucky for me you remembered the way."

I listened for a telltale shift in his voice, a give-away nuance that would let me know he was on to me. But he sounded steady. Calm. Perhaps even a little flattered. He couldn't know that I'd found the ruby earring or that his mask had slipped, exposing his true nature.

Panic welled at the back of my throat, but I swallowed it down and managed a tremulous smile. "Thank you for being so understanding, but now I'm embarrassed. This isn't like me. I'm never impulsive. I should go and let you get back to your evening." I reached into my pocket for the car key and my fingers brushed up against the cool metal canister of the pepper spray.

"Stay," he said. "You can go out in the boat with me."

The thought of going with him into the swamp sent a fresh wave of terror spiraling through me. "Thank you but another night. I really do need to get home to Angus."

"He won't miss you."

"How do you know?" Too late, I realized I'd fallen for his bait. I saw something glimmer in his eyes as he reached for my hand, gently removing the car key from my fingers and placing it on the step with my phone. I couldn't keep the fear from my voice now, but it didn't matter because he knew. I could see it in the gleam of his eyes, in the smirk that tugged at the corners of his mouth.

An image came to me then of a young Kendrick, naked and bound, eyes glowing with the flame of devotion as the fiery brand of the Brotherhood scorched a triskele at the back of his neck.

He had purposely lowered his guard, letting me see what he wanted me to see.

"My mother first took me to see Atticus Pope when I was just a child. I was frightened of him at first. I could see the beast inside him and I tried to run away, but in time, I came to accept my destiny. I came to see that our union was inevitable. I had the sight and he, the power. Together we would be invincible. Immortal. My father tried to stop it by taking me away, but he was too late. I had already been chosen. I was the only one who could hide Atticus from his enemies. For two decades he lay dormant inside me until the time came to rebuild the Brotherhood."

He was letting me see other things now. Allowing me into his memories so that I could fully comprehend Pope's evil, so that my terror would strengthen his magic.

I saw the young female *Congé* prone on the ground beside the mortsafe as Kendrick snipped the old lock and opened the gate. Then she was gasping and choking and trying to claw her way up out of the grave as the gate clanged shut and a new padlock was snapped into place.

That image faded as older memories surfaced. Pope and Mary Willoughby entwined in her bed. Pope leaning over Annalee, touching her, mesmerizing her, blowing a powerful dust into her lungs so that she would do his bidding.

He showed me other victims, too. The homeless and the lost. Children that had been taken from their families. He wanted me to see them all. He wanted me to look upon those innocent faces as their screams echoed through my head.

And then the images faded, replaced by even older, darker memories dimmed by time and space. I tried to block the visions, but Kendrick laughed at my futility.

"It would be easier if you would come into the swamp willingly, but…" He shrugged. "Either way, your blood will flow just as freely."

He plucked my car key from the step and rose to fling it into the shadows. Then he tossed my phone to the ground and cracked it with his heel. He turned his back to me for just an instant, so certain was he of his dominance and my submission.

But he had misjudged me. He had underestimated my power and cunning. By the time he faced me again, I'd flipped open the pepper spray and aimed the fiery irritant straight into those strange, golden eyes.

Thirty-Five

I didn't call out to Rhapsody. The only way to save her was to lead Kendrick away from the house, buy her some time so that she could get to the road, find a phone and call for help. As soon as the effects of the pepper spray wore off, he would come after me, and so I raced across the yard and plunged into the trees, letting moonlight guide me through the ground mist.

The silence of the forest closed in on me. I could hear nothing beyond the rasp of my breath and the rush of blood in my ears. Panic robbed me of my sense of direction and I had no idea where I was or which way to head. But I kept going. On and on until a tangle of vines caught my feet and I tumbled down an embankment, twisting a knee and grazing my head on a rock.

I lay there dazed as blood trickled into my eyes. Wiping the back of my hand across the wound, I tried to rise, but the knee gave way and I sprawled facedown on the hard ground. I heard him then, coming up fast behind me. So close I could detect the thud of his boots as he raced through the woods.

Hitching myself over a dead log, I flattened myself on the forest floor, letting the mist roll over me.

Everything went deadly silent. Even the birds had scattered. I couldn't hear so much as a footfall now but I knew he was nearby. If I concentrated hard enough, I would be able to pick up the saw of his breath and the excited hum of his blood. He was undoubtedly listening for me, too, and it was all I could do to quiet my pounding heart.

I was scarcely hidden by the mist and the log. He would be on me soon and I needed to keep moving, needed to put as much distance as I could between us.

I flexed my knee, wincing at the pain, and then, rising to a crouch, I slipped deeper into the trees. I moved in silence, or so I thought, but he must have heard something—the crunch of a dead leaf, the catch of my breath. He vectored in on the minuscule sound and came at me, making no effort to conceal his approach.

He was a powerful man and even uninjured, I couldn't hope to outrun him for long. I needed to outwit him. Evade him. Snagging the lowest branch of a sweet gum, I swung myself up and scrambled from limb to limb until the thick foliage concealed me. Then I cleared my mind so that he couldn't pick up so much as a stray thought or telltale emotion.

Not a minute later, Kendrick sprang from the woods as silent as a panther and paused in a patch of moonlight, sniffing the air and listening to the night as he moved his head from side to side. He was so close I could have leaped down upon him from my perch and the thought did cross my mind that surprise might be my best weapon. But he was quick and far stronger than I. I may have caught him off guard with the pepper spray, but he would be ready for me now. Time was my only real weapon. I had to wait him out.

He hovered beneath me for so long that I began to think he knew I was there. He was toying with me, prolonging the inevitable so that he could use my fear against me.

Finally he took to the trees again and I waited several beats before climbing down through the branches and lowering myself to the ground. I stood with throbbing head and trembling knee as I listened to the night in much the same way that he had. I sniffed the air, turning from side to side as I tried to pick up his trail. He had gone north so I headed south, back to the house. Rhapsody had surely gotten away by now, but I had to make certain.

I chose stealth over speed, but the pace was risky. If I lingered too long in the woods, he could intuit my plan and rush back to the house ahead of me. A momentary panic made me quicken my steps, but a snapping twig drew me up short. I couldn't afford to get careless.

Stay smart, stay focused. Concentrate on your breathing and your every footfall. Don't make a sound. Don't make a mistake. One misplaced step and you die.

The first thing I saw when I came out of the woods was the raised hood on my vehicle. He had taken the time to disable it before coming after me.

I ran across the yard to the porch, calling softly to Rhapsody. When she didn't answer, I whirled to survey the yard. She would have made for the nearest house, I felt certain. Which meant I needed to keep Kendrick away from the road.

Without a moment's hesitation, I plunged down the embankment, slipping and sliding and scrabbling like a crab to the bottom. Then I dashed to the boathouse, yanking helplessly on the padlock. My gaze lit on the owl emblem and I flashed to the locks on the mortsafe and shed. Someone must have bought up a supply, Martin Stark had suggested that day in the circle. Now I knew that Kendrick had been that someone.

I didn't waste time trying to break in because I knew he wouldn't have been so careless as to leave the key to the outboard. Instead, I headed for the rowboat.

Still operating as silently as I could, I untied the rope and carefully climbed in, settling myself on the middle bench facing the house and the woods. I used an oar to push off and then set both oars in the grooves and paddled.

I was an inexperienced rower, but what I lacked in technique I made up for in strength from all my years of toiling in cemeteries. My rhythm established, I steered the boat toward the bank, gliding through shadows to put distance between myself and the black soul of Atticus Pope with each stroke.

Thirty-Six

My shoulders ached and my knee grew stiff. I kept to the shadows as night sounds assailed me. The buzz of mosquitoes, the croak of a bullfrog.

More sounds came to me. Distant sounds. A car engine out on the road. A jet flying through the night.

And then the terrifying rumble of the outboard.

He was coming.

I'd stopped paddling to listen and the boat drifted out of the shadows into full moonlight. I tightened my grasp on the oars and guided the boat back to shallow water, putting my back into the strokes until the outboard grew louder and the waves from the prop sloshed against the bank. Then I steered the boat into the bank, letting the prow run aground as I spotted the death's-head.

The wings spread across the night sky as the skull face grinned down at me in the moonlight. Once I had imagined that effigy coming to life. I had seen the thing swoop down from the treetop and dive toward me, but now I knew that the animation was a mind trick. Even then I had been under Atticus Pope's influence.

I sank ankle-deep in mud as I climbed out of the boat. Pulling myself free, I trudged up the bank to solid ground, pausing just beyond the tree line to get my bearings. If I could find my way to the caged graves, I could follow the trail to the cemetery and from there I could make my way to the house and look for Angus.

I tried to keep my defenses up as I limped along, but there were too many obstacles along the way, too many dead branches and treacherous vines that tripped me up and tested my weak knee as well as my focus. But I kept going, ignoring the pain as I gathered speed and maybe even a little confidence.

As I came out of the woods onto the path, I heard the sputter of the outboard as Kendrick pulled to the bank. The engine died and, in the ensuing silence, fear and doubt crept back in. I had distance on him but I didn't know how long I could outpace him. I felt certain he would make for Seven Gates. He would go through the cemetery, out to the road and up to the Willoughby house, which had been my original destination.

I left the path and waded out into the tall weeds toward the mortsafes. Toward Atticus Pope's twelve buried disciples. I almost expected to see them rise up out of their prisons and form a circle around me, but they were silent tonight. Silent and waiting.

I lowered myself to the ground and kept an eye on the path, praying that Kendrick wouldn't think to look for me in the circle. He would go to the cemetery and up to the house. I desperately wanted to believe that. I lay flat on my stomach, chin on the ground as I watched the woods and waited for him to emerge from the trees.

He didn't come. Not for the longest time.

Had he taken a shortcut through the woods to the cemetery? Was he lying in wait for me in the church ruins?

Heart thudding, I listened intently to the darkness. The disciples were silent, but the dead woman wasn't. She was with me in the circle, inside that caged grave, clinging to the grate as she allowed me to glimpse her last terrifying moments. I was trapped with her, gasping and sputtering and trying to claw my way up through the dirt. By the time I managed to shake off the vision, Kendrick was almost upon me.

He burst out of the woods and paused on the path, clutching the hilt of a machete. For a moment, I thought he might do exactly as I had predicted. He even started along the path toward the cemetery before he whirled and plunged through the weeds at a dead run.

I stumbled to my feet, but he was too quick. He seemed to sail across the mortsafe, machete lifted over his head. I turned to flee, but the flat side of the blade hit the back of my head and I crumpled. Rolling to my back, I looked up into the night sky as I slid backward into oblivion.

I opened my eyes and blinked as the scenery moved around me. It took a moment to clear the cobwebs from my brain and then terror crashed down upon me. Kendrick was dragging me through the grass toward the open mortsafe. I clutched at the weeds, but his strength seemed superhuman. And maybe he was. I wondered if anything was left of Lucian Kendrick in that powerful body. Atticus Pope seemed in full control now.

He dropped my legs and threw open the mortsafe gate. I tried to crawl away from him, but he pulled me back, picking me up and throwing me into the cage, into the still-open grave where the *Congé*'s body had been recovered. Where the remains of one of his disciples still lay restless.

He stood over the cage grinning down at me as he reached for the gate. A movement on the path caught his attention and he turned with bared teeth, his countenance contorting into something primal and savage. I heard a low snarl as Angus slunk through the weeds. The dog halted and canted his head as if trying to pick up the scent of the man who had once soothed him. But Kendrick was gone, and in the blink of an eye, Angus lunged, going straight for the jugular.

I scrambled out of the cage and grabbed the machete. When the man with two souls finally managed to free himself from Angus's teeth, I was more than ready for him.

Lifting the machete, I swung, but the blade never made contact. A shot rang out and then another. Pope staggered back, stopped and then toppled into the open mortsafe.

I realized then there were people all around us,

converging on the clearing. Tom Malloy. Annalee Nash. Martin Stark. Angus growled a warning as they formed a circle around the mortsafe but he needn't have worried. They weren't there for us. They had come for vengeance. They had come to make certain that what had been done to them as children would not be done to others.

I huddled beside Angus as Annalee clanged the door shut and Stark knelt to fasten the padlock. I didn't know if Pope was still alive, but Malloy kept his weapon drawn just in case.

But he needn't have worried, either, because justice was coming. A cloud moved over the moon as a deeper darkness crept in from the woods. Shadow beings surrounded the mortsafe waiting for Pope's spirit to transcend. Waiting to carry him down, down, down into that place of torture and misery reserved for the blackest of souls.

Thirty-Seven

One month later

With the help of Annalee Nash and Tom Malloy, I finished the restoration of Seven Gates Cemetery by the end of summer.

An investigation had been launched into the shooting death of Detective Lucien Kendrick, but once sufficient evidence had been collected and witness testimonies gathered that linked him to the brutal slaying of Darius Goodwine and the still-unnamed woman who had been buried alive in the caged grave, Officer Malloy had been exonerated and reinstated. Kendrick's house and property had been thoroughly searched and among the strange and disturbing items recovered was a human skull, no doubt taken from the center grave in the circle.

The authorities had been a little too anxious to accept the explanation of a psychotic breakdown. They didn't want to be pulled back into the shadowy past of kidnappings, torture and human sacrifices. Of black magic and witchcraft and secret ceremonies conducted in the old church ruins.

Some in Ascension would continue to harbor doubts about Annalee Nash and her role in her parents' murders, but I knew the *Congé* had killed Mary Willoughby and perhaps George, too. Just as I knew the townspeople would continue to protect and watch over Annalee because that was their nature.

I couldn't help but wonder if there were others like Annalee and Officer Malloy and Martin Stark. The children and relatives of Pope's followers who had been used in the rituals against their will. Were they out there even now plotting revenge or were they leading normal lives, still waiting for Pope's resurrection?

The one bright spot in all the darkness was Rhapsody Goodwine. She had made her way home that night and now bristled under Essie's watchful eyes. She had been told of the lengths her father had gone to to protect her, but whatever she felt about his sacrifice lay hidden beneath her passive demeanor and the path she would ultimately choose remained a mystery.

As for me, I was only too happy to leave Seven Gates Cemetery behind and return to Charleston. The dog days of August and September had finally given way to the milder temperatures of early October. One evening not long after my return, Dr. Shaw and I sat on the porch of our favorite restaurant on Queen Street sipping our drinks as I filled him in on everything that had happened since last we'd talked.

Afterward, I fell into a pensive silence as I watched the street.

"Is something wrong?" he asked over the flickering candle.

"I'm feeling unsettled," I admitted. "Like I have unfinished business."

"You've been through an ordeal," he said. "Sometimes I wonder how you manage to keep your sanity."

I smiled. "You're assuming that I have."

He studied my features in the candlelight. "We still haven't discussed the ghost in the room. Or on the porch, I should say."

"And whose ghost would that be?"

He looked troubled. "You saw the announcement in the paper?"

"I did. His intended is very striking. Will you go to the wedding?"

"What makes you think I'll be invited? Jonathan Devlin has never been a fan of me or my work, and that's putting it mildly," Dr. Shaw said with an unexpected trace of bitterness.

"You'll be invited. John will to see to it."

"Then I'm afraid I shall have to decline. I'm well past the age where champagne and small talk hold even the slightest fascination. Give me a good book and a strong Scotch any evening of the week."

"Dr. Shaw…" I leaned in. "The last time we had dinner you told me about a young man you once knew, a traveler who had looked down into an abyss on the other side and was so frightened by what he saw that he tried to convince himself he'd experienced nothing more than a nightmare. Do you remember his name?"

He glanced away. "It was a long time ago and my memory isn't what it once was."

"I figured as much."

He gave me a sage appraisal. "Perhaps it's just as well. I've always thought it best not to knock on doors you don't want opened."

"Maybe you're right. Some things are best left a mystery."

No matter the identity of Dr. Shaw's traveler, I would remain convinced that Devlin had somehow been with me at the bottom of those porch steps warning me of danger. I would always wonder if he'd been the watcher in the woods, observing me from another plane because he couldn't be with me in the physical world. Maybe the disappearance of the young *Congé*, undoubtedly his colleague, had prompted him to come and find me. To lead me to those mortsafes and to the death's-head in order to warn me of danger.

Or maybe I was indulging in a little wishful thinking. Obviously, I wasn't ready to let go yet despite Devlin's pending marriage.

A little while later, I walked alone on Tradd Street, savoring the delicate scent of the tea olives that drifted on the night air like a memory. When I arrived at the wrought-iron gate where I had last seen Devlin, I paused, tempted yet again to try Rose's key in the lock. But how could a skeleton key that had been left for me years ago on a headstone in Oak Grove Cemetery and had later turned up again on my nightstand be connected in any way to this gate or to Devlin or to the deadly *Congé*?

Maybe some things really were best left a mystery.

Still, I lingered in front of the gate until headlights drove me across the street where I hid myself in the shadows. Devlin's car pulled to the curb and he got out, striding down the sidewalk to the gate where he once again turned to scan the darkness. The gate swung open and a woman appeared on the other side. I could see the shimmer of her silvery gold hair in the moonlight and the gleam of her blue eyes as she took Devlin's arm and drew him through the gate.

"You're late," I heard her say. "Where have you been?"

"I had business to attend to," Devlin replied. "But surely I'm not that late."

"The others are already here and you know how they hate to be kept waiting."

"Too bad."

"Shush. Don't let them hear you say that."

Their voices died away as he wrapped an arm around her slender waist and drew her to him. I glanced away, wanting desperately to escape but not daring to reveal myself. When I chanced another glance, the woman had disappeared down the fragrant alleyway, but Devlin hovered just inside the gate, peering through the darkness until his gaze lit upon me. I felt his presence as strongly as though he stood at my side. I heard his drawl as clearly as if he had whispered into my ear.

Careful, my love. You're still in danger.

* * * * *

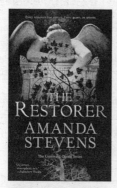

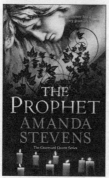

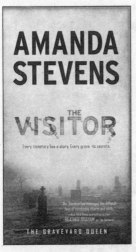